Born in Pali Village, Bombay, **Godfrey Joseph Pereira** finished High School at Saint Andrew's School. He graduated from college with a degree in English Literature and Philosophy. What followed was a career in journalism. He was Assistant Editor at *Society Magazine*, Principal Correspondent at *Sunday Magazine* and *India Today*, and worked as a War Correspondent covering the First Gulf War from Israel. His first novel *Bloodline Bandra* was published by HarperCollins in 2014. The novel made the 'Top Ten' List at Oxford Bookstore. His novel *Four and Twenty Blackbirds* is a work of historical fiction. He has lived and worked as a journalist in New York City and New Jersey and now works and resides in West Palm Beach, Florida.

FOUR AND TWENTY BLACK BIRDS

The Insane Life of an English Smuggler in Bombay

Godfrey Joseph Pereira

SPEAKING TIGER

SPEAKING TIGER BOOKS LLP
125A, Ground Floor, Shahpur Jat, near Asiad Village,
New Delhi 110049

First published by Speaking Tiger Books 2021

ISBN: 978-93-5447-217-6
eISBN: 978-93-5447-222-0

10 9 8 7 6 5 4 3 2 1

Typeset in Garamond Premier Pro by SÜRYA, New Delhi
Printed at Shree Maitrey Printech Pvt. Ltd., Noida

For The Nazarene
What Is Truth?

For My Sister, Maria; Mother, Olive; Father, Victor—
who all reside in one grave
'La Tristesse Durera Toujours'

Contents

AUTHOR'S NOTE

From England He Came

Danny Strongbow had read my first novel *Bloodline Bandra* in London. When he visited the United States, he called me in New Jersey. We met at the Boilermaker, a bar in the East Village in New York City, on 5 June 2015. We talked of trivialities, and somewhere between the fourth and fifth negroni, Danny handed me a large cardboard shopping bag and said, 'You need to read what's inside this bag; maybe, you can do something with this.'

Danny is ashamed of what his grandfather did in India. He cannot forgive; he will not forget. He said he suffered from an immense guilt by association and was afflicted with an 'unfortunate genetic gift' inherited from his grandfather. He refused to explain. Danny grew up in Wyman's Brook, north-west of Cheltenham, England with his mother Doris, who was Charlie Strongbow's first illegitimate daughter. When he began working as an advertising executive, he bought a home on King's Road in Chelsea. He tried often, but never did manage to comprehend his grandfather's tortured psyche. Occasionally, he would sit at the Chelsea Harbour Pier for hours, trying to communicate with the ghost of Charlie Strongbow riding a renegade boat to Cross Island, Bombay. These self-conducted séances were frustrating futile endeavours.

As we were leaving the bar, Danny whispered, 'I heard, I have my grandfather's deep blue eyes. I have to live with that; see my world through that.' He touched his old bag in my arms and stared at the bar's exposed brick wall, 'Maya died last year,' he said. At that time, I did not know who Maya was. Before I could ask, he turned and walked into the East Village without saying goodbye.

The next day I began reading Danny's grandfather Charlie Strongbow's letters, which detailed what had really happened on Cross Island. There were also letters describing his incarceration at the asylum for the insane in Southall, England. Like Francisco Goya's fourteen 'Black Paintings' in the latter years of his life, Strongbow's letters painted a horrorscope of his hallucinatory mutilations. The bag also contained Danny Strongbow's vivid recollections of what his mother and mother's sister had told him. I remember Danny saying, 'It all really started on Cross Island, this glorious, insane, tragic story.'

At the edge of Ferry Wharf in Mumbai today, garishly painted boats are moored, swaying in slow-motion lullaby, like a child's cradle being rocked, gently. Cross Island is four hundred metres away perched in the bay, brown, deserted and ugly, squatting in the Arabian Sea. The Navy has thrown a secretive cordon around Cross Island. You cannot go there. How did the island get its name? Christian missionaries? Or the simple fact that ships have to cross it to enter the dock area which lies to its right? It's a short sail between Cross Island and the docks. This played a pivotal role in what is narrated in these pages. The island's history is undocumented, but the folklore that surrounds it is well known to locals. Some still call Cross Island, Chinal Tekdi. Literally translated from Hindi, it means, hill of whores, and that, like the old folk say, 'is a 'nuther story, for a 'nuther time'; gristly child sacrifices conducted under the cloak of nocturnal obscurity, is another dark whisper from the island's past.

As the years rolled on, I had forgotten about the island. Then I met Danny Strongbow in New York City, and the voice and life of the 'big bearded' Englishman came alive from a forgotten pauper's grave in Southall, England, and travelled across dark waters, back to Cross Island.

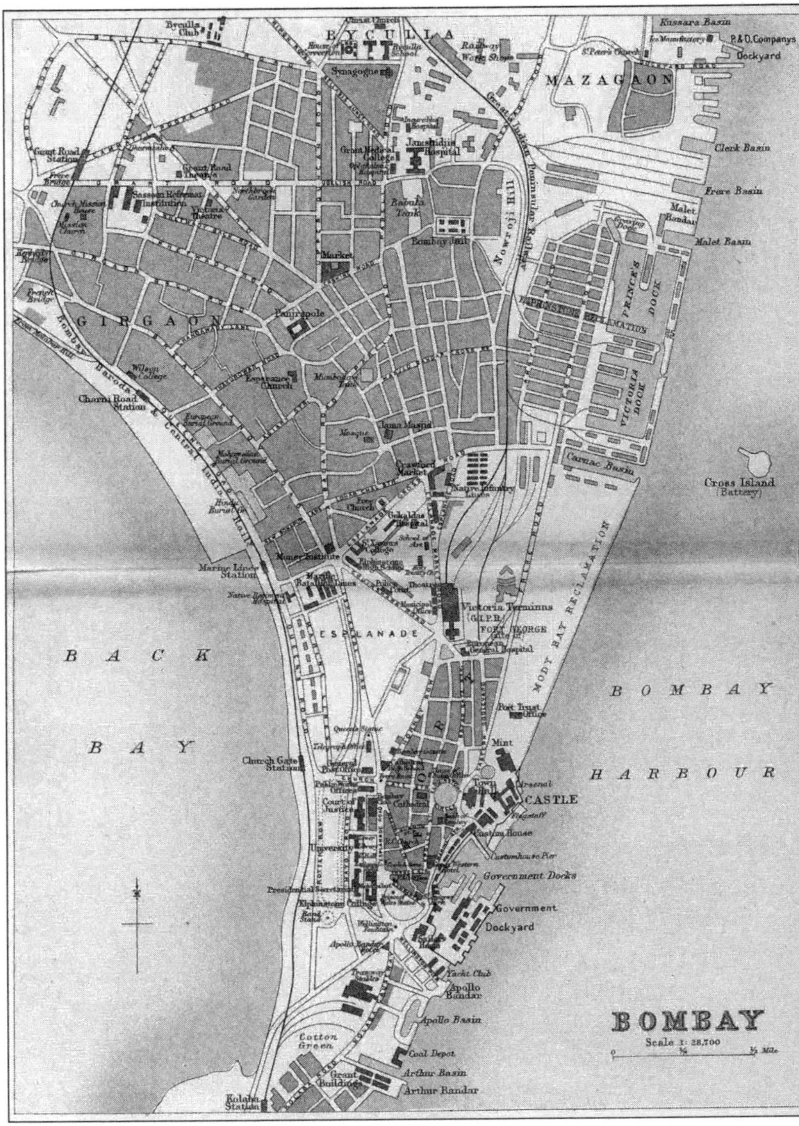

A Map of Bombay from Maps of Constable's, 1893.
Source: *Wikimedia Commons*

BOOK I

Chapter 1

The Karma Curse

Charlie had been an exceptionally intelligent child, born in the shadow of the serpent bearer, Ophiuchus, the forsaken thirteenth Zodiac sign. As a boy, he had often heard his parents' friends and acquaintances whisper, 'What's the matter with the boy?' The local physician had informed his mother, 'A secret imaginary friend is not an abnormality,' and had concluded, 'it will pass as he gets older.' And then later, when Charlie was twelve years old, the hallucinations began. After an attack, Charlie would creep up to his room, read fairy tales, get under his blanket, curl into the foetal position and talk to Dodo in the darkness.

His childhood had been traumatic. At the Immaculate Heart of Mary School in Fort, Bombay, the nuns scourged him because of his inability to grasp simplicities. They maintained that, 'The child has a brilliant mind, but he refuses to apply it to formal education.' They called him an 'idiot' and 'stupid' and other bad names. When he cried, they whipped his bottom and wrote stern notes to his mother, which he handed over. His mother subconsciously denied the fact that Charlie had medical problems relating to his mind. She knew that her child's learning disability emanated from her family line. But the social stigma of having given birth to a feeble-minded child prevented her from informing the Mother Superior, priests and teachers. 'The boy, if he fails to improve, is headed for the dustbin,' they informed her. 'We have been praying for him to improve, but now we see that he has begun a quiet stubborn rebellion. This is the wrong place for something like that. We will not let that happen.'

Day after excruciating day, Charlie reluctantly attended school, where he was often punished with thrashings on his palms, cheeks and buttocks. Once in the fifth standard, Sister Rosemary pontificated on 'The Father, Son and Holy Ghost' in the religious education class. 'The Blessed Trinity,' she thundered, 'is what our faith rests on.' And then Sister Rosemary paused, took off her glasses, polished them with a handkerchief, put them back on, smiled sardonically and asked the class the holy trick question. 'How many Gods do we have?' Sitting on a back bench, Charlie raised his hand. 'There are three Gods,' he told Sister Rosemary who went into instant ecclesiastical shock. Charlie was politely asked to leave his desk and come forth to face the inquisition of Sister Rosemary. There was absolute silence in the class. The frightened class watched as the thick Roman blade of Catholic righteousness swooshed down to an apostate beheading. Sister Rosemary crossed herself reverently, slapped him viciously three times, called him an 'ignorant heathen' and commanded him to kneel in penance for half an hour. 'Have you been listening to anything I have been saying?' she snarled. 'Good Lord Almighty, there is One God, you fool.' 'The Blessed Trinity' had confused Charlie, who did not dare tell her that her explanation had been inadequate. Sister Rosemary loomed like a swelling thundercloud of Christian wrath before the kneeling Charlie; and the boy lost control over his bladder. Charlie felt the warm wetness. He did not look down at the floor. He began to whimper, gazing at

Sister Rosemary; his eyes pleading, his voice a forlorn beggar's whisper for forgiveness. He folded his hands in prayer as he cried for an end to the excruciating torture and humiliation. Sister Rosemary turned her laser-beam-like stare from Charlie, looked at the class, raised her eyebrows in amusement, and smirked. And the whole class jeered and laughed.

What the nuns, in their misguided missionary zeal could not comprehend, is that they were meticulously manufacturing Charlie into a product with no heart. The snivelling boy would grow up to be an unconscionable man, whose morality would justify a way out of situations by savage and unethical means if possible.

When Charlie finally left school with a disgraceful passing grade, he often had dark fantasies of violently stripping the religious habit off Sister Rosemary, forcing her to prostrate before a Pagan court, and then crucifying her...naked, her rosary dangling between her bleeding breasts.

In a trance, Charlie would stare at these apparitions with vengeance.

Chapter 2

Between House and Home

Charlie: *There's no going back; not now...after all these years... We've been here for almost two hundred years. We built this goddam country. I was born here, and I will die here. I am entitled...Do you understand?*

Dodo: *There is a time to keep and a time to cast away, Charlie.*

Charlie: *Don't throw Christianity at me, Dodo, I am a Brahmin. They say we have lost our moral legitimacy to be here; but this is home. I was born here in Bombay, thirty-five years ago. Today, Friday, the 15th of August, 1947, I woke up to a new reality. They have divided this land into Hindu India and Muslim Pakistan. The Hindus, Muslims and Sikhs have begun a trail of murder. I won't be surprised, if they begin murdering the British next. Why not? They have centuries of grievances...I see this new insolent glare of independence in their eyes, they want us all to leave, but this is my home, I have family here...somewhere out there is Maya...I lost my first daughter Doris; they took her back to England, I think...now Maya is all I have. I have a gut feeling; Maya is here, somewhere...*

Charlie is a six-foot-seven-inch Gulliverian entity. His white body is sun scorched, sculpted, lined and honed by the intense labour that he has had to endure at the Bombay Docks. His long black hair parted in the middle reaches his shoulders, his moustache and flowing beard seem to grow wild. A slender aquiline nose sits between high cheek bones and his piercing eyes have rutted crow's feet by their sides. A European Moses, with a faint sympathetic aura of the crucified Nazarene, his demeanour and deep blue eyes appear to possess learnings beyond his years. His almost reverential physicality, if confronted with antagonism, suggests a retaliatory possibility of fire and brimstone, still, no one can recall a time when Charlie used his physical prowess to win a fight. Even the lofty, sturdy Pathans eye him with respect.

When he speaks, he communicates with confidence; even if the subject matter is alien to him, Charlie talks with an authoritarian decisiveness. And always, behind the calm of his countenance and body language, there lurks a subterranean warning; an area where the antagonist can get lost, even ambushed. But he walks on the streets of Bombay with a Maharaja's regal authority.

Through the festive streets around Ferry Warf, Charlie wandered, pensive, thinking about the Hindu-Muslim savagery. He has heard the murderous rumbles reverberating throughout the country. 'These people must know that the borders of partition have not yet been revealed. The mood is strange, given the circumstances. They should be joyous and reflective, not so celebratory. Nobody seems to care right now of what would, or could, happen when the borders are made public.' Charlie buys *The Times of India* from a street vendor. As Charlie hands him two annas, he looks at the banner headline: 'Birth of India's Freedom' and scans the first fourteen members of the new cabinet of India. There is no mention of the still unknown borders between India and Pakistan on the front page.

Reeling from the intoxication of independence, people dance on littered streets. A megaphone blares the hot favourite, 'Yahan Badla Wafa Ka' from the Hindi film *Jugnu*; the badly amplified voices of Mohammad Rafi and Noor Jehan blasts through Gunpowder Road. A billboard with actress Leela Chitnis endorsing Lux Toilet Soap says, 'Here Is a Lovely Tip from Leela Chitnis' another proclaims 'Horlicks Overcomes Weakness' and another one for Colgate toothpaste says: 'The Test of Love Lies in Your Kiss'. The advertisements in English seem incongruous in the now Hindu India.

Ambling cows chew on rotting garbage, stray dogs scamper in the heat. He inhales vapours of sweat and sour body odour. Blaring loud cacophonous music and locomotive horns compete for attention. And the crowds swell like boiling water. A Muslim man leads a reluctant goat to slaughter; his burqa-clad wife follows. A Hindu touches a cow's head between the horns and places his hand on his heart in a gesture of reverence. Sweets pass hands. Slum kids are dancing, raucously appreciating the free entertainment. A street vendor selling pungent fried beef yawns and scratches his groin. Leprous beggars cry for alms, eunuchs in ill-clad saris clap their hands and offer ersatz blessings and good luck prayers for the future. They demand money in gruff tones from shopkeepers, because, after all, this is a momentous joyous day. Suddenly a skirmish begins, but it is thwarted by a rare appearance of the police before it turns ugly, and the festivities continue.

Charlie sighs. 'This festival of fools will end in calamity. It seems like just yesterday, Hindus, Sikhs and Muslims collectively put aside their gods, and complex social and caste differences to fight British rule, and now that they are triumphant, they turn cannibalistic. They are eating each other, and simultaneously dancing on the streets! How do you explain this paradox?'

On a crumbling wall, an old filthy poster of the Muslim leader Jinnah proclaiming a united India flaps in the wind. A scurrilous graffiti artist has drawn a pair of decorative green horns on his bony shoulders, and scrawled violent obscenities beneath the poster.

He looked at the poster, smiled and remembered, years ago when he had first encountered Kanji Dwarkadas on a hot summer afternoon in October 1936. Charlie who worked at the docks had been loitering around the unloading area when he noticed a man arguing with the Loading Supervisor. What surprised Charlie was that the man was clearly agitated, but his mannerisms were calm, his arguments mild and explanatory. There was a low tide receding atmosphere about him that seemed contradictory to the situation, whatever the situation seemed to be...What was this man doing here anyway? Charlie asked himself. This was a restricted area. Charlie walked up to the English supervisor, physically pulled him away by his arm and led him away from the man who was explaining his frustrations in a low, calm voice. 'What's going on here, Marty?' Charlie demanded. 'Who let that man in here? And... what the hell is he protesting about?' It was the young Loading Supervisor's fourth day on the job. He had just arrived from England two weeks ago. Harried and short fused, he sputtered: 'He's some bigwig Congress man...demanding to know where his shipment of Italian marble is. He says his friend, who is some tinpot leader, will get agitated if this marble is not there. It's not my fault if that damn marble is not on the cargo manifest! Still he insists...' 'What is his friend's name?' Charlie asked. 'I don't know his friend's first name but this man says the last name on the customer bill is Gin-Naa,' the Loading Supervisor answered. 'This man says that his friend has the power to make big trouble. Do you know...have you heard of this fellow, Gin- Naa?' Charlie smiled and nodded, 'Yes,' he said, 'I know who he is. I will take care of this problem, don't you lose sweat over this.'

When Charlie talks, thumb and forefinger of his left hand smooths the ends of his unruly moustache; then the hand opens and strokes his beard gently. He looks you in the eye as his head bobs up and down in slow motion, agreeing or disagreeing with whatever is being discussed. He never raises his voice, even if sparks of an argument seem imminent, or if a threat is being issued. If an insult and challenge of a gauntlet are thrown at his face, Charlie backs away in an apologetic dignified retreat, folding his hands in a namaste. By the next sundown, the challenger is in a hospital contemplating the unfortunate crippling accident that has befallen him. Charlie does not believe in handling violence personally. Although he has the capacity to separate balls from sockets, he hires other people to do the bone crushing. Something to do with his reading of the three treasures of Taoism: compassion, frugality and humility; he once confided in a friend with a twinkle in his eye.

Turning around, he faced the agitated man.

He was aware that 'South Court' or 'Jinnah House' as locals called it was being constructed. It was located on Malabar Hill on Mount Pleasant Road on ten thousand square metres (2.5 acres) of prime sea-facing property. It was rumoured that this was a house being built to British regal proportions. It was a stunning collage of exquisite Italian marble. The impeccable slabs were carefully selected by stonemasons and brought all the way from Italy. There was walnut woodwork from Romania and Belgian crystal, all conceived and designed by the famous architect Claude Batley and personally supervised by Jinnah. Charlie knew precisely who Muslim leader Muhammad Ali Jinnah Bhai was.

Charlie located the shipment of marble, refused the

considerable bribe that K.D., as Charlie called him, was offering, and told him that if ever he needed help, he hoped K.D. would use his contacts to help Charlie in the future.

At the docks, he has built an unshakeable reputation with the wheelers and dealers as a man you can trust implicitly. Underground contacts know that Charlie possesses a Socratic stubbornness. He would rather drink the cup of poison than recant, apologize or turn informer. He builds and stores contacts like a philatelist, constantly cataloguing, sorting and trading for a better stamp. Much like a Godfather in the Cosa Nostra, he dispenses help with a solitary string attached. He makes a mild suggestion that one day, maybe, he may ask for a repayment of the favour. And the debt has to repaid, or else…Charlie shook K.D's hand and apologized for the inconvenience.

And that was how Charlie met Kanji Dwarkadas, Jinnah's right-hand man, who was destined to tutor him on how to use back alleys and dead ends to survive and thrive in India.

Through the years, they had kept in touch through back doors. Charlie was aware that many Indian movers and shakers were constantly receiving shipments of expensive material from all over the world. 'Where are they getting all this money from?' Charlie had often wondered. It did not take him long to figure out that there were powerful people siphoning some of the struggle for freedom funds to wood, brass, feather and tile their sumptuous nests and personal projects. Charlie had filed K.D. as a 'contact-friend' if he ever needed help in corrupt, hard-to-access high places. And K.D. through the years had supplied Charlie with intimate details about the enigmatic, secretive Jinnah, and the complicated workings of the Indian political systems. It was K.D. who taught Charlie how to manoeuvre, weave and duck and crawl through the open sewers of Indian politics. He also provided Charlie with character sketches of the rich and powerful and connected him with low-life human cogs that were used by the powerful to make the wheels of corruption turn silently in the dark after normal business hours.

Charlie looked at the poster with the horns again. The sunken cheeks, the high bony cheekbones, and the dark inscrutable eyes lent an appropriate lifelessness to the taut-skinned unsmiling death mask. 'The father of Muslim Pakistan,' Charlie thought. 'Born on Christmas Day, 1876. A brilliant walking contradiction, a man who had scourged Mahatma Gandhi and the Congress with a Muslim whip, and used the threat of Hindu majority vote in India to win his Islamic kingdom, and who liberally indulged in Western haraam habits, was the face of Islam in a breaking India.'

Like Jinnah, Charlie has a passion for music. He acquires records from sailors at the docks. There were times when Charlie had to pay for records; but mostly he would trade his knowledge of the best bars and whorehouses in Bombay in exchange for the music to seamen desperate to dispense their semen and flesh out their masturbatory fantasies. Charlie had learned and fine-tuned the ability to barter and haggle like an Indian housewife at a fish market. He could be tenacious, conniving and mildly intimidating in incessant waves as he slowly whittled down the price. His mind stored an encyclopaedic rolodex of names and places, prices and pleasures offered in Bombay. Sailors approached him all the time, looking for expensive watches sold cheap in the black market, gold, hashish, ganja, heroin and prostitutes who were willing to perform out-of-the-ordinary *Kama Sutra* positions. From underage boys and girls, to influential madams, pimps and transvestites, to girls from continental Europe, Japan and Nepal who were trafficked into Kamathipura, Charlie knew the flesh market, warts and all. He seldom volunteered information without a payback.

Charlie had heard that the outwardly taciturn, grim, stone-faced Jinnah had a soft, almost melodious human side to him; he loved the swing of Jazz, but there were also dark metaphysical alleys. His wife Ruttie, a Parsi, was just eighteen when she married forty-two-year-old Jinnah, who was ostracized by her community and family for marrying Jinnah, a Muslim and an 'old man' to boot, whose political aspirations had no time for her love and affections. Later, their marriage in tatters, Ruttie's loneliness turned to melancholy and then snaked into depression. Weary of playing solitaire with her seventy-eight Tarot cards and tired of placing her fingers on the planchette of the Ouija Board, she began tapping at the trap door of darkness. She soon turned to 'The Other World', became obsessed with the occult, spirits and séances. Embarrassed, disillusioned and privately ashamed of his wife's acquired mystical characteristics, Jinnah lamented, 'She was a child and I should never have married her.' 'The Flower of Bombay' had withered and now resided with bitterness behind a self-imposed fence of impenetrable thorns.

Jinnah, a staunch rationalist, tells his inner circle that mysticism is a ruinous depravity, but the couple's close associate K.D. confided to Charlie, that in a moment of marital weakness, perhaps tempered by frivolity, Jinnah may have consented to make a deal with Mephistopheles to quieten his strong-willed wife's nagging insistence that the occult would protect him and guide him to his goals. Charlie was sure that he had. Otherwise this man, Charlie reasoned, with his flamboyant alternate anti-Islamic lifestyle, so blasphemous to his holy book, could not have survived. Behind the Koranic curtain, Jinnah, a Shia Khoja Mohammedan, led a life that Sharia Law abiding Muslims would abhor. He was known to savour smoked ham, was a chain smoker, and occasionally attended Jazz concerts by Ken

Mack or Antonio Xavier Vaz, the Goan trumpeter who went by the name of Chic Chocolate in the Bombay Gymkhana and the Royal Bombay Yacht Club. These were the same clubs that Charlie used to frequent. Charlie had often sidled up to Jinnah at The Taj Mahal Palace to try and make contact, but Jinnah was always aloof, haughty...almost dismissive. Once when K.D. was with Jinnah, Charlie ambled up to their table. He was greeted warmly by K.D., while Jinnah looked away. Invited by K.D. to join them, Charlie had sat at the table, while Jinnah stared at the Jazz quartet blowing Charlie Parker. Finally, the band took a five-minute break. Charlie had been talking to K.D. when Jinnah interrupted. 'You don't seem to have a pukka British accent?' he observed, 'How come? Or are you acting a part to suit your present company? Is this your performative persona?' Charlie smiled at the sarcasm. 'My name is Charlie Strongbow, sir,' Charlie explained, 'I was born here in Bombay...I am not...' 'Oh, I thought you were an actor,' Jinnah retorted. 'You have the personality...When I was studying to be a barrister in London, I had dreams of playing the role of Romeo at The Old Vic. I had even signed a contract with a Shakespearean theatrical company. I was ready to give up law; but my father went ballistic when he heard about my stage aspirations, so, I had to abandon that ambition. I still like Shakespeare, but unfortunately these days, the Bard has to take a back seat to the Partition.' Charlie looked at the gaunt cold face across him and tried to imagine Jinnah as Juliet's passionate lover but all he could conjure was an embarrassing cardboard caricature of Jinnah as Romeo. Charlie silently quoted the Bard: 'For never was a story of more woe than this.'

Charlie decided to change the subject to Jazz, but Jinnah seemed uninterested, disconnected, aloof and hostile. Charlie knew then, that anything he said, even if it was pleasant or complimentary would be weaponized by Jinnah and slingshot back in a full-frontal verbal assault designed to denigrate and damage. Charlie felt acutely uncomfortable with Jinnah's contemptuous hostility and decided it would be prudent to retreat in silence. Charlie muttered a polite goodbye and walked away. Jinnah did not even deign to glimpse at Charlie's humiliating retreat. He focused on the band, as they returned to the small stage and began playing Scott Joplin's 'Maple Leaf Rag'.

Despite the tumult, upheavals and killings that the Partition created, jazz in Bombay continued playing on the sidelines for many British dandies, who were joined by rich and upper middle-class Indians. Jinnah would surreptitiously sneak into jazz joints, letting Western improvisations wash over his pseudo-Islamic life for a while.

'This enigmatic man,' thought Charlie, 'a man as far away from Islam as I am from Christianity, is going to be the leader of a Muslim country.'

He felt the raw energy of the crowds who had taken advantage of the free transport that the government had magnanimously announced. 'The nation is on the move,' somebody shouted. 'Finally we are all one, we are free. Jai Hind.' 'Not for long,' Charlie thought. He wondered what his old friend K.D. would have to say about this, and about India's new prime minister.

Jawaharlal Nehru, born into a Kashmiri Pandit Brahmin family, was a rabid agnostic. He would now lead a nation where Hindus were a vociferous majority. He had an acute dislike for Hinduism and its traditions, and he was not afraid of offending the many gods. Nehru's legendary anger and angst were well known, and Hinduism for him is not a Holy Cow that has to be revered or respected. 'Much is said about the superiority of our religion,' he thundered with anger and bitterness. 'Your religion has become a thing of the kitchen, as to what you can eat, and what you cannot eat, as to whom you can touch, and whom you cannot touch. The spectacle of what is called religion,' he explained, 'or at any rate organized religion, in India and elsewhere, has filled me with horror and I have frequently condemned it and wished to make a clean sweep of it. Almost always, it seemed to stand for blind belief and reaction, dogma and bigotry, superstition, exploitation and the preservation of vested interests.' Nehru's words were a dark prophetic harbinger to the bone-breaking, throat-slitting carnage that were to follow.

Nehru and Jinnah were diametrically opposite personalities. The one common denominator they shared was that both men were tobacco addicts, heavy smokers who inhaled only British cigarettes. Nehru and Jinnah, it seemed, had failed to read the swadeshi memo to boycott British products and 'Be Indian, Buy Indian'. Jinnah chain-smoked cork-tipped Craven 'A', while Nehru smoked State Express 555, popularly termed as 555. Between the two leaders, one a pseudo-Muslim, the other a lapsed Hindu, there was literally and figuratively a cloud of toxic smoke.

Now despite the raging fires they knew were coming, there was no place left to backtrack. Like Jinnah, Nehru had made a tryst with destiny long years ago and now the time had come to redeem that pledge.

Behind the opaque bureaucratic curtain, partition lines were being chiselled.

A Himalayan holocaust was to come for the living, where sights of the mutilated and dying were going to be worse than the putrefying stench of death. A jaw-grinding hate was beginning to swirl under Indian skies like the swollen dark ominous monsoon clouds that could trigger deluge and death.

Charlie wondered, 'This bloody aftermath that will surely

come, this colossal turgid mess, how much of this lies on the uneasy head of The Crown and British leaders in India?'

The next day, on the streets of Bombay and the rest of India, fear, anxiety and jubilation swirled in the diseased communal tin cup that had always been held in India's right hand. In Bombay, near Rampart Row, an insignificant complaint about too much sugar in his tea led to an argument, which prompted a Hindu customer to verbally abuse the Muslim tea stall owner. Hearing the argument, a small crowd of Hindus began gathering around the stall. 'Go make your filthy tea in Pakistan, you pig,' a fanatic voice from the crowd snarled. A stone was hurled at the tea stall owner, and in the melee that erupted, someone knifed the Muslim. As a crowd watched, they set fire to his stall. Shop owners in the whole area quickly downed their shutters. Muslims began arriving, and the now familiar two fanged riot raged. Hundreds watched as the carnage occurred. No one bothered to help the tea stall owner. Stabbed and sobbing, his life seeped out of him in a slow bleed. The police arrived. Crowd and murderers dispersed; the grievously injured were carted off to the nearest municipal hospital, the dead to morgues, and the new normal went about the chore of living in a free India.

At the Wayside Inn restaurant, nestled in a corner of Rampart Row, sat a man born an untouchable. He was dressed in a rumpled three-piece suit. His spectacles had a thick black frame; and his dark eyes appeared to view the world with quizzical reflection. An unusually high forehead, impeccable black hair combed back, a strong hint of a growing double chin and a smooth-shaven face angled to a pudgy roundness, completed his rather stern countenance. On his table was a pot of tea, his teacup and saucer, three pencils, four pens and a sheaf of papers. He had been busy writing when the ruckus of the riot disturbed his concentration. He quietly observed the

Hindus and Muslims attacking each other. As the owner, Pervez Patel filled his cup, the bespectacled man said, 'The sovereignty of scriptures of all religions must come to an end if we want to have a united integrated modern India.' Patel nodded and smiled, 'Dr Ambedkar, my friend,' he said, 'those are very nice words, but that will never happen. We will be killing each other over religious differences long after you and I are dead and gone. Religious leaders need the "sovereignty of scriptures" as you call it to enslave the masses; and the politicians need these religious leaders. That is the way we were, this is the way we are, and that is the way we will be, now and forever.' Dr Ambedkar looked at him silently, then transferred his gaze to his foolscap sheets and picked up his pen to begin writing. Patel moved away to serve another customer. But Dr Ambedkar just stared at his papers; words seemed so inadequate, suddenly. He sat immobile at his customary table number four; the paragraph that he had been working on now seemed irrelevant. Finally in a stupor, he gathered his papers, his pens and pencils, paid Patel, said goodbye, and walked out of the Wayside Inn. As he passed the now destroyed tea stand, the architect of the Indian Constitution stopped and stared at the blood stains on the road. 'Maybe a hundred years from today,' he thought, 'what will happen if a Hindu leader emerges who is a rabid anti-Muslim? Can the Indian Constitution stop him? What will happen if he receives a massive mandate by the majority Hindus and the not-so-subtle persecution of Muslims becomes a new and accepted reality? By then, the Muslim population will have increased and they will fight back. Can the country withstand the bloodbath? Was it wise for India to stick to secularism? Can the Hindu and Muslim cultures ever live together in harmony in India, or am I just being a fool by hoping that one day that Golden Age we once had will return?' Dr Ambedkar hung his head in sorrow and confusion as he turned away from the bloodstains. A crowd of Hindus and Muslims were beginning to hurl vile slogans at each other. He heard the words Allah and Ram. 'There between the two gods,' he thought, 'somewhere between them, lies the mystical socio-political solution to this problem, but that is a place where angels and demons fear to tread.'

Chapter 3

A Crack in the Divide

The Christian world contemptuously spat on the Indians as 'the heathens' slaughtered each other. In Bloemfontein (Orange Free State), South Africa, apartheid capital of the world, the leading newspaper printed a patronizing and sarcastic message by administrator Doctor S.P. Barnard, titled 'Go Back to India'.

And Winston Churchill stated: 'The Indian political parties and political classes do not represent the Indian masses. It is a delusion to believe that they do.'

In Bishopstown, Cork, Bob O'Callaghan owner of the *Mug & Brush* was having a conversation with a regular client. O'Callaghan said, 'Well, we don't have to care anymore, do we, it's their bloody mess now. But remember I said this—they will blame us for all their problems. I don't know how or when, but they will, you mark my words.'

Cyrus Dinshaw a Parsi gentleman, who was an editor at a local newspaper, was having a drink with his old friend Dr Homi Bulsara, at the Metro Bar, in Colaba, Bombay. 'These Hindus and Muslims are like animals, don't you think? They cannot put their stupid differences aside,' said Dinshaw. Bulsara nodded and sipped his whisky.

Charlie wondered, 'How could the political leaders have

embraced and accepted this?' Mahatma Gandhi, defeated and disillusioned was in Calcutta. He had refused to take part in the 'celebrations'. The Partition had wrenched the old, tired heart out of his frail chest, and nobody seemed to really care. A sidelined Gandhi was powerless against Cyril Radcliffe, the London lawyer who had been handed the job of partitioning the tumultuous country. What made Radcliffe an outstandingly unsuitable candidate was that he had never been to India.

Given a life choking deadline, questionable data and outdated maps, Radcliffe hurriedly used a rule of thumb approach, instead of cartographic callipers. He split Punjab in the West and Bengal in the East. Then in his self-imposed solitary confinement, he incinerated all his work papers and official documents, leaving smouldering ashes, death and mayhem behind. It was ironic, Charlie thought, that Cyril Radcliffe is literally a short-sighted man. Conscripted in World War I, his poor eyesight had him demoted to the Labour Corps. Radcliffe was publicly unapologetic for his actions in India, but he knew that he had been part of a historic indefensible bloody blunder. Languishing in acute guilt, he refused his salary of forty thousand rupees (then three thousand pounds). After he drew his line, Radcliffe recalled with distaste, 'When I arrived in India, I was told by all the political leaders that the time at my disposal was very short. All the leaders like Jinnah, Nehru and Patel told me that they wanted the line before or on 15 August. So...I drew them a line.'

This disastrous cartographic blood line set fire to the existence of three hundred and fifty million people living in India. It displaced around fifteen million, thousands of women were abducted, and over a million people lost their lives in the brutality. Trains filled with mutilated corpses, women defiled, raped, murdered, foetuses pulled from wombs, children knifed, men dismembered, homes torched and burnt...the stench of wrath roamed the streets, free and independent, holding wild fire and long sharp knives.

Reading this in *The Times of India*, Charlie was ecstatic. This breakdown of law and order, this senseless uncontrollable communal war, was the perfect diversion he needed to put his plan into first gear.

Cyril Radcliffe left for London on the day of Independence. Two days later, when the Radcliffe Line was made public, he was resting in his Bond Street apartment, far from the decapitation of his imperfect surgery.

The great English poet, Wystan Hugh Auden summarized the British blunder in a stinging snarky poem titled *Partition*. Without naming Radcliffe, Auden, famed for his pithy lines, painted the process of the Radcliffe Line with unwavering historical accuracy:

...in seven weeks it was done, the frontiers decided,
A continent for better or worse divided.
The next day he sailed for England, where he could quickly forget
The case, as a good lawyer must. Return he would not,
Afraid, as he told his Club, that he might get shot.

Like millions on the day of Independence, people of Bengal's Muslim-dominated districts in Murshidabad and Malda joyously strung Pakistani flags on the porches of their homes, but two days after Independence, when the borders were finally announced, the terrifying unsettling realization dawned that they were now part of Hindu India. And a mass migration began on both sides, as terrified people scurried to the places they wished to belong to for the rest of their lives. And their perilous journeys, on foot, bullock carts, trains and buses turned into an odyssey of bleeding and dying.

Hell opened its brim-stoned maw of fanged savagery. The Muslims did not want to be in a Hindu-dominated India, and the Hindus and Sikhs did not want to be in a Muslim Pakistan. There was no visible police force out on the streets to stem the incessant flow of bloodshed; and the army appeared to be floundering.

In what was perceived as an insult to India, military hero, Lieutenant Colonel Mahmood Khan Durrani, who fought with the British Indian Army in North Malaya during World War II, and who was a recipient of the George Cross for heroism, while a Prisoner of War of the Japanese Army, opted to live in Pakistan and serve in the army.

Charlie was worried that the Indians would target the British next. He arranged a meeting with his old friend K.D. They met for dinner at The Taj Mahal Palace. Charlie wanted information. 'Are British subjects going to be attacked in India?' He asked K.D. 'Is there any underground group that is planning this? I know that through your sources you will be aware of plans like this.' 'My sources state that there have been a few minor incidents,' said K.D. 'but nothing serious. I can assure you that there is no organized group in India that is planning any subversive moves against British subjects. We...they all know that most of you are heading back to Britain. That does not mean that it could not happen, you know that, Charlie.' Sitting at a table nearby, a group of Indians were raucously discussing the current state of affairs. One snarky voice brought up Colonel Mahmood Khan Durrani and his move to Pakistan. He referred to Durrani as a circumcised ungrateful stray dog. 'And what about that?' Charlie asked K.D.

'Let me explain,' said K.D. with a sigh. He lowered his voice to a whisper, so that the men at the next table would not be privy to his conversation. 'On 15 August 1947, India's Independence day, Scottish-born war veteran Rob Lockhart was appointed commander-in-chief of the Indian Army, with the acting rank of general, by Nehru, despite the availability of Indian military operation planner Lieutenant General Cariappa, who in my opinion, is a man of outstanding military capabilities. But maybe it is a good thing that Cariappa was not chosen. Sometimes the gods work in ways we cannot comprehend.

'I know from my sources that when Robert Lockhart offered Nehru a precise plan to strengthen the numbers of the Indian Army, Nehru flung his carefully calibrated papers to the floor. He pointed his forefinger at Lockhart like a gun and shouted, "We don't need a defence plan. Our policy is non-violence. We foresee no military threats. You can scrap the army. The police are good enough to meet our security needs." These are the words of a fool, who has absolutely no futuristic vision. I am talking about the security and defence of this nation.

'Many people are not aware of this right now. On 16th September, our "Uncle Nehru" directed that the army of two hundred and eighty thousand be slashed down to a hundred and fifty thousand. This is a tragedy, because the Indian soldiers, returning from fighting Hitler's armies, could have been a mighty force of deterrence here. They would have stopped a lot of bloodshed that is happening.

'Do you know that by the end of the war, Indian enlistment in the British Indian army was a staggering 2.5 million men? Eighty-seven thousand dead, eleven thousand, seven hundred and fifty-four missing in action, presumed dead; almost thirty-four thousand critically wounded and sixty-seven thousand, three hundred and forty Indians were prisoners of war? This even momentarily melted the hardened jowls of that despicable fat India hater, Winston Churchill, who chomped on his *Romeo y Julieta* Cuban cigar and grudgingly admitted to "the unsurpassed bravery of Indian soldiers and officers". Now these trained-to-kill men are coming home, with absolutely no future prospects. These are tough soldiers, who fought Hitler's armies, and the Japanese. They now have nothing to do, but look at the trenches painted with communal blood. Muslim soldiers can go to Pakistan and enlist in the army, but Hindus have to live here, jobless. How long do you think it will be before they are pulled into the ditch of this madness? That is what the ignorant, arrogant Nehru does not understand.

'Now you know why the army is not out there preventing the killing; and the police force is inadequate. They don't have enough personnel, and they are not trained to put out the fires of this hell. The Indian army has been castrated by their "Uncle Nehru". That is the reason why this war hero defected to Pakistan. If the Indians start attacking the British here, there will be nothing this new government can do to protect you, even if they wanted to. My advice is, go back to England. Nothing good can come out of all this Charlie, at least for people like you.'

Charlie had listened in silence. 'I will take this as it comes,' he told K.D. 'This is home, for better or worse, and I have good friends like you here.' K.D. smiled, 'You don't have to wait, till death do us part Charlie,' he joked. They continued eating in silence. After dinner, K.D. thanked Charlie for footing the bill; he then grew momentarily pensive, and said in a low voice, 'There is big trouble coming Charlie...blood is going to flow, like the river Ganges.'

Confusion led to rumours...A Muslim child was knifed, a Hindu woman raped, her breasts hacked off, a Sikh's testicles burnt, the hair on his head ripped from his scalp...stories ricocheted like shrapnel from a bomb, and the rabid fangs of hatred meandered into massacres, as old touchstones of terror rumbled down mountains of hatred, twisting logic, rationality and common decency into a crocodilian death roll. Religion, as always, was the sacred paranoid instructional manual behind the gristly human sacrifices.

In London, Winston Churchill snarled: 'I hate Indians. They are a beastly people with a beastly religion.'

Chapter 4

Changing of the Guard

Charlie needed to talk to his friends; this was a new world now. He was sure they would be there, drinking and talking about the long journey home. The Mulberry Bush at Ferry Wharf on the east coast of Bombay was crowded. 'Hey, Charlie,' the bartender said, 'getting ready to leave, are we?' Charlie paused and then smiled, 'This is my home,' he replied. 'I don't have any other place to go.' 'Enjoy your drink,' the bartender said, 'I will be closing this place down. You may or may not have heard—there is going to be a total ban on alcohol soon. Prohibition is coming. For me, that is the end and anyway all hell is happening; this fire will last forever with these people.'

Charlie walked to a corner table. 'Ahaaaa...Charlie,' a tipsy Timothy Blackwell hissed, 'Come on in, join the farewell party.' Charlie smiled. 'Good to see you Thommo,' Charlie said, patting him on the shoulder. There was an easy familiarity between the men. They all worked at the Victoria Docks in Bombay. Everybody called Timothy Blackwell 'Thommo'. If Thommo looked like someone who had spent a considerable amount of time in jail, the assumption would have been correct. Thommo was English white trash, a yobbo, lost between the bars of a jail and the open space of nowhere. India was a place where he could get away with murder; and now, he would have to return to strait-laced England and its stiff upper-lip morality. Thommo was born on Rushdale Road near Meersbrook Park in Sheffield in South Yorkshire, England. His father worked at Portland Works, the famous Sheffield steel company, something Thommo was inordinately proud of. When the family visited relatives in 'Andytown' a suburb of West Belfast in Northern Ireland, Thommo always bragged, 'I was born in a place where the best knives in the world come from.' He grew up tough and developed a laconic sense of humour as a teenager which he sometimes used to hide his social awkwardness. When an acquaintance in High School questioned his ability to grasp a simple math equation in class and called him 'thick as two short planks', Thommo had cornered the boy in the school lavatory. 'I am not smart,' he said, 'it's not my fault, you see me godparents had me wisdom teeth pulled out. It's an old Catholic thing, you wouldn't understand, you being Protestant and all, you know.' He then broke the boy's jaw. When once asked why he added so much milk to his tea, Thommo faked a serious expression and mumbled, 'Me Mum had only one tit, did not breast feed me, I need to make up for all that calcium I lost.' Unable to control the revolt brewing inside him his mother had watched from afar with helpless trepidation as he graduated from petty theft to aggravated assault and armed robberies. His father, after a few initial talks with Thommo, ignored his only child's existence. Thommo was arrested and sent to reform school when he was sixteen; his parents were not surprised. Repeated incarcerations were the self-education learning institutions where Thommo studied the nuances of how to be a good criminal. He graduated *summa cum laude*, a distinction he was proud of. Life was leading him to a solitary dead end when on a whim he took a job as a 'grease monkey' aboard a ship travelling to Bombay. He did not visit his parents to say goodbye. His small travelling bag contained one change of clothes, a toothbrush, and a tempered and honed stainless steeled *Wade & Butcher* stag handle carving knife to remind him of home; and here he was, a stevedore at the Bombay Docks sailing to nowhere.

Charlie glanced at William Watson, sitting opposite Thommo. Willie was a mild-mannered deck supervisor who had once been an accountant. His job was to plan, direct and control the loading and unloading of freight. Pilfering merchandise was an occupational hazard that he accepted because it brought him a steady monthly illegal bonus. He looked like a priest with his hair parted in the middle, a thick moustache and a compulsive habit of bringing his palms together as if praying and touching them to his lips when he listened to something he thought was serious. His round face and kind brown eyes made you want to confess your sins to him. His obsessive attentiveness to minute details, however inconsequential, impressed Charlie. Willie had once been an expert at cooking the books till they appeared legit and palatable. He could move fragmented numbers around till they appeared whole. He also organized, conducted and executed most of the stolen trade business that the dock rats ran. From the time goods were stolen at the docks and store houses, to their journey by trucks to their illegal destinations, Willie set the time, tracked the loads and made sure that the merchandise did not disappear en route. The denizens of the underbelly of Bombay respected and trusted Willie; and Willie did the job with ruthless efficiency. When one of the trucks was hijacked, Willie had tapped his network of informers and discovered who the leader of the gang was. The next day the tough gang boss was moaning and whimpering in an intensive care unit. Here he was with purple swollen eyelids, broken kneecaps, a shattered jaw, and both kidneys dispensing sporadic gusts of blood into the urine in his bladder which trickled through a catheter and dripped crimson misery into a plastic drainage bag hanging from a rusty stand by his bed. Willie was like Charlie, he rarely got his hands dirty. Jobs were farmed out to shadow mobsters who mingled in Bombay's darkness. They, in turn, made contact with a third person who then picked a petty hoodlum to do the job. Charlie had decided that if his dream was to be achieved, he would need Willie as his logistics manager. Charlie said, 'I don't want to go to England.' Thommo laughed, waving his arms. 'You don't...we don't have a bloody choice! This game here is over.' Willie looked at Charlie, 'Things are going to change, and they are in charge now.' Charlie looked steadily at both men, 'I have a plan. We need a boat.' Thommo roared with laughter, even Willie looked perplexed, and as he smiled his voice took on a patronizing tone. 'A boat...you did say boat, didn't you? It's a long way to London, Charlie.' Charlie smiled, *if they only realized* he thought, *how long I have been nursing this idea and how difficult it has been with this disease...all that forced education, those books I had to read to arrive at this point.*

His crippled scholastic record lead to a literary path of self-education and a self-exploratory analysis of what 'the experts' considered his irrational mind. The doctors he had been to had arrived at a series of grey diagnosis that confused him. Unable to accurately define the hallucinations and outbursts, he learnt to live with them. Acutely aware that he was ignorant and unlearned after school, Charlie effectuated an almost martinet routine of self-education. He began reading paperback crime fiction novels by Arthur Conan Doyle, slowly graduated to authors like Joseph Conrad, and later dissected the metaphysical and ethical systems of Arthur Schopenhauer and the revolutionary thoughts of Friedrich Wilhelm Nietzsche. He read *The Prince* by Niccolò Machiavelli and concluded that the

Italian's conniving philosophy was palatable. That it was okay to piss in the public pasta sauce bowl, as long as the masses were conditioned into acceptance through fake news and fear. In his quest to understand the human mind, Charlie often found fault with Dr Sigmund Freud and his approach to psychoanalysis, and concluded that the analytical psychology of Carl Jung and his concept of 'Collective Unconscious' made more sense.

Charlie had often tried in vain to comprehend the elusive psychological complexity of the Indian mind. Many of the essential Indian mannerisms, actions and reactions had always flummoxed Charlie. And although he was born in Bombay, the subtle nuances of many head wobbles and hand gestures still eluded him. To try and better comprehend the Indian psyche, he read *A Passage to India* by E.M. Forster, R.K. Narayan's *Malgudi Days* and *The English Teacher*. Charlie glimpsed shades of himself in Krishna, the protagonist whose relationship with his daughter Leela, after his wife Susila died, underwent a startling metamorphosis. Intuitively, Charlie felt a distinctive parallel analogy. He also delved into Indian and British history, studied Hindu religious works and was fascinated by the novels of Munshi Premchand, translated from Hindi-Urdu into English. Sometimes late at night, he had fiery literary discussions with Dodo on the interpretations and conclusions of writers from William Shakespeare to Walt Whitman and David Herbert Lawrence. He read what Lawrence once said: 'I want to gather together about twenty souls and sail away from this world of war and squalour and found a little colony where there shall be no money but a sort of communism as far as necessaries of life go, and some real decency...a place where one can live simply, apart from this civilization...[with] a few other people who are also at peace and happy and live, and understand and be free.'

These lines were the infestations that germinated in his mind in a slow boil, and eventually started the Cross Island brain fever inside Charlie's already diseased head.

And then, the change that was to come walked into The Mulberry Bush.

Two Indian men sauntered in and up to the bar. They ordered whisky. Thommo looked at them and smirked. 'This is an English bar,' he shouted. 'You are not fokkin' welcome here.' One of the Indian men yelled right back, 'Arre...this is not your country anymore, bada sahib. Better you be going back to your Ing-Land, gora.' Charlie placed a warning hand on Thommo's knuckles, 'Let it go, he is right.' Thommo uncoiled like a serpent, slid out of his chair and hit the Indian on the right side of his skull. The man's body was momentarily airborne by the intensity of the blow as he crashed into a table. The other Indian put up both hands in a sign of surrender. Thommo spat in his face and kicked him in his groin as he whimpered to the floor, sobbing in pain and disbelief. The crowd in the bar had fallen silent, transfixed by the sudden violence. The bar man, a giant of an English man, with tattoos on both arms pointed at Charlie and his friends. 'You three, out, now.' For a drunken moment it looked like Thommo was going to attack the bartender. His Rasputin eyes flashed thunder. Charlie held Thommo as he began guiding him to the door. The bartender bent over one of the fallen Indians, helping him up he said, 'Sorry about these three hooligans. You shall be served, sir.'

Outside the bar, Willie turned to Thommo and said, 'That was the one of the changes I was talking about.' Thommo snorted in rage at the humiliating reality of diminished power that the English were now facing. 'This would not have happened in the past,' he lamented.

In 1901, the British viceroy of India, Lord Curzon had said,

'As long as we rule India, we are the greatest power in the world. If we lose it, we shall straightway drop to a third rate power.' Now, that time had arrived, and all over India, a white exodus had begun. From the plains to the hill stations, the British, feeling powerless, were packing and getting ready for the long journey home.

There were myriad stories of how servants grieved at the loss of employment, and the measured kindness that an English family had shown them. In Shimla, Ram Lal and his wife Bhagwanti were in tears. They had been with the Andersons for twenty years, taking care of the family's summer home. Through the years, the Anderson's fourteen-year-old daughter Pamela had grown close to Meena, Ram and Bhagwanti's daughter. Now the girls sat on the verandah of the house and talked about keeping in touch, remembering shared moments over the years when the servant-mistress line had been blurred momentarily. There were wet eyes and promises made, to keep in touch, to write...but they both knew; this was the end. The Andersons had to leave.

CHAPTER 5

Supernatural Shadows

The next weekend, Charlie called a meeting. This time they met at his home near the Victoria Dock area. 'Where's the bottle?' Thommo growled. Willie complained that he was hungry. Charlie ignored them. 'I need the both of you to listen to what I have to say. We'll drink later, after I'm finished. What we are going to do is open a supply of British and other European goods. From Quaker Oats to Cow and Gate baby milk, French wines, cheese, perfumes, Scotch whisky and cigarettes. We all know that the prohibition is on its way. That is good news.' 'How are we going to get these products?' Thommo asked. Charlie smiled, stroked his beard and waved his right hand in the air. He looked at Thommo. Before you attacked those Indians at the bar, remember I said something about a boat? Willie laughed, 'Yes, yes...a boat to England, flying the Union Jack.' Charlie ignored him. 'Just off the Bombay harbour, is Cross Island. It sits in the water about four hundred metres from Ferry Wharf. It is not far from Elephanta Island. There's a crumbling fortification on this island built by the British or Portuguese during the First World War, but nobody lives there, as there is no known water source, but we'll get to that problem later. The locals believe that it is haunted. Murders have happened there, so they say…it is perfect for us, because the locals avoid the island. Cross Island is going to be our home. And this is how it is going to happen: we will bribe the dock authorities, who will bribe the captains on various ships. I have contacts in Southampton. I can fix things there. They will drop the merchandise onto our boat before they cross Cross Island to the Bombay Docks. We will row the goods onto our island and then sort it all out for distribution. Our boat will be used to deliver the goods to the mainland. We need British folk, without Christian morals, and who do not want to leave, for this to happen.'

For many of the approximately eight hundred thousand British leaving India, it was a question of what to take and what to leave behind. Mary and Daniel Carrington lived in a bungalow on Pali Hill in Bandra, Bombay. They were booked to leave on the *RMS Franconia*, a troopship that was scheduled to sail in a month from Bombay to Liverpool. Their home was filled with antiques, from rose wood furniture to glass lamps, exquisite four poster mahogany beds, Mughal paintings and carpets from Persia and Afghanistan. Then there were the two horses in the stable behind the bungalow, and the car, and jeep that Daniel used for hunting. He looked at the two stuffed tigers in his living room—should he leave them behind? And what to do about the three cats, two dogs and the Blue Fronted Amazonian talking parrot? Then there were the six servants who were hoping to covet what the Carrington's left behind. Should they take a few of them back to England too? It would be posh to have native servants back home. And finally, the house itself had to be sold. How much could they ferry to the docks in Bombay and onto a ship? There were load limitations, even if they bribed people at the docks, they could not take it all, or maybe they could…?

The docks in Bombay were streamlined for corruption. From dock bosses to cargo handlers, stealing merchandise brought them a sumptuous second salary. Working as a loader at the docks, and operating with arrogant impunity, was a small-time hoodlum, Abdul Karim Sher Khan, who people called Karim Lala. He was a six-foot Afghan man mountain, who had murdered his way from the Kunar province of Afghanistan to Bombay. He controlled a few illiterate but loyal Pashtun minions, who were willing to die for him. Like most crime organizations all over the world, one had to have common blood to belong. You had to be a Pashtun from Afghanistan to be included in Karim Lala's operations. Like his Italian criminal counterparts in New York City, Lala cast a suspicious eye on anyone whose blood did not run parallel to his own. As a Pathan, he despised Hindus for their idolatry and only tolerated Indian Muslims because the Koranic knot of Islam bound them together. The Pathans were regal looking: tall, broad body frames, aquiline noses and bushy beards made them a distinguished sight on Bombay streets. Legends of their physical prowess preceded them in the cities and towns they chose as their adoptive homes. A Pathan was rumoured to satisfy several women, one after the other, with his legendary well-endowed manhood. They were also indomitable fighters, perpetually armed with a curved butcher's knife hidden in their loose clothing. Their loyalty was never questioned and 'honour' was the rustic iron template which patterned their existence. They were known to stand by their word even if it culminated in death. An Afghan Pathan's 'promise' put an English 'gentleman's agreement' to shame. Charlie did not know Karim Lala personally. He had heard that he was a small-time gold and hashish smuggler but since they were going to be operating from the same geographical domain, Charlie had talked to him, and Lala had given Charlie his word that if the articles of Charlie's business did not involve gold or hashish, there would be no problems.

Back at his home, Charlie looked at the two men and his deep blue eyes twinkled. 'I know this, with a bribe, we can do this. The British have been doing this for almost two hundred years. These Indians have a backbone that supports corruption; it is the way they do business here.' Charlie looked at the two men, 'Well, what will it be? Cold rain in muggy England, or hot sunshine and wealth in India?' Thommo held out his arm and shook Charlie's hand, Willie did the same. Charlie smiled; they had reached a gentleman's agreement. 'Now, we drink,' he said. Charlie walked to his bar and came back with a bottle of Scotch. The men toasted each other.

'I'm going to tell you a story that is connected to Cross Island,' Charlie said as he settled in his rocking chair. 'What I am about to describe is documented fact. In 1553, Luis de Camoes, a Portuguese poet with strong royal connections was forced to leave Portugal. He left for Goa aboard the *São Bento*. Before he left, he raided the national treasury and loaded the ship with bar after bar of Portuguese gold. This was his poetic revenge on the royal court. He was arrested when he reached Goa, but by that time, the gold on the ship had disappeared. They had to let him go. What the poet had done was transfer the gold in the middle of the sea to a vessel bound for Bombay. They were then going to rendezvous in Bombay and sell the gold in the black market.

'Of course, when they reached Bombay, the ship's captain was nowhere to be found. He buried the gold on Cross Island while he bartered with the Bombay underground. One evening, drunk in a bar, he was killed in a knife fight and the gold...well, that's where the gold is. They say that there is no fresh water on

Cross Island, but my research says that he dumped the gold in a well that was later filled in.' Willie pointed his index finger at Charlie, his tone was argumentative: 'Someone would have tried finding it. I am sure you are not the only one who knows all this.' Charlie waved his hands in frustration. 'Yes, people have tried, many of them, but they were digging for gold. We will be digging for water—the source of that natural spring is where gold is. I am going to use the best water diviner that lives in India.'

The next morning Charlie called his foreman, said he was sick, a stomach ailment. He had to go see his doctor. He finished his eggs and bacon, took a long bath, grumbled about the heat and dressed himself in his Sunday best. He drove his car to Churchgate station; he had to know what she thought. Victoria Fernandes was an old friend, a retired nurse. Her two daughters had married Englishmen and were getting ready to sail to England. 'Ahaaa...Charlie,' she squealed, 'Good to see you. What happened? What are you doing here? You got sacked at the docks, or what?' 'I need to talk to you,' Charlie explained. Victoria pursed her wrinkled lips, rubbed the loose skin over her right cheekbone. 'Come in, Charlie,' she said, turning to her easy chair which sat before a decorative frame that held an English pastoral scene. She settled in and asked, 'Do you want some coffee? You never were the tea kind. Now that's not English, is it?' Charlie laughed. 'I don't feel English, Victoria, never have, you know that.' She smiled. Charlie looked at her: *She had been beautiful when she was younger; time is a thieving bastard, look at her now. Wonder what I will look like when I get long in the tooth?*

'Well, time's up, Charlie, I am going to miss you,' she said. 'All the King's horses, and all the King's men, could not hold this country together.' 'Yea,' Charlie mused, 'London Bridge is falling down, my fair lady.'

Charlie walked into her kitchen and came back with whisky and ice. 'I am not going to England,' he said. Victoria looked at him, through her round wire-framed glasses. 'Sit,' she ordered. 'Talk.' So Charlie told her. When Charlie mentioned Cross Island, Victoria's hand fluttered as she massaged her left breast and began rocking in her chair. Alarmed, Charlie thought she was having a heart attack. Victoria took off her glasses, and began polishing them with her handkerchief. She looked away from Charlie and said, 'I am not having a heart attack, but your idea of living on Cross Island feels like one.' Victoria peered at Charlie, 'I am going to explain this, just once. I have never talked about this; not even to my husband, God rest his soul... but you are my friend, and there is danger here, and you need to know.' Charlie nodded. 'I was seventeen years old, when I fell in love with an English boy. His name is not important. One night, we hired a boat and travelled to Cross Island. We made love, or had sex—whatever you want to call it. Then something happened for which I still have no explanation. Naked, lying there, I thought I saw something in the darkness, something moving without sound. We left soon after that. A week later my lover was dead. The post-mortem could not explain how he died. Nothing. A month passed and I received the stigmata.' 'The what!' exclaimed Charlie. 'This is a cock-and-bull story Victoria. What the hell are you talking about?' Victoria nodded, 'Perhaps, Charlie, perhaps...who's to tell...' Charlie was now visibly ruffled. He began massaging his beard, his nervous fingers squeezing the hair like he was trying to stop an involuntary muscle flutter. Victoria slowly began unbuttoning the top of her flowered dress. 'Aye, what are you doing?' Charlie gasped. Victoria smiled, a sad woebegone remembrance glinting from behind her glasses. She unhooked her black brassiere. Her shrivelled breasts hung down her chest. And there, there on the left side, was what seemed like a crude birthmark. 'What does it look like, Charlie?' She asked softly. 'Can you tell?' Victoria took her time as she got out of her chair. She stood before Charlie, who was now standing, a look of mortification on his face. Charlie looked at the mark; it looked like a small black hill. Victoria took his right hand and placed it on the disfiguration. 'This,' she said, 'is Cross Island. You can even see the one tree on the left side of the island, that's where I lost my virginity.'

Charlie averted his eyes as she fixed her brassiere and buttoned her dress. She smiled at his discomfort and said, 'Have another drink, Charlie. You might as well have lunch here, my friend.' Charlie walked to the kitchen and came back with the bottle of whisky. Victoria looked into his eyes. There was sadness in her voice. 'I am Catholic, Charlie, there is a crown of thorns on Cross Island, don't let them place it on your head.'

Charlie sat transfixed. Was the old girl losing her mind? She would not lie to him, Charlie knew that, and that's what made him uncomfortable. Perhaps, she is like the other Indians, she just wants us gone. After all these years of us being friends, this is what it comes down to.

***Charlie:** Dodo, what do you think?*

***Dodo:** If you don't like the facts being presented, Charlie, and you cannot refute them, you attack the credibility and morality of the person presenting the facts. This is one of the benchmarks of trial law; a tried and tested manoeuvre that lawyers employ. Sadly, it works, always. And that is what you are doing right now.*

***Charlie:** Shut up, Dodo...*

***Dodo:** Let me know what conclusion you come to. Attack your old friend, see where it goes.*

The bottle was half gone when Victoria returned and

began setting the table. 'Who were you talking to Charlie?' she asked. 'Oh, Charlie,' replied, 'It's an old habit. I talk to myself sometimes.' He moved to the dining table, clutching his bottle and glass. Victoria sat opposite Charlie. 'You're my friend, Charlie; I wouldn't lie to you. I don't need to, I don't have to. Do you understand?' Charlie nodded as he poured another drink.

'You know Bombay,' she said. 'Look at the crowds here. They sleep on the pavements; occupy any stretch of vacant land illegally. They live besides gutters and filth. Why, Charlie, why do you think that no one, no one has built their tin huts on Cross Island? It is a short boat ride away from mainland Bombay. What is stopping them from living there?' Charlie offered a lame answer. 'There is no water source there.' Victoria looked at him and shook her head. 'No, Charlie, they can ferry the water there.' 'That mark...it could be a skin disease,' Charlie tried to explain. 'I have been to five doctors. There is no explanation, except that it is a birthmark. But I know, it was not there when I was born. I am not going senile, Charlie.' There was a long uncomfortable silence before Victoria spoke again, 'I do not understand what is going on in India right now, politically or socially...I mean, how do you explain all this?' The meal finally over, Charlie said that he had to leave. He promised her he would return soon. As he shook her hand, Victoria said, 'Maya wrote me a letter.' Charlie froze. 'Yes, Charlie, she has always been in touch with me, I could not tell you all these years, I know you will not understand. I like her. I cannot tell you where she is. She made me swear I won't, years ago, when you...well...you know your history, Charlie. She is comfortable and happy. I think she felt, that maybe...you would go to England. She asked how you were.' Charlie heard her words, they seemed to be elongated and delivered in slow motion.

Charlie was mumbling now. 'After all these years, now you tell me this, you knew all along...Does she want to meet me? Is she here in India; she is here, isn't she?' Victoria took off her glasses and looked at Charlie in silence. He wanted to ask Victoria a final question about Maya although he knew what the outcome would sound like. Charlie waved a half goodbye, turned to leave...and then, a thunderbolt came out of the sky: 'Is Maya the reason why you need to stay in India?' Charlie could not differentiate the origin, or the male or female characteristics of the tone. Had Victoria spoken? Was it him talking aloud? Was Dodo intervening again? Charlie walked out of Victoria's home.

Alone in her home, feeling nostalgic, Maya decided to write another letter to Victoria.

Dear Victoria,

I suppose you received my letter. Thank you for writing back to me. The older I get, the more I seem to want to turn away from the threads that bind me to my past. I don't mean you, you know what I mean.

Maybe it is fear. Let sleeping dogs lie, that sort of thing. But, unfortunately, Charlie is a part of me and so is Caitlin Rafferty, my mother. I have no idea where she is. Maybe she is back in Ireland, or still in India. I don't know my parents; I will never know them, so, sometimes I think, what is the point in trying to go back into that world where there is, at least for me, the colour of darkness.

I had a dream the other night that I was standing alone on the Cliffs of Moher in Ireland, calling out to Caitlin. I have never been to Ireland, but like many people, I have seen pictures of this beautiful place; so why did I have this dream? Maybe because Caitlin was Irish? I don't know...

There is a legend about the mermaid of Moher. A local fisherman was fishing from the Cliffs of Moher. He noticed a beautiful mermaid sunbathing. He fell in love with her. Beside her, was her magic cloak that she needed to wear to go back to the sea. The fisherman snatched the cloak ran to his home and hid it. She followed him to his house, begged and pleaded for her cloak, but he refused to tell her where he had hidden it. Since she could not go back to the sea, she accepted his proposal, married him and they had a daughter. She had always longed to go back, and one sunny day, the mermaid discovered the cloak and went back home to the sea. The fisherman, when he got back, wept for her, then went out to sea and never returned. The daughter lived on the Cliffs of Moher, all her life in solitude, watching the sea, waiting. Hoping...

Victoria, there are times when I feel like that girl from the Cliffs of Moher; watching, waiting, hoping...

Sometimes, as I sit in my living room or in a park, I wonder what it would have been like to live with Charlie and Caitlin. From what you have told me, it would have been hell, so there goes another fantasy. My adoptive parents are as normal as it gets, boring but normal. It is not that I don't appreciate them but something is missing. I don't know what it is. From what you have told me, I have my father's deep blue eyes, and some of his rebellion. You have not seen me since I was taken away. That seems like such a sad line. I feel that loneliness sometimes. The fact that I was abandoned adds to the misery and pain.

Victoria, if I met Charlie at this stage, I am afraid that I would want to stay with him, and from what you have told me, his life is still wild and unpredictable. I do not want to be trapped in that situation. I think that it is enough for me to know that he is alive, happy and free. I wish him well, but do not want to be a part of his life, much of which is in direct confrontation with things that I believe in.

Do I come across as selfish? Perhaps I do. But Victoria, I am just trying to protect myself. I do hope that you understand.

Maybe one day, Charlie and I will meet, maybe. I am aware through your letters, how much he wants to see me. I think it is his guilt that he wants to erase in some way. I don't know. I am just guessing here.

When I go to the park and see families...the father, mother, a little child giggling as she swings, I want that. I could have had that. Why I was denied that experience, we will never know. Some part of me sometimes wants to sit with Charlie, understand him, talk to him, lay my head on his shoulder and cry, love him... but that fantasy will never happen, because...it is better this way, I think, because...I don't know, Victoria, I don't know.

I will write you another letter soon. I have been seeing a boy, I will tell you about him in my next letter. I also have a new job. More of that later.

I wish you well. I hope your health is good. Bye for now.

Sincerely,

Maya

Chapter 6

Voices of Graveyard Flowers

The next morning, *The Sea Horse* docked alongside. Charlie, who was the captain of the port, was busy; Thommo and Willie were on the ship's deck supervising the unloading. When they met for lunch, Charlie said, 'Tonight at my home. We need to talk.' 'What happened to you yesterday?' Willie asked. 'We heard you were sick.' 'Oh! It was nothing; I had to go see a woman.' Thommo smirked, 'You dirty dog.' Charlie let it slide. 'Tonight, be there, eight.'

Charlie had the bottle out. After the men settled in his living room, Charlie told them what Victoria had said about Cross Island. Thommo slapped his thigh, he laughed so hard that he spilled his drink. Willie looked perplexed, 'Come on, Charlie, don't tell me you believe what this old cow is telling you. This is superstition mixed with ignorance. She has some skin disease and she's making up this Cross Island story.' Thommo pointed at Charlie, 'You've been here too long, ol' chap, their fokkin' brown skin is rubbing off on you.' 'Yes,' agreed Willie, 'You are beginning to sound like an ignorant coolie.' Charlie stroked his beard, 'I don't know,' he said, 'I've known her since I was a twenty-one-year old lad. She knows things about me that no one else does. She is my friend. She really cares about what could happen to me.' Thommo looked at Charlie and said, 'Do you want to do this, or don't you? Think about it. It really is that simple. You get us fired up and then you invent a problem. This is a ghost story, meant to frighten little children. What the fok' do you want Charlie? That old lady probably needs a bat in her attic. I could satisfy that urge, one for the cause, you know.' 'Don't talk about her like that,' Charlie growled. 'She's better than all three of us.' Willie shook his head in amusement. He looked at Charlie the way you look at an imbecile and Charlie began to feel anger welling up from the humiliation and open scorn he was being lambasted with. 'We'll talk about this tomorrow,' he said, 'I need to get to bed. It's been a long day.'

Lying in the darkness, listening to the rotation of the fan blades, sleep would not come. The black mark on Victoria's breast kept flashing in his mind. The real Cross Island appeared, then that dark mark, that one tree on the island, the shadow of that one tree on her breast, exactly where the tree on the Island was...'What do you think, Dodo?' Silence. 'Dodo!' The fan above whirred its wind song and eventually Charlie drifted off into slumber. A nightmare rudely awoke him at six in the morning. A lunatic, with enlarged pupils, had been whispering in his brain; as the whitewashed eyelashes fluttered, the albino face smiled displaying a decaying mouth, and from that rot, a small voice...'The happiness of a mad man, only a mad man will know, only a mad man...' Years later, this fractured whisper would take over Charlie's reality and destroy his sanity.

Charlie knew many of the locals in Bombay; he understood their sentiments, their nuances, their actions and reactions. The fact that he had converted to Hinduism made him a compatriot in faith. He was close to many of them and often helped them out by supplying them with small things, like tools, paint and cement that they needed for their homes. Charlie now decided to test market Cross Island.

Dev Kumar was a friend who now worked for the new government in the Bombay municipality as a civil engineer. He was an educated man, a smart man who always applied logic and reasoning to any given situation. A well-read man, he loved English literature. Lord Byron and John Donne were his favorite poets. 'I heard someone talking about Cross Island,' Charlie said hoping the sentence would appear as nonchalant jibber-jabber. Dev looked sharply at Charlie. 'The place is haunted, you know. That's what everybody says.' 'What do you mean?' Charlie asked. 'There is this story that my father told me,' Dev said. 'My father had once gone out to Cross Island. This is what he says he saw.' 'Did you believe him?' Charlie countered. 'I don't know, Charlie. My father used to drink a lot but he never exaggerated; anyway I never asked him what he was doing out there, and I am sure he would not tell me. What he saw was a woman walking naked and alone. Her menstrual blood left a trail, and her feet made no sound. Also, there were no footprints on the soft mud on Cross Island. Naked and lonely, sad and frightening she looked, that is what he said. He told me this because I had mentioned that I was thinking of taking my family on a picnic to Cross Island. I've always been curious about that place. No one lives there and I wanted to see that canon. It seemed like a harmless place. My father took me into another room because he didn't want my wife listening to what he had to say. If his story was meant to frighten me, well, it did.' 'Was the woman Indian or British?' Charlie asked. 'I don't know,' Dev replied, 'that was the story I heard, and he never talked about it again. I took my family to Elephanta Caves instead after hearing his story. I mean why take a chance, Charlie? You're going to ask me if I believe it is haunted...Well, my reasoning will say no; but there are too many stories, and that is why the locals leave it alone. They say many murders have taken place there, child sacrifices...horrible things, Charlie, bad things, very bad...Anyway why do you want to know about Cross Island? There is nothing there and, Charlie, I'm sure you'll be leaving India soon, won't you? You have to come home and have a meal with my family before you leave; promise.' 'Yes, I will, Dev,' Charlie said, 'Say hello to your wife and children. Tell them Uncle Charlie will see them soon.' The men shook hands and as Charlie half turned to walk away; he looked at Dev and said, 'Do you really believe all that? You're not a superstitious man. I know you.' Dev was silent. 'This is clash of education and culture, Charlie. My answer is yes and no. In the end, my friend, I don't know.' Charlie nodded. He knew Dev was being as truthful as his upbringing, religion and immediate society would allow.

Another local, Mukesh Saxena, a Hindi-language teacher at the local college that Charlie talked to simply referred to Cross Island as bhooth bangla, the haunted house. When Charlie asked him why, he said, 'Char-lee, many people say so, my father, mother, grandfather...everyone. People say, you go there, you die. Many people say suicides happened there. Bad place, that Cross Island.' 'How do you know this is all true?' Charlie asked. 'I don't know, Char-lee?' Saxena said, 'I cannot prove nothing.' 'This is all ignorance and superstition. You know that...' Charlie tried to explain. Saxena interrupted Charlie, 'Once my mother told me that her mother went to Cross Island and some months after that she got a bad black mark on left side of chest. I don't know, Char-lee, I just heard that when I was little boy...' Charlie's voice emerged from his open mouth as a horrified croak. 'Whaaat?' Saxena became alarmed. 'Char-lee, arre why for are you shouting?' 'Are you sure, Mukesh? That is what you heard?' Charlie asked. 'Yes,' Saxena replied, 'our whole family knows that.' Charlie looked at Saxena silently for a long time. 'You are making me very much afraid, Char-lee, what is problem?' Charlie had managed regain his composure. He smiled at Saxena, 'Nothing, nothing. Just the heat, I guess. I will see you soon.'

The next day Charlie arrived at The Mulberry Bush early. The bartender peered at him with an evil eye, 'If you intend to start a fight here with those hoodlum friends of yours then you had better keep walking the other way.' Charlie smiled, 'No trouble,' he said, 'I promise.' To his surprise there were six Indians sitting at one of the tables. Charlie walked to the bar and ordered a whisky. The Mulberry Bush had been his 'local pub' for years now. He liked the owner who ran the place. Charlie downed his drink and ordered another. As the bartender served him, Charlie asked his question in what he hoped was a non-committal voice: 'Hey Tom, what do you know of Cross Island?' 'What everybody knows,' Tom shot back. 'That it is haunted and no one lives there, and it's a dry dung heap that nobody gives a damn about.' 'Nah,' said Charlie, 'that's all ignorant superstition that comes from poor education and fish-wife chatter, you know that.' 'I hear what I hear Charlie,' Tom said as he moved away to serve an Indian customer who had walked to the bar. He then walked back, tapped Charlie on his left shoulder and said, 'Let me tell you a story. November 1922. Howard Carter, the English archaeologist discovered the tomb of Tutankhamun, you know...King Tut, the Boy King?' Charlie nodded. 'What you may not know,' Tom continued, 'is that the famous Egyptologist James Henry Breasted who worked with Carter on the tomb later said that during this excavation, Carter had dispatched a young boy to his house to get something he needed. When this boy entered Carter's home, he heard a soft far-off childlike lament. When he looked at the bird cage that held Carter's pet canary, there was a cobra in the cage, and from its mouth dangled the bloody canary. You know what the symbol of Egyptian monarchy is Charlie? Make an uneducated guess...' 'A cobra,' Charlie answered. Tom nodded menacingly, bent low and whispered theatrically into Charlie's ear, 'Twelve men who worked with Carter when he opened Tutankhamun's tomb died soon after, including the Earl of Carnarvon, who had the nerve to finance the entire excavation. This tomb had remained undiscovered for three thousand years. They could not, and did not, and would not, let the dead king rest in peace. There is a price to pay for disturbing the lives of the dead, Charlie. Remember that.' As Tom walked away, Charlie heard an Indian voice say, 'Excuse me, sir.' Charlie turned and looked in the direction the voice was coming from. It was a man from a table close to Charlie's bar stool. 'So sorry, sir,' he was saying, 'but I could not help listen to what the bartender was saying. I also have a story like that.' Charlie was about to snub him. Tell him that it was impolite to eavesdrop on conversations he was no part of, but he decided to listen, he had time.

The Indian moved to the stool besides Charlie. 'See sir, the Hope Diamond is the most famous diamond in the world, no...I am sure you know that, sir. It is the biggest deep blue diamond in the world and it was stolen from our India, from a temple dedicated to Sita, you know the Hindu goddess who was the wife of Rama. The Hope Diamond was in her forehead; her third eye, some very bad person robbed it. I don't know how, but it landed in the hands of King Louis XVI of France. Princess de Lamballie and Marie Antoinette both wore this diamond. All their heads were chopped off during the French Revolution. You know, I am studying French at college, my teacher was just saying this the other day. After that, fourteen people who were connected with the Hope Diamond died, just like that, my teacher told me this.' Charlie sighed, called for another drink, thanked the young man and hoped that he did not have any more stories. The man nodded his head, 'Just thought that you might like to hear the story.' Charlie thanked him again, looked away, hoping that he would leave. The man seemed to sense that Charlie wanted to be left alone now. He turned and joined his friends at their table.

Soon Thommo and Willie walked in. Thommo looked at the Indians and stopped, then walked to their table. The bartender approached Thommo, the cricket bat in his hand swinging. Thommo slapped one of the Indians lightly on his shoulder, laughed at nothing and walked to the bar. Charlie shook his head and smiled. Willie said, 'Well, seems like old Thommo does not want to play cricket today!' They moved to a vacant table, ordered drinks and Thommo looked at Charlie, 'Well,' he said, 'Are we going to do this?' Charlie looked at both men. 'Yes,' he said. Charlie began talking, outlining the plan. The three men were first going to contact Englishmen who wanted to live in India 'dead or alive,' Charlie said. 'All the materials we need are there in the docks. We steal it all. I can arrange that. We need a large boat with a good engine to ferry us across the mainland to Cross Island; that is there too, sitting pretty, stored in one of the warehouses. I've been planning this for years. This is the time to do this, the Indians are engulfed in this mindless communal violence, hopefully the riots continue, it is a great smokescreen.' They discussed the start to the Cross Island venture for another two hours.

At the far corner of the bar, the group of Indians was raucously arguing about independence in loud drunken voices. 'These gora baas-turds made all this dirty mess and now they are going.' Waving his whisky glass of ice cubes and Dutch courage, his amplified insult was heard by everyone in the bar. Momentarily Charlie's anger flared at the open disrespect, but he calmed down, walked across the bar to the Indians and poked one of them on his left shoulder. 'You people were being buggered by your corrupt bloody rulers before the British got here,' Charlie said through clenched teeth, 'read your Maharaja and dynastic history before you give me "the Goras are responsible for all the corruption cow shit".' Charlie turned and began walking back to his friends. One of the Indians shouted an obscene comment. Charlie heard the word gora that was spat with venom again followed by a vulgar Hindi obscenity that suggested he fornicate with his mother. Charlie understood Hindi; Thommo too understood the vile insult. He was out of his chair like a stone from a catapult. Willie moved fast and shouted, 'This is not worth a fokkin' fight, we have better things to do. Let's go.' He stopped Thommo's rush, grabbed Charlie by his arm and hustled them towards the door as he watched the bartender swing his bat.

As they walked out, Thommo casually said to the bartender, 'Hey Tom, you have the bat, but I have the balls, hard fast ones.' Tom laughed, 'Anytime you want to play Thommo, anytime.'

Chapter 7

A Choir of Corruption

The next day at the docks Charlie was summoned to a meeting. A letter had arrived from the new chief minister of Bombay State, Balasaheb Gangadhar, popularly known as B.G. Kher. In a year's time, the letter stated, all 'foreign nationals' would be replaced by qualified Indians at the docks in Bombay. The Indians were moving fast amid the chaos, Charlie thought. On the day of Independence, J.S. Bharucha was asked to head the Bombay Police Force. Charlie had seen a photograph in the newspaper as he formally took over from the last British Commissioner A.E. Caffin. Charlie had read about Kher and Bharucha. He needed the cooperation of their departments if he were to survive on Cross Island. Word on the street had it that the two men were incorruptible. Not good, Charlie thought, but they both had assistants and Charlie knew he could make a deal with them. When he met Thommo and Willie at lunch time he told them of the letter. The men were not surprised. 'Well, it had to come,' Willie explained, 'They don't want us around anymore and even if they did, professionally, it wouldn't look good for them to be seen relying on us. They need to show the world that they can handle this thing on their own.' Charlie led them to a large tin shack which had a heavy padlock on the door. He inserted the key and swung open the double doors; and there, resting on a wooden custom cradle was their boat. 'This here used to be a supply boat, to ships that were too large to dock alongside,' he explained. 'The engine went out and so they abandoned her. I've asked an engineer to repair her. Willie, I will need an invoice from the office authorizing this repair. State that we need her for supply reasons. I don't care what you say; just make it official so that we can get the money for the repairs, a new paint job and anything else that needs to be replaced. I need you to inspect the boat and make a list. Change everything, seats, lights, everything. It is not our money. Can you do it?' 'Sure,' Willie nodded. 'And,' Charlie continued, 'paint a big India flag on her starboard.' 'We need to call her something,' Thommo mused, 'Maybe an Indian god or goddess or maybe we should just fokkin' call her "Jinnah of Pakistan".' The men laughed at Thommo's black humour. 'Yes, great idea,' said Charlie with scorn. 'Nice name for a Hindu funeral pyre.' As the men walked away from the shed, Charlie said, 'We have six months to get everything done here before we move permanently to Cross Island. We'll meet a week from now at my place and coordinate. And remember,' Charlie cautioned, 'no women on the island. We don't need girlfriends or wives, even if they are Anglo-Indian.'

In anglicized places like Calcutta, Bombay and Madras 'dark blood' and white skin often cohabited. It was no secret that many young British men, far from home, distraught by rivers of hot molten wet dreams, sought to sow their hard white oats by having 'a taste of the natives'. Sometimes, these dark lusty dalliances metamorphosed into love and marriage, and produced little Anglo-Indian babies, at other times it led to disaster, considering the general Indian mentality of social and religious conservativeness and white British racism.

Saturday night, Thommo and Willie sat at Charlie's home. Charlie's eyes twinkled. 'I can't believe we're going to do this. It's really going to happen. I know it now. Look here,' he said, jabbing at a note pad. 'I have the type of men picked out and I have added four women.' Thommo looked startled. 'Women? I thought you said no women.' Charlie smiled. 'I thought about it, we need these women to do chores and help around, do the laundry, cook, but the main reason I am bringing them along is...' Charlie paused. Willie and Thommo looked at him quizzically; and then Charlie raised his forefinger and said, 'They are the brothel. We need them for that, to ease tensions, to have some fun, you know. I am aware what English bachelors in Bombay do. I have talked to the four girls. We have arrived at a salary for them.' Thommo threw back his head and slapped his thigh so violently; Charlie thought he was having a seizure. 'Ahaaa...' he shouted, 'Charlie, you fokkin' dirty diseased dog, fok'...what a brilliant idea.' 'Are they Indian or English?' Willie wanted to know. Charlie smiled, 'Irish,' he said, 'let's keep this British.'

It took three weeks for the boat to be repaired and painted. The engineer assured Charlie that the boat's engine was as good as new. She now glistened with white paint, and the Indian flag on her starboard seemed to flutter in the wind. 'What are you going to call her, boss?' the painter asked. Charlie smiled and his eyes had a faraway look. '*S.P. Maya*,' he said softly, '*Sea Princess Maya*. Paint that in red on the upper part of her port side. God, she's beautiful.'

Victoria had written to Maya detailing Charlie's Cross Island venture. Maya replied, quickly this time.

Dear Victoria,

I have to thank you for not letting Charlie know where I am. I know that it is a difficult position that I put you in, but I think it is the right thing, for now at least. This Cross Island business that Charlie is involved with can only bring disaster. It is illegal and wrong. There is something criminal about it all, Victoria. I don't know what else to say.

As promised in my last letter, I will tell you about my job and the boy I have been seeing. First the job. As you know, I graduated college with a degree in English Literature. I think Charlie's fondness for reading has somehow rubbed off on me. I have found a job as a trainee sub-editor with a publishing house that deals with children's books. One day, I hope to write one, maybe many. I have always liked writing.

Now about the boy. He is around my age. His name is Burt Slater. We get along with a few disagreements. We have been seeing each other for about eight months now. It seems to be going well. But, I still have not told him that I am adopted. If I did that, I would have to tell him what happened and why my parents abandoned me. I don't know, Victoria...I don't know what I am ashamed of—the fact that my real father is what he is; a dangerous man without morals or conscience? That he does not care who dies, so long as he gets what he wants. I mean, what will Burt think of me? With a father like that...Burt comes from a very conventional, religious family and the fact that I am a bastard child might be a problem. Victoria, I have to live with the consequences of what my parents did, whether I like it or not! I can lie to Burt about my real parents, but that I would never do. In many ways, I am not like Charlie and I must confess that I despise his ways. I know you tell me the truth about him in your letters and I know that you love him in your own way, and so do I, but there is no way that I am like him and perhaps that is the reason why I do not want to see Charlie. If we ever met, I would have to tell him how disgusted I am, at the way he has chosen to live his life and still...he is my father. What a tragedy this is, Victoria!

I must stop writing now, as this is very upsetting and it is filling me with a sadness that I do not want, but have to deal with.

Victoria, maybe if I met Charlie I could manage to put some common sense into his brain. I have to think about this.

Sincerely,
Maya

At the docks, Charlie and Willie began earmarking the things they needed to steal. They contacted the burgeoning black-market shadow people in Bombay's underground, and supplies began moving out of the docks on a regular basis. This was their savings account. Charlie stashed the money, the old-fashioned way, under his bed.

And then came the hard part. Charlie had to get through personnel at the office of the chief minister. He needed an official document that stated that Charlie's company was going to lease Cross Island for five years to export Indian goods to Europe and import foreign goods back to India. He had to prove to them that this was an official venture of the Victoria Docks. He then had to submit this document to the police department, who would certify all the documents and then hand them over to the State. It took him three weeks of working through a contact and a local lawyer to get the paperwork done. He visited the police headquarters and walked into a concrete wall. Charlie discovered, much to his consternation and chagrin that his money could not talk here. He would have to wait. 'Where is the registration for this new company?' An assistant to the police chief demanded. 'What you have here, is not a proper official document. This will not do.' When Charlie contacted the lawyer who had helped draw up the various documents, the lawyer scoffed, 'These people are just trying to make trouble. I will arrange for the registration.' When Charlie returned to the police station with the registration, the assistant was on 'sick leave'. They informed Charlie that he would have to wait, as the assistant was the only one who could authorize anything to do with the Cross Island venture. After a week Charlie returned to the police station. The assistant was there. Charlie politely asked about his health as the assistant thumbed through the papers. 'We need proper authorization from Victoria Docks, stating that they are sanctioning this,' he said. 'You will have to get that from the Bombay Port Trust.'

Charlie explained the problem to Willie. 'We will never get the Bombay Port Trust to sanction this on behalf of Victoria Docks,' Charlie said. Willie smiled. 'Yes, we can,' he said quietly, 'I know someone who works there. Through Willie's contact, Bombay Port Trust stationary was stolen; a letter of authorization and the appropriate signatures were forged and Charlie went back to the police station. As he handed the document over to the assistant Charlie thought, 'If this idiot cross checks this, we are doomed.' The assistant worked in slow motion, checking each page in the Cross Island file. Finally he seemed satisfied. 'Come back in three weeks,' he said, 'I will get all this authorized and cleared; and one more thing...' Charlie sighed, 'Now what?' he thought. 'I need a written authorization from the docks that this project is insured by the same company that represents Victoria docks. I will also need the insurance papers. That is all.' 'Why couldn't he have told me all this in the beginning,' Charlie thought, 'My God! How are these people going to govern this country?'

Anglo-Indian Rory Dawson was the Administrative Manager at the Victoria Docks. Charlie also knew that he would refuse to sign a document of insurance using a fake company. Once again, Willie's conniving mind helped solve the problem by unearthing Dawson's corruption. Dawson was involved with innumerable schemes at the docks that paid for his luxurious lifestyle and debts incurred due to his gambling addiction. Thommo cornered him on the deck of a ship, flashed his knife, told him that if he did not consent to this, they were going to expose all his corrupt dealings. Dawson smiled. He had heard of Thommo's violence. Dawson was no choir boy. The knife did not bother him. He was used to the corrosive acid that flowed through the intestines of the underbelly at the docks. He explained the logistical foolishness and the danger behind Thommo's request. 'For this to happen, the insurance company will have to be bribed, the head of dock operations will have to be bribed, all the signatories on your fake document will have to be taken care of, it's too complicated.' 'Do it,' Thommo hissed, 'I have the money.' Dawson shook his head, said it was impossible. Thommo smiled as Dawson argued; and then brutally cut into his remonstrations. 'I know where you live,' Thommo said in a low growl, 'I know you have four children and a nice English wife, a girl from Croydon, right?' If Dawson refused, Thommo snarled, his wife was going to be brutally assaulted and raped. Thommo explained in excruciating detail what he would do to her. Dawson began sweating in the shade. He was numbed by Thommo's Luciferian moxie, but he knew, as his nerve ends perspired that Thommo's evil was no empty threat. 'And after I am finished with her, what are you fokkin' going to do? Complain to management? Go to the police?' Thommo laughed. Eventually, Dawson drew up the document of insurance, and signed a letter of authorization. Thommo handed Dawson an envelope for his cooperation and said, 'Thank you Rory, now don't go spending this shuffling marked cards, buy the children something nice and say hello to the Missus for me.'

And so, the Cross Island venture began; a house of sand, in the middle of the heaving Arabian Sea.

When they visited the island, Charlie was surprised that it was bigger than it looked. He gazed at the far end and spied the lone tree on the left of the island, and thought of Victoria Fernandes and her stigmata. On the island, Charlie began jotting down notes: 'Have to build proper stone steps. Wider. Stronger.' They walked to the edge where an old cannon lay, disgraced by nature's elements. 'What did they use it for?' Charlie wondered aloud. 'I heard,' Willie exclaimed, 'the English built this fortification to defend ships going into the harbour from sea pirates.' As they walked to the far left of the cannon, Charlie noticed the edge of a flat stone protruding through the leaves of a thicket. He began tearing the branches away, helped by Thommo and Willie; and there, what had been obscured by the thick bush for decades was now partially visible. It was a square stone altar, set on a four-foot pedestal of bricks. They quickly tore away the rest of the foliage. On the altar was a weather-beaten cracked black statue of Goddess Kali, dancing on the body of Shiva. Her dead shark eyes gleamed with vengeance, ten bejewelled arms flailed, and her large protruding crimson tongue stuck out of her mouth like a blood-soaked sponge.

Charlie stared at the altar, stone cold.

Full moon. Deserted island. Kidnapped six-month-old baby girl crushed to a man's chest. She struggles, whimpers, cries. Child placed on stone. Flowered frock torn from body. Sandalwood paste smeared. Jagged knife rips; from tip of sternum to pubic area. Child's eyes widen; mouth snaps opens. Gurgling sounds. There is blood. Warm. Bubbling. Spurting. Flowing down tender brown skin. Child shudders involuntarily, small fingers flex. One hand moves. Last helpless reflex; towards gaping stomach. Man forces hand into chest cavity. Baby still alive. Grabs infant heart. One strong wrench, a twist. Heart offered to Kali. Folded hands. A prayer. A bow. Body stuffed into gunny sack. He dips forefinger in blood. Reverently anoints his forehead, and leaves. Cannot look back. Sacred sacrifice Tantra scripture warns: 'Kali eats while humble offering still warm. Do not disturb. If satisfied, the wish of the person, in whose noble name the sacrificial offer has been made, will definitely be granted.'

Charlie felt sweat trickle down from the nape of his neck and travel down the skin of his spine. He touched his abdomen. 'My God! The stories are true,' he thought, 'this is where child sacrifices used to take place.' Around the statue's neck was a garland of fifty small white plastic skulls. Thommo was watching. He saw the frigid immobility, the flash rigor mortis set into Charlie's body; instinctively he knew what Charlie was thinking. Affectionately, Thommo wrapped his arm around Charlie's shoulder. 'Let it go mate,' he said softly in a rare tone of sympathy. 'We will come and live here. There will be no more dying.' On the way back, Charlie wrote in his book, 'Ask contractor to destroy altar, take Kali away.'

Chapter 8

A Thorn in the Cross

Charlie first heard about Detective D.H. Desai through a police contact. In many ways he had been anticipating this; still what he heard was disturbing because it could spike the momentum that the Cross Island project had attained. Desai had begun investigating what was happening on Cross Island, cross checking all existing documents. Charlie knew that the spotlight would expose the cover up, and if this got out through the smoke tunnels that he had constructed, it could mean trouble. Desai worked with the police department as head of the detective branch and Charlie's source whispered that Desai wanted to 'make a name for himself'. When he heard that Desai had a little team who regularly discussed Charlie Strongbow and Cross Island in the back rooms of the police headquarters, Charlie decided that he had to do something.

He concluded that he needed to provide a derailment, fire and death, that would throw the police department off his track.

The next morning, Desai's name was in all the newspapers. The detective swore to reporters that he would find the culprits who had done this.

Dodo arrived.

Dodo: *So my boy, happy with your handiwork? A masterpiece painted by Caravaggio, full of subtle light and deep darkness.*

Charlie: *It was that or lose all that I have been working for.*

Dodo: *Ahaaaa...oh! You didn't know that this would happen? After all your time here in India, you didn't know that this would be the reaction? You did this to your own people? You consider yourself an Indian, a holy man; Brahmin. You have lost all moral right to be here. Go back to England or whatever shit-hole your filthy murderous heredity comes from, you don't belong here. This is a mortal sin.*

Charlie: *I am not a Christian. How many times do I have to underline that?*

Dodo: *So you are a Hindu, eh? Brahmin...Hindu...yes! If reincarnation is a reality then you will be born a diseased cow in your next life and my god, I hope that someone slits your throat and throws your carcass into a sewer.*

Charlie: *Don't get dramatic, little man. You sound like a bad Shakespearian character. This conversation is over.*

The next week, Charlie met with the architect that the contractor had recommended. He showed him the scribbles that he had done. All the structures, Charlie explained were going to be constructed of wood with asbestos roofing. The architect promised that he would have the blueprints ready in three weeks. Six days later, the architect's son arrived to meet Charlie. The architect had died. Heart attack.

Sunday morning, Thommo was at Charlie's home when they heard three knocks on the door. Charlie walked to the door, opened it and suppressed the surprise he felt. 'May I enter, sir?' the uniformed man asked, ever so polite. Charlie instinctively knew who he was. He feigned astonishment and inquired 'Who are you?' 'I am from the police department, Detective D.H. Desai.' Charlie invited him in, shook his hand saying, 'I am Charlie Strongbow.' He introduced him to Thommo and asked, 'Why are you here? What can I do to help you?' Desai smiled as he sat down on Charlie's couch. 'I am looking into the case of a pig's head thrown into a mosque, I want to know why and other things and...' 'Why are you here?' Charlie questioned, rudely interrupting Desai. 'Eight people died in riots that followed, many poor people injured, many people's property destroyed,' Desai explained patiently. 'A vendor at slaughter house, he is saying that he sold pig to a big English man. Not full pig body, just head. He is sure, sir, that he can identify the face of fellow who he sold pig's head to. Somehow, what he is saying fits your good self, sir. I would much like to arrange meeting between two of you. Will not take very long.' 'We English eat pork all the time, you know that, don't you?' Charlie said; his voice was gentle. 'There are so many Englishmen in Bombay who have a beard like I do,' Charlie said calmly. 'That may very well be case, sir,' Desai persisted, 'but still, we be needing to do this. If you are not minding very much, sir, we have to have meeting, otherwise you and me have to go police station now.' Charlie wanted to smash the fake politeness from Desai's countenance. Thommo was glaring at Desai, a murderous look in his eyes. Charlie hoped that Thommo would keep his mouth shut, and his fists to himself. Suddenly Charlie exclaimed, 'Sure, sure, fix the meeting for the end of the week. I will accompany you to the slaughterhouse Friday evening, not a problem. Thank you for coming.' 'Many thanks to yourself,' Desai said as he got out of the chair and headed for the door. When the door closed behind Desai, Charlie looked at Thommo and laughed, 'We are not going to kill him. That would complicate things.' Thommo sat still, just looking at Charlie. 'You have a better way?' he asked. 'Yes,' confirmed Charlie, 'Yes, I have. He is extremely clever, Thommo, see, he did not mention Cross Island, not once. That is what this is all about. You will have to help me here. It's a job tailor made for you.'

Monday morning, Charlie citing official dock work requested a meeting with Desai's boss, Mr S.V. Raman. A meeting was scheduled. Raman was a busy man. 'You have five minutes,' he growled, 'What is the problem here?' Charlie had his briefcase of documents, but Raman was not interested in them. 'What is the problem?' he repeated. 'One of your detectives, Desai, is a drug smuggler,' Charlie explained. He has been obtaining hashish from the docks and storing it in a shed in his garden. He then sells it in the underground market.' 'Is he getting this from the Afghan, that Karim Lala fellow?' Raman wanted to know. 'I don't know,' Charlie said. 'What I know is that I opposed his small business and presence at the docks, and now he is making trouble for us. Unnecessary harassment. He is interfering with official dock work, using his position and authority. This has to stop. I have come here to you for help.' 'How do I know what you are telling me is the truth?' Raman asked. Charlie was ready with his answer. 'Raid his home tonight. Check the shed in his garden. I have heard through my sources that he is going to make a deal tonight. I have witnesses who are ready to state that Desai is dealing with them.' Charlie was lying about the witnesses and hoped that Raman would not call his bluff. 'I hope,' Charlie continued, 'that you will treat this as confidential, otherwise my life could be in danger.'

Fortunately for Charlie, Desai had not conferred with his superiors about his suspicion that Charlie could be behind the pig's head incidence. Desai made one fatal mistake. According to police protocol, he should have filed an official report about his suspicions. Raman needed to keep this under wraps. If a politician heard about this, there would be questions, and maybe an uncomfortable inquiry of his department. 'I will see what I can do about this,' was all Raman had to say.

After Charlie had left, Raman summoned two of his trusted aides. He instructed them to go to Desai's home, with an official search warrant. Desai was not at home when they arrived. They searched the house, then moved to the garden. His wife unlocked the garden shed and after a five-minute search they found a gunny sack hidden behind some boxes of cement. Inside the sack was half a kilo of hashish. The same night, his pet, a magnificent purebred German Shepherd was discovered by Desai's four-year-old daughter, dead in the garden. When Desai got home that night, his wife told him what had happened. 'They said that you have to report to the police station in the morning, otherwise an arrest warrant will be issued,' she said through tears. Desai's daughter was hysterical with fright and sadness. He walked to the dog kennel and saw the dried yellow froth on his dog's mouth. He knew with certainty that his pet had been poisoned. Desai sank to the grass, cradled his pet's head in his arms and wept.

He now knew that if he persisted, and went after Charlie, his daughter would be in danger, then his wife. He knew that the hashish had been planted in his shed. When Desai stood before Raman, he was asked if he had anything to say. Desai hung his head and decided to stay silent. Raman was a shrewd intuitive man. 'There is something going on here, I don't understand right now. Your silence and refusal to defend yourself, or explain...it is rather strange. I have heard that you are an honest man, a man who wanted to do your job, and do it well. So what happened...?' Desai looked down at the floor, silent in his misery. Frustrated, Raman said, 'This is what I am going to do. I am going to issue a temporary transfer for you to Calcutta until I can sort this all out. Something tells me that sacking you will not solve this problem. There is more to this, much more, I feel that. If all goes well for you, after the inquiry, you will be reinstated. Once again I ask you, do you have anything to say?' Desai shook his head indicating a negative reply.

Desai warned his two associate detectives to lay off the pig's head case and Cross Island. He told them what had happened. The men needed their well-paying jobs. Desai's wife, trembling with raw fear and anxiety asked, 'Is this worth our lives? What is wrong with you? Moti died. We are Hindu; let Muslims take care of pigs in their mosques. And why do you care what those goras do?' Desai did not answer but continued to pack. The personnel at police headquarters had been told that Desai was being transferred because he had been interfering with the legitimate work the Victoria Docks was conducting on Cross Island; and the only two people, the associate detectives who thought that Charlie might be connected to the pig's head in the mosque, shut their mouths and continued with their daily routines. Back at the docks, Charlie heard the news about Desai's transfer. Charlie smiled and thought, 'It's just the way things are here, it's easy to manipulate the system. Thank God, there is no cure for it.'

Back in his home, Charlie began to pace in his living room contemplating his next move.

One, two, three, four.

Turn.

One, two, three, four.

Turn.

Somewhere a rooster crowed, he heard the motor of a truck growling. The pace quickened.

One, two, three, four.

Turn.

A Stone Age rhythm began. Sounds of pulverizing primitivism, sticks on animal skin, drum rolls ascending, as warning smoke signals spat crackling electrical charges.

The beginnings of a good old-fashioned auditory hallucination.

'There is a pattern here; there is danger here, Charlie.'

'This is not Dodo,' Charlie thought. 'Who is this?'

Stressed syllables bounced in his larynx, squeezed through his throat, and ricocheted out of his mouth like a stutterer consumed by high anxiety pleading to be understood. His body metamorphosed into a spasmodic marionette; and from afar he heard the woman at the control bar laugh. Suddenly she was there, staring into his anguished eyes. Her clawed fingernails penetrated his skull. Charlie fell to the floor like an animal in its death throes, moaning and twisting with agony. As the woman turned to leave, she sniggered, 'Thank God, there is no cure for it.'

Chapter 9

Shadows of Darkness

The next day, he visited an ayurvedic doctor. The doctor listened to his symptoms. The diagnosis was one word: *Unmada*. 'Schizophrenia.' The doctor explained. 'Imbalance of energies on an inner level. Schizophrenia is a disorder of the mind caused by a million things, many of which we are ignorant about. I am going to give you three powders. Take these with cold water or milk three times a day. No fried foods. No alcohol. Try to meditate. Come back and see me in two weeks.'

'Are you sure that what I have is schizophrenia?' Charlie asked, 'I have been to many doctors and always, the diagnosis is different.'

'I cannot be a hundred per cent certain,' the doctor confessed, 'even in conventional medicine, doctors do not know enough about this disease. Maybe it is a tumour in the brain... it could be so many different things. Take the powders I have prescribed. Let us see what happens.'

When self-doubt arrived, it fluttered like a candle placed in the path of a small wind stream that seeped through a cracked windowpane. One moment he was sure, the next undecided. Alone in his home, Charlie, for the first time in his life, was thinking about going to England. 'I don't know where Maya is,' he thought. 'This sickness that I have is getting worse, soon this will get unmanageable, I know. They would treat it better in England, and really what is it that I need here...I am getting older; eventually they will want us all out. My white skin makes me an outsider. What's the point in fighting this anymore? Had the architect died because of his connection to Cross Island? That's nonsense, then I should be dead, Willie should be dead, Thommo should be dead...the hell with all this madness.' Dodo arrived in silence watching the flame of indecision dance to the mindless direction of a fickle wind.

Chapter 10

From Portugal She Came

While he tried to deal with his dilemma, Charlie was unaware that on a side street in Bombay, the searing ballad of Dona Maria and Thommo had begun. She was mysterious and unfathomable, lusty and unreachable; a Portuguese alpha she-wolf. She was aware that her predatory brown eyes flamed with the promises her supple body advertised. From Lisbon, she had journeyed to Goa to join her rich Portuguese lover who was now working with people from India. When she returned from the Mapusa Market one Friday afternoon, she had found him in bed with one of his servants, a young boy. It was then that he had finally confessed that he was homosexual, and was using her to make people believe that he had a conventional relationship. She smiled, said she understood, and in two weeks, left for Bombay. To recuperate. To plan the next move. To see what the present held for her future. She ran into Thommo outside her hotel on the causeway in Colaba. Without a word being spoken, they both knew. They looked into each other's eyes, Thommo's gaze then moved to her ample breasts, she let him look, moving her posture every so lightly in an enticing motion, then turned, and began walking away. Thommo raced to catch up with her. 'Are you hungry?' he asked the back of her head. She did not turn around. 'Hungry for what?' She asked. Thommo laughed. 'Food,' he said, 'good Portuguese food.' She turned around to face him and looked into his eyes. She smiled. 'Sure,' she said, 'why not?' Thommo knew the best Portuguese restaurant in Churchgate. He hailed a taxi and soon they were sitting in Bonjardim tavern sipping Port and nibbling sweet bread, while Thommo explained what Bombay was all about. When the bottle was over, Thommo ordered another. She smiled that beatific smile and said, 'I don't get drunk, so if you are thinking about *relação sexual*, I think you should reconsider.' Thommo mouthed the two words, '*relação sexual*?' like it was a mantra. She laughed when he finally figured it out. 'Oh,' he exclaimed, 'you think I am doing this so that I can fok' you?' She smiled, nodded. Thommo looked at her and said, 'How fokkin' right you are. Cheers. Now that you mention it, I will hold my dragon.' They ate Cozido à Portuguesa, the famed Portuguese stew, and Dona Maria sketched her life for Thommo. He watched her mouth moving, watched her slender hand movements and luscious breasts. He wanted her, was willing to pay the price that she quoted. The problem was, she knew it, could sense his desperation. Dona Maria had been in this kind of situation before, many, many times. She was comfortable with the destruction that she was intentionally causing as Thommo painted the ruins of his catastrophic life for her.

Dona Maria was going to put Thommo through her test. She had decided that if this did not work out, she was going to return to the family farm in Lisbon. Thommo was a tough nut, reinforced with steel and tempered by fire. She was going to make him her slave for a full two months. If he could endure, and she could stay alive, she knew this union would last. She was aware that she could lose her life here; he would knife her if she moved the line too fast or too far. It was a chance she was willing to take simply because that is the way she was, that is the way she had always been, even as a child.

When she was ten years old, her neighbour, a twelve-year-old boy had been given a fancy air rifle for Christmas. A relative had brought it all the way from far away America. It was powerful enough to kill a small bird with its lead pellets, and the fact that it was from America, land of the real cowboys, made the boy feel extremely fortunate. When he showed it to Maria and boasted that he had superhuman aim and could knock a fly off her wall, she concocted a plan. She told Aloisio, 'I will stand on the first floor and poke my finger through a hole. You stand on the ground below and, if you can shoot my finger off, I will kiss you, if you cannot, you will have to steal your sister's doll and give it to me. You are allowed just one shot.' He looked at her pink lips and the offer of intimacy in her deep brown eyes, and agreed instantly. Aloisio squinted through the gun sight at her tiny finger protruding from a hole in the balcony. He took his time. He pulled the trigger. A popping sound was heard; then derisive laughter from above. Aloisio knew that he had missed. Maria got her doll.

Now here, gazing at Thommo and the glint of insanity in his personality, she decided that this was a play she had to make, it might mean more than losing a finger, but as always, she kissed the cube for good luck and hurled it on the gambling board. 'You throw the dice,' she thought, 'sometimes you get the ladder, sometimes the snake.'

'Why do you like living on the outside?' Dona Maria asked him.

'Why did you not stay in Portugal?' Thommo shot back.

'I was in love,' she explained.

'Don't make me laugh,' he said, his voice double coated with sarcasm. 'A woman like you...and love?'

Her eyes flashed in anger and resentment, 'You don't know me,' she said defensively.

'I hope I never do,' he explained, 'If I really, really knew everything about you, understood you completely, if we both moved in perfect harmony and all that horse shit, we would be bored silly, living our lives finishing each other's sentences. Know what I mean?'

In the taxi back, Dona Maria made her first move. 'If possible, can you find me a small bungalow where I can live? Can you do that, and pay for it?' 'What if I don't?' Thommo answered, not looking at her. She was silent. He repeated the question and added, 'I am not a pimp, you know.' She nodded. 'Then,' she mumbled a hint of pain in her tremulous voice, 'I must go back to the farm in Lisbon, and you will never see me again.' It was now or never. Thommo grabbed the shiny silver barbed piece of metal, bobbing and glinting in the murky water, shoved it into his mouth and swallowed it—hook, line, bait and sinker.

For two months, Thommo obeyed the bidding of Dona Maria. He fought it like a cornered animal but eventually he was subdued; still snarling and vicious, he finally lay down at her feet. She asked for an expensive bathtub. Perfumes. Clothes. Wines. Furniture. A well-stocked bar. She demanded it all. She commanded, degraded, humiliated, scorned and belittled him constantly. She acted like she was entitled, like she was royalty. He was the peasant holding the peacock feathers to fan the queen. He argued with her, threatened her, tried to say no, but in the end, Dona Maria prevailed. At one point, Thommo could not take the manipulation anymore. He decided to slit her throat, but when she looked at him, he knew he could not follow through on the murder, not her, he told himself. Then, after a painful two months, she commanded him to get into her bed and made love to him, passionately and violently. She possessed his body, caressing it, kneading it expertly. After it was over, Thommo knew she was his kind of animal. It was then that she told him about the two-month test that she had put him through. 'Daughter of a bitch,' Thommo shouted, 'Do you realize that you almost lost your life?' Dona Maria nodded. 'I was ready for that; I knew your knife could come. It's over now, Thommo. We are now one, win or lose. From this night on you will see a different woman. I have a lot of money; my ex-lover gave it to me when I left Goa. I asked you for all those things because I needed to test you. I wanted to see if your endurance could stand this...'

Then, there in bed, exhausted and satiated, Thommo called her a 'crazy cow' and told her about Cross Island. He also explained that Charlie had stated that he wanted no women besides the prostitutes on Cross Island. 'Let me meet Charlie,' Dona Maria said. 'I will explain why I have to be there.' Thommo laughed nervously. He lied to her, told her that he had talked to Charlie, and Charlie did not want her living on Cross Island. 'You say we are one. I have a dose of arsenic. I want you to slip it into Charlie's whisky when we visit him. We are going to kill him, and then, we will take over the operations of Cross Island.' She looked at him. 'You want me to murder for you?' Thommo stared into her eyes and nodded.

The next day, Thommo introduced her to Charlie who had absolutely no idea that Dona Maria was Thommo's girlfriend and that she wanted to live on Cross Island. Charlie welcomed her to his home and offered her some wine. He poured whisky for Thommo and him, and then excused himself to go to the kitchen to get some ice. Dona Maria looked at Thommo and slipped the arsenic into Charlie's whisky. When Charlie got back, they began discussing life in Bombay. Thommo had warned her not to bring up Cross Island.

Two hours later, when Thommo said they had to leave, Charlie was still alive. On the way home, Dona Maria asked, 'Well, what happened? He is still alive.' Thommo let out a roar of laughter, slapping his thighs. 'That was your test, my lady. Now we're even. That was plain old sugar you slipped into his drink.' She shook her head in dismay.

Later when they were in bed, she made him swear that now, the games would stop. No more tests, they both agreed. Dona Maria looked at Thommo and said, 'I think I am in love with you. Please do not laugh.' Thommo patted her right breast, kissed her, turned around in bed and drifted off to sleep.

Chapter 11

Passions of the Mind

Dona Maria knew that the next meeting with Charlie was going to be an exercise in futility if she did not play her cards shrewdly. She spent the week plotting and planning on what would be the most effective approach. When they met at Charlie's home, Dona Maria looked into his deep blue eyes and said, 'I am going to be living with Thommo on Cross Island. The decision is not yours to make.' Charlie smiled, turned away and said, 'No, my lady. You are not.' They both knew then that this meeting was going to be fractious; a bristling goddess against a calculating sage. Thommo squirmed, uncomfortable with his middle-man position. This was not his way of dealing with a disagreement. Thommo's solution to any opposition was a snarling threat: a fist to the face or a knife in the gut. That usually decided things.

Charlie looked at Dona Maria like she was an insufferable affront. He was seeking a vulnerability he could exploit. 'I have a ruthless efficiency...' she was saying. He cut her voice off savagely. 'There are no decadent privileges on Cross Island,' he explained. 'I can live like a slut, work like a slave,' she swore. Still Charlie shook his head in disagreement. He looked at Thommo for help saying, 'I thought we had an agreement. No one brings their women to the island, and now you bring this, here. What's this really all about?' Thommo was silent. Dona Maria knew she was losing the debate. Charlie remained calm and firm. She would not be making that journey to Cross Island.

Charlie knew this was trouble. Her smoking sexuality would be kerosene on the men's hot fantasies, and the women would resent her, but Charlie knew that if he stuck to his guns he would lose Thommo. Dodo came through laughing uncontrollably at his dilemma.

Dodo: *What you are really scared about, Charlie, is that she will take control. She is that kind of alpha she-wolf. What are you going to do about it? And deep down, like a lot of men, you want her, don't you? Sure, she can help, but at what cost? She is a woman who will want more than just one pound of flesh. She will want lots of warm blood to wash that flesh down her pretty throat. And then there is Thommo, you make one wrong move and she will command him to use that knife. You need Thommo, for all the rough stuff that is going to come, so your acceptance of her is what the French call 'fait accompli'.*

Charlie: *Dodo, I know something that they are not aware of. I am going to give up Cross Island. I am going to England.*

Dodo: *Well, why did you not tell her? Why did you go through that ridiculous charade?*

Charlie: *I like the game, Dodo. Verbal fencing stimulates me. I must admit, she did win but of course, I will never admit that to her. What I am going to tell her is that if she still insists on coming to Cross Island, I will drop out of the project. There is no way this can be done without me. She knows that and Thommo does too. I will lay the guilt of the failure to start the Cross Island project on her beautiful bosom. Then, let's see what her lover boy Thommo does. There is nothing more to discuss, is there? Good night.*

He thought about his decision to go to England all week. At the docks, he maintained a stubborn silence when he met Thommo and Willie. Sunday arrived and Charlie was sitting in the home of Victoria Fernandes, he had come to say goodbye to his old friend. She surprised Charlie when she said with her usual gentleness, 'There is a small chance that Maya would meet with you in the near future.' Charlie's hand that held his glass of whisky and ice trembled visibly. The only sound in the room was of the ice cubes clinking against each other. Charlie just sat there, mute as buffalo with a colossal load on its back. 'No questions, Charlie,' Fernandes warned, 'that's what she told me in a letter I recently received.' They both knew now that Charlie would have to drastically alter his plans because he believed that Maya was still in India. Victoria, who knew the truth about Maya's whereabouts, stayed silent. Charlie's decision to stay or go was not for her to decide. She could not say more than what she had already revealed. Charlie sipped his drink. Dona Maria was now a real problem that he would have to deal with and resolve.

Charlie had forgotten that he had to go back to the ayurvedic doctor. When he did think about it, he dismissed the doctor's diagnosis and continued drinking. The next assault came while he was at work. It paralyzed him.

That night, alone at home, Charlie was thinking about what had happened to him at the docks. He made a fatal decision. He was going to handle 'these disturbances' by himself. He was going to meditate and control his mind. He thought of Dona Maria and decided that one day he was going to claim her as his own. Another decision that had the gristly noose of death around it.

The next morning at the docks, Charlie talked to Thommo and Willie. 'Tell Dona Maria,' he said, 'that she is welcome on Cross Island.' Thommo smiled and patted Charlie on his shoulder. 'I need to know something,' Willie said, 'why have you been avoiding us for the past three weeks? Is there a problem?' Charlie shook his head. 'There were some personal things that I had to fix. It's alright now.'

When they met again at Charlie's home, an atmosphere of reconciliation prevailed. The outer edge of this new conciliatory handshake was however gripped by a fast-cooking sexual tension between Charlie and Dona Maria. Thommo watched like a cobra, hood spread in primordial defense. He looked at her; she appeared nonchalant. Willie watched the palpable passion play and Dodo hovered around passing snarky comments. The conversation was perfunctory until Dona Maria suddenly exclaimed, 'Já chega, let's talk about what we are really going to do on Cross Island. How much, in terms of money, is the first consignment going to be? Have we got our distribution system layout?' Charlie, calm and collected, explained with precision, looking straight into the brown eyes of Dona Maria. 'How much of a credit line are we willing to give?' she wanted to know. An argument began. Now Willie and Thommo joined in. No credits, they both proclaimed. These bloody Indians will make you run after them for even a rupee. Charlie sat silent, like a good judge listening to the arguments and rebuttals. Dona Maria stated that it was good business practice that could be extended to customers who bought large amounts. She argued, cajoled, pleaded with passion and finally, she managed to win. They agreed that eventually a credit line would be offered.

Through it all, Dona Maria stayed by Thommo's side; but when Thommo walked to the lavatory in the kitchen she asked Charlie for a map of Cross Island, and almost by accident her right breast brushed against his left arm. It happened so fast that Willie did not notice the interaction. Charlie smiled. She smiled. They both looked at the topography of their future, finger tips on the map, studying the surroundings of Cross Island. When Thommo got back, Dona Maria said, 'I know that you all are busy at the docks right now. I would like to supervise the construction on Cross Island. I will be there every day seeing that the new contractor is doing his job.' 'That's a tough job,' Charlie explained, 'what you are not taking into consideration is the fact that Indians do not like being bossed by a woman. They might not want to work under you. It will embarrass them.' Once again, a heated discussion began. Again, she prevailed, when she assured Charlie, 'If you do not see progress in one month, not only will I stop going to Cross Island, I will also drop out of this project. That's how serious I am. I can work with these Indians, Charlie. I used to work with donkeys and pigs on my farm. You have to have some faith in me, Charlie. We have to all work together, or this is not going to happen.' She squeezed Charlie's arm gently. Thommo saw their eyes meet.

It was close to midnight when they decided to end the meeting. In the taxi home, Dona Maria held Thommo's hand gently, caressing it with her thumb and forefinger. Back in the house, she said she was tired, was going to bed. Thommo eyed her back as she headed for the bedroom. Something made her turn around. He was standing there, relaxed, and in his hand was a knife. His instinct had flashed a red light that warned of her interest in Charlie. She stared at the serrated blade. She knew that she was minutes away from being knifed. His black eyes had that soulless shark look. She walked up to him as he stared at her. He hissed laconically, 'What is this fokkin' game?' She stood there, inches away from the knife and explained her strategy to get Charlie to comply. She told him that for the first time in her life, she was willing to die for a man, and that man was him. She swore on her mother's grave that infidelity would never come between them. Finally, Thommo put the knife away. He was still seething with anger and doubt, but the raging waters of his wrath were slowly beginning to recede from the crimson overflow line. She held his arm and led him to bed. He thumped the knife on the nightstand, the sound of metal on wood cracked like a whiplash in the silence. Thommo undressed and drifted into sleep, his lithe back to her body. She knew she dare not hide the knife. He did not need steel to end her existence, he could always strangle her. A sardonic thought flashed through her fear. What would be better, being knifed or being strangled? Dona Maria did not know if she would wake up to see the next morning. Her last thought was a prayer, 'And if I die before I wake, I pray to God my soul to take.'

Back home, Charlie sat at his kitchen table staring at the whisky in his glass, recalling the paranoia in Thommo's eyes. Dodo was still around, offering unsolicited advice.

Dodo: *Is this two-bit gutter snipe whore worth anything?*

Charlie: *Yes.*

Dodo: *Are you willing to put Cross Island at risk because you want to...*

Charlie: *It's not just the sex. Her very being, her attitude...I have never encountered a woman like her. Never. Do you understand? I could spend the rest of my life with her. I don't know what love is, but what I am feeling, is close to the definitions I have heard ever since I was a child.*

Dodo: *And what about Thommo?*

Charlie: *Eventually he will have to go.*

Dodo: *You mean, he will have to die.*

Charlie: *I never said that. I mean he will have to go. I need to plan for that eventuality, not now, but somewhere down the line, he will have to go. For now, I need him, so he stays till the time arises, and then, with her permission, he will disappear.*

Dodo: *Charlie, do you realize how mad this all sounds, how irrational, how stupid! And what, may I add, if she prefers him?*

Charlie: *I know in my gut, my heart, my blood and soul, she wants to be with me. I just know. I cannot explain.*

Dodo: *You are behaving like a love-struck idiot.*

Charlie: *Well, what do you think I should do?*

There was no reply. Dodo had left.

Chapter 12

A Faustian Bargain

Dona Maria, Charlie and Thommo met the new contractor and Charlie explained that now, Dona Maria would oversee the construction at Cross Island. The contractor visibly balked and began a litany of protests. Charlie assured him in Hindi that this would not last. 'Find her a husband,' the contractor mumbled, 'that's what she needs to keep her out of construction. This is man's work.' Charlie nodded. Dona Maria and Thommo wanted to know what the contractor had just said. Charlie explained: 'What he is saying is that maybe, maybe you might not be able to control the men.' Dona Maria poked the contractor in his chest with her forefinger and said, 'Tell him I have been controlling men ever since I started menstruating. Tell the bastard that. Tell him I can write that down in blood if he wants.' Charlie waved the argument away. The next day, at six in the morning, Dona Maria was at Cross Island with a crew of fifteen workers and the contractor. She was dressed in jodhpurs, a loose blouse and a large hat; Roman sandals completed her outfit. Dona Maria did two things immediately. She picked out a man on the crew who could translate for her, and hired a chaiwala who doubled as a paanwala. She knew by now that Indians liked their tea breaks and some of them loved chewing betel nut leaf, laced with slaked-lime paste and tobacco. Dona Maria christened him 'The Chef' since he was also in charge of dispensing vegetarian meals and water. Through her interpreter, she informed the crew that all this was for free, if work carried on as per the timeframe she desired. If they fell behind schedule, they would have to pay for it all. The first week, all went well. She began using the interpreter as her spy, paying him extra and letting him get an occasional glimpse of her breasts when she bent low to pick up something. By now, even the contractor who had been a sneering bystander began to have a newfound respect for the way she handled the men. She drove them like galley slaves, smiling as she pounded them.

In the fourth week, hell erupted. A Hindu worker made an ugly comment about Prophet Mohammed, while the Muslims prayed. Suddenly, it was the old Hindu-Muslim confrontation. Dona Maria had to throw herself between the two groups who were ready to kill and maim. All work stopped. She knew that this was the beginning of a riotous end. She told them that if there was any more trouble, she would report it to the police and they would not receive their weekly wage. She then packed them all back into the boat, separating the Hindus and Muslims, and headed out to Ferry Wharf. Once they landed, she told them that she did not want them working for her anymore. The contractor was livid. This was his crew. But Dona Maria was determined. No threat could change her mind.

The next day Dona Maria walked into the construction site of a building near Ferry Wharf. She picked out her crew, offered them better wages and whisked them away. This was now an all-Muslim crew. No more communal grandstanding she told herself. It was then, after she had solved the problem that she informed Charlie. She talked to the contractor who was a Muslim, and told him that she respected Prophet Mohammed and now he would have no problems. However, when the contractor heard the daily wage that she had generously offered he went berserk. He was the one whose pocket was going to be dented by Dona Maria's magnanimity. He complained to Charlie, who asked Thommo to deal with the contractor. Thommo did not say much. He produced the knife and the contractor crumbled like a house built with termite-eaten wood. Work on Cross Island began, again.

Occasionally, Charlie, Thommo and Willie journeyed to the site. Charlie was astounded at the dexterity with which Dona Maria handled the work and crew. He could see that she was a politician who would lie, cheat, offer the world on a plate, shake your hand with a sincere smile, then do exactly the opposite of her initial promise, if that was what suited her. Her spy, who she had retained, kept her abreast of the complaints and grumblings of the crew. She cajoled, manipulated and offered rewards once all work was completed. By the second month, Dona Maria knew the histories of the crew's families intimately. She offered them advice and stroked them into conformity. She got a decent physician to attend to one of a worker's sick son and told them that if they were ever threatened by the Hindus, she would get them physical backing to repel any attack. She put down Hinduism when convenient and quoted lines from the Koran, let them take their prayer breaks and overlooked the occasional cigarette doctored with hashish that some of the men smoked.

When she heard that one of the workers, Abbas Aleem, had refused to send his two daughters to school, she visited the family in the slums off Ferry Wharf. She covered her head with a shawl as a mark of respect, wore a long skirt that came down to her ankles and a loose blouse that hid her arms. She asked around the slum and found a young man who agreed to act as a translator. She ignored Aleem, who stood in his hut, mortified and embarrassed, and talked to his father, who as patriarch was proudly responsible for the girls being banned from attending school. Dona Maria talked of the glorious things the girls could do in new India if they were educated. She begged, pleaded and used logic when necessary as she explained the new age, and the role educated women would play to make the world a better more peaceful place. The old man refuted some of her arguments, but mostly listened in silence. Finally she quoted scripture: 'Acquisition of knowledge is binding on all Muslims, male and female, the holy prophet Muhammed, peace be upon him, said that,' she told the old man. And then, to dull the edge from what she had just preached to the patriarch, she whispered, 'But my wise old friend, you already know that.' Something in Dona Maria's tone and manner touched him. The patriarch looked at Dona Maria, who sat before him on the floor, cross legged, her eyes lowered in submission and humility. He listened as Dona Maria said she would pay the girls' fees at a private school for Muslim girls for a full year. The stern old patriarch finally turned to his son and nodded in affirmation. The girls would now have an education. Their mother smiled.

She whispered to the crew leader that once Cross Island was complete, there was more work to be done elsewhere. Victoria Docks, she explained, would be expanding their operations to different places around Bombay. This would mean permanent employment, better salaries, maybe even free housing. Dona Maria lied when she deemed it necessary, but she also helped her workers with a sincerity that was astounding.

Day after day, except Sundays, Dona Maria worked on Cross Island. On Sundays she went to church and pleaded with Jesus Christ for forgiveness. The Faustian bargain she had accepted, she told her Lord and saviour, was a necessity for her survival.

She hoped that in his infinite wisdom, he would understand her predicament.

When Charlie asked her how she managed to cope with the rigours of work on Cross Island, she smiled, 'I do what my workers do,' she joked. 'Shit behind a rock, wash in the sea, it's a glorious ancient Indian left-handed tradition.' Charlie smiled. 'It's not easy, Charlie,' she said softly, 'but I am doing it for me...and you.' Charlie looked at her silently and placed his hand on her waist. He could see that the long tedious hours were taking a toll on her body. Her face, neck and hands had gone a deep-nut brown. Lines were beginning to form on her beautiful countenance, but her wild, untamed animal quality remained intact. She never complained and managed to solve all operational problems on her own. Once a troubling situation was solved, she told Charlie about how it had started, and explained the deviant methods she had used to remedy it. Her deception amazed Charlie, her pragmatism, and the steel-handed ferocity with which she pushed petty morals into the gutter astounded him. This was a Portuguese Catholic woman who had the soul of a Roman pagan goddess. This was his woman he told himself. Thommo was an ignorant peasant who did not deserve her magnificence.

Charlie now began meditating with the religious fervour of a Himalayan monk; he was sure he could control and lower the schizophrenic attacks to a manageable level by fine tuning his brain and nervous system. He would wake up at five every morning, often with a hangover, sit in the full-lotus position on his carpet and chant, '*Ehyeh ašer ehyeh.*'

On 22 October 1947, Charlie's heart soared when he heard that India and Pakistan were at war; they were feuding over the princely state of Jammu and Kashmir. This would be a great distraction from their Cross Island venture, he thought. Now that the Hindus were in India and a majority of Muslims were ensconced in Pakistan, one would think that they would have settled down. But a tribal insurrection broke out in Poonch in southwest Kashmir; and the Pakistani Army had entered the conflict in support of the tribal forces, the Indian army retaliated. Here we go again, Charlie smirked, there was no difference in this new slaughter. Except that this time the killing was official, approved by governments on both sides.

And then, the bad news. On 30 January 1948, a .38 Beretta semi-autmomatic pistol spewed three bullets. Seventy-eight-year-old Mahatma Gandhi was assassinated at 5.17 p.m. in the compound of Birla House, a large mansion on Albuquerque Road in New Delhi where he was conducting a prayer meeting. Nathuram Godse, the assassin, was grabbed by an American, former naval Lieutenant Commander Herbert 'Tom' Reiner Jr of Lancaster, Massachusetts. Reiner had recently arrived in India and was working as a vice consul attached to the American Embassy in New Delhi. Hearing that Gandhi would be holding a multi-faith prayer meeting not far from the diplomatic enclave, Reiner decided to attend, hoping to meet him. He nearly did. Reiner was standing close to Gandhi and Godse, seconds before Godse pulled the trigger. Thinking that Godse was now going to try and shoot himself out of the situation, Reiner pounced on him, tried to get at his gun, failed, put a lock on Godse's neck and shoulder, frog-marched him and hurled Godse into the arms of some stunned Royal Indian Air Force men standing nearby.

In Bombay, Charlie heard the BBC correspondent Robert Stimson, who was present at the prayer meeting, talk about Reiner's heroics; and read a front-page report about Reiner by another eye witness, Robert Trumbull of *The New York Times*. But mostly the Indian press, government and people ignored

Reiner; and the *Pakistan Times* sub-headline read 'Crowds Seize Assailant'. Reiner had already been relegated by India and Pakistan to the back of the book glossary of history. Charlie did not really care who had apprehended Gandhi's assassin. All he hoped for was that the colonial claw of the British Secret Service had not clandestinely aided in the planning of the assassination. If even a hint of a connection was unearthed, it would be the end of Cross Island.

Chapter 13

The Way of the Cross

The undercurrents of communal violence were now the new normal and the war continued in the Kashmir region. The small town on Cross Island was near completion. Charlie called a final meeting of all who would be living on the island.

Finally, the generators that were going to provide electricity were stolen from the docks and ferried to Cross Island. Dona Maria had done a great job supervising the work. Now she ran through the list of people who had enlisted to receive the smuggled goods. This list had been painstakingly prepared through Charlie's contacts. She arched her eyebrow when she discovered that most of the recipients were people in power: politicians, police, businessmen, small-time smugglers, top brass at the docks and informants who supplied Charlie with crucial underbelly news made up the soiled list. Packages would be hand delivered; cash on delivery was the slogan. Dona Maria reminded Charlie that he had promised her that 'good customers' would get a line of credit. Charlie grew visibly irritated. 'All that will come later,' he scowled, and walked away.

The government of India, besides handling the early teething problems, was busy handling the first Kashmir war. The officials had bigger fish to fry. They had no time to zone in on the activities of a small bunch of renegade Englishmen on a deserted island. The move to Cross Island had to be made now! Willie, in charge of logistics, had worked out the time and day. A week before the big move, Charlie, Thommo and Willie applied for their annual month-long 'Vacation Paid Leave', after which, they would apply for 'Sick Leave'. This would still give them unfettered access to the docks. The men they had recruited at the docks did the same. Given the amount of social chaos, corruption and incompetency, they were sure that it would be a long time before they were officially relieved of their jobs.

Charlie and the islanders were openly contemptuous of corruption in the Indian rank and file, but were also aware that it was this manipulative cancer that helped them operate and survive. Thommo often joked that the universal India symbol should be a greased thumb and forefinger rubbing each other, with the words chai-pani embroidered in a saffron arc above the symbol. When the 'Jeep Scandal', the first big corruption case exploded, Willie smiled. Discussing the scandal with Charlie, Willie shrugged his shoulders, 'What these Indians don't seem to realize,' Willie explained, 'is that this corruption was prevalent from the time of the Maharajas. It is part of their daily lives, they accept it. The people are not shocked or surprised when asked to pay baksheesh. Everybody is so used to it, they just carry on. Of course, now they say we invented it all.' Charlie laughed and sneered, 'Indians...born into manipulation; bred for corruption. This is an ancient culture, but this country has shown the world that like good wine, a civilization does not get better with time; India is the degenerate proof of that. We should all be thankful how she has nurtured her cradle-to-grave corruption.' Even Mahatma Gandhi seemed to agree. He had, when alive, helplessly observed the open corruption and distanced himself from the crooked managerial machinations. At its very core, the Congress party was corrupt. A sickness that had attained critical mass in 1939 when Gandhi had observed, 'I would go to the length of giving the whole Congress a decent burial, rather than put up with the corruption that is rampant.' Later, when the malaise worsened, he wanted to dismantle the whole Congress but by this time, his honourary position had lost its once reverential moral and political clout. He wore the mantle of 'Father of the Nation' in quiet solitude; his family had moved on and abandoned him.

The 'Jeep Scandal' proved to the world that Mahatma Gandhi had been right in his accusations. The Indian High Commissioner to Britain, V.K. Krishna Menon, who the British had christened 'Mephistopheles in a Savile Row suit' had ruthlessly dismissed every written political protocol rule, and secretly signed a deal with a UK company 'Messers Anti-Mistantes' to buy two thousand refurbished second-hand jeeps for the Indian army. The deal was worth eighty lakh rupees, and only a hundred and fifty-five jeeps had been delivered. The army termed the jeeps as 'second rate', mechanically and structurally unfit for offense or defense. The Jawaharlal Nehru government began spinning its political wheels, hoping an elongated quasi inquiry would calm people and the corruption would soon be forgotten. The Indian government was aware that the secret British intelligence unit MI5 had Menon under a microscope. MI5 had begun extensive surveillance of Menon's questionable commercial transactions, especially the defense contracts he was handling. MI5 followed the stench of the crooked money trail and painted a stark picture of how money from various contracts eventually ended in accounts that Menon controlled. Still, Nehru joined Menon in his foxhole, and fought with him; shooting a barrage of inconsequential blanks on his behalf, intended for public consumption at home and to quiet the howls of international condemnation. Even when it was discovered that for that same amount of money, brand new jeeps could have been purchased from the United States or Canada, Menon remained unchastised. The deal had been signed. The money had been paid. The kickbacks had been pocketed. The incomplete, imperfect assignment was accepted; and the obvious monetary kickback and political skullduggery was consigned to a 'File and Hopefully Forget' governmental godown. The British perceived Menon as Jawaharlal Nehru's 'evil genius', while the Americans openly branded him a 'poisonous bastard', still Menon was allowed to soldier on. Later, when Menon appeared on the cover of *Time* magazine accompanied by an Indian snake charmer's flute and a hooded cobra his reputation at home stayed untarnished. Menon was the second most powerful man in India, lagging just a step behind Nehru, and although MI5 in Britain characterized Menon as, 'A sick man whose relations with fellows can never be normal or happy...and utterly unscrupulous...impairing the whole conduct of India's foreign relations,' Menon 'the snake charmer' stayed, for the time being, untouchable; privately arrogant about his public corruption. Reading this in *The Times of India* Charlie smirked, 'And they tell me, I am manipulative and corrupt. Brown-washed history has always reiterated that the British were the creators and perpetrators of this vile social and political maleficence called corruption. The truth is that the British built on, reinforced and exploited the already set up structures of corruption. There is enough historical evidence that suggests corruption in India was birthed by the Rajas and Indians long before the British arrived at the port of Surat. Did you know the Mughal emperor, Nuruddin Salim Jahangir, was extremely corrupt, a drunk and an opium addict? He was the one who sold India to the British after Sir Thomas Roe bribed him. Corruption here goes way back in time.'

Menon was not a solitary reprobate, a string of corruptions followed; the movers were shaking their corrupt cudgels with impunity. Rao Shiv Bahadur Singh, a politician from the Congress party from Vindhya Pradesh [later Madhya Pradesh] was apprehended with forged documents and accepting a bribe of twenty-five thousand rupees for renewing a gem trader's lease on the Panna diamond mines. In a rare display of justice, he was imprisoned and died there but the corruption carried on. Clearing the way for Cross Island.

BOOK II

Chapter 1

Eating Blackbird Pie

Midnight, 14 May 1948: nineteen English men, one Portuguese woman and four Irish whores sailed to Cross Island on the *Sea Princess Maya* flying the Indian tri-colour. For them, it was the birth of a new state, whose illegal status did not really matter.

On Cross Island, Willie was in charge; he designated, argued, made promises, agreed and disagreed. Charlie, Willie, Dona Maria and Thommo had their own shacks, the sixteen Englishmen who had accompanied them shared residences, while the four Irish prostitutes had their own place. Charlie christened the whore house 'The House of Tarts'. The girls squealed and performed a little jig, the men laughed and all was well on Cross Island. The next day, the carpenter created a decorative signboard that advertised the brothel in red. On the bottom of the sign, the girls insisted that he carve 'Home Baked, Hot and Fresh'. Charlie laughed and thought of the old English nursery rhyme:

Sing a song of sixpence,
A pocket full of rye.
Four and twenty blackbirds,
Baked in a pie.
When the pie was opened,
The birds began to sing;

'Singing blackbirds baked in a pie!'—the line sounded like one of his many schizophrenic hallucinations. Perfectly irrational in its mindbending imagery. An afterthought flashed through his mind. There were twenty-four people on Cross Island, so the four and twenty mentioned in the poem seemed appropriate; and if you stood the individual numbers hip to hip, you got the figure four-twenty. Now Charlie chuckled with mirth. For Indians, the number four-twenty had derogatory connotations. It was bestowed on a person who had questionable morals; a four-twenty was not to be trusted. This number could apply to each desperado on Cross Island. Charlie laughed out aloud. 'Yea,' he exclaimed to no one in particular, 'four and twenty blackbirds!'

All the personal belongings of the islanders were already there. Willie had done a magnificent job of coordinating the herculean effort. The girls tested the beds, the men their equipment. Dona Maria inspected the communal kitchen looking for flaws that she might have overlooked. Charlie looked with satisfaction at the store houses that would hold the merchandise and Thommo walked the perimeter of Cross Island, surveying the mainland and wondering if and when an attack would come. As he looked at the huge drums filled with drinking water that had been placed beside the now-demolished Kali altar, he was reminded of the rumours of child sacrifices. Spitting on the ground, Thommo told himself, that even he would never stoop to that level of senseless murder in the name of a goddess.

That night, Bob Johnson, one of the three electricians told Willie that he needed to go home as he had forgotten to bring his passport. Willie scowled. This would mean an unnecessary trip to Ferry Wharf. The next morning, Willie sailed to the Wharf; told Bob that he would wait while he retrieved his passport. An hour passed, two hours, three, four... Willie gunned *Sea Princess Maya*'s engines and rode back to Cross Island. The same evening, Charlie and Thommo accompanied him to the Wharf. They took a taxi to the electrician's home. The door was locked, lights out. Thommo broke into the darkness of the house. In the kitchen, Bob was sprawled on his back, a gaping crimson gash in his stomach. Charlie flicked on the kitchen light. Near the body, they found a small duffle bag containing his passport. 'Who would want to kill him?' Charlie asked no one in particular, 'Why...?'

The ride back to Cross Island was dark and silent. Their meeting that night at Thommo's shack was sombre. 'Perhaps, he owed a loan shark money,' Dona Maria said. 'He could have had enemies, how are we to know?' Charlie shook his head. 'The timing bothers me. If this is a contract killing, then that bastard Karim Lala has to be involved. If that is the case, we are in deep trouble. There is no point in me meeting him. He will deny it. But again, he gave me his word that he would not interfere, and Lala is a man known to stick by his promises. But, he is a low-life; he could have changed his position.' They talked for an hour. There were no answers, only questions that led to Johnson's kitchen and the dead bloody body. Charlie insisted they replace Johnson because he wanted to maintain the number of people on Cross Island at twenty-four. 'It is a neurologically powerful number,' he explained. 'There is a reason why pure gold is called twenty-four carats, it is also the symbol of harmony between sky and earth and there are twenty-four hours in a day and the Ashoka Chakra has twenty-four spokes...' Willie held up his hand and laughed, 'Enough, oh wise one! Verily, I say unto thee, thou surely were born in bloody superstitious India.' He promised Charlie that he would contact Liam O'Riordan, an electrician who had been dropped from the original list. 'He's a good man,' Willie confirmed, 'I know him well.' They continued to discuss Johnson. They were sure that once the body had been discovered by the police, his place of work would be contacted and his family informed. They decided to tell the rest that Johnson had left because he wanted to reconcile with his wife.

Back in the city the next night, in a house off Ferry Wharf, a man was paid for taking Johnson's life. This man was one of the shadows of Bombay. His family had been pavement dwellers and had abandoned him as a child. He had spent his youth in brutal remand homes for children, where he was taught to read and write, learnt carpentry, learnt to fight, and heard glowing stories from the older boys about the fast-buck road of crime. As a young adult he decided that wood was not his forte, and that the life of a petty criminal best suited his temperament. He started off selling movie tickets in the market and slowly worked his way up the ladder of well-paid crime jobs. Like many others of his trade, he operated alone. He was the last contact in an underground chain that could not be traced. People of his ilk were useful. Besides the occasional murder, he had handled stolen goods from the docks for years. He was a low-down professional career criminal, but also the spine of organized crime. He did his job, got paid and then waited for his next assignment. If arrested, he genuinely knew nothing, and could not finger the person who had given him the job. A note detailing the operation would be shoved under the door to his house; he would memorize it and then destroy it. When the job was done, his fee would appear the same way as the note. It was that simple. He had no idea how many people he worked for, or who they were. No ties. No complications. No questions. Murder was just a job that helped him sustain.

They found Willie discussing the logistics of their first consignment for the black market with the men. Nobody questioned his authority on this, not even Charlie or Thommo. Everybody knew that he knew precisely what he was doing. The crew from Cross Island would meet a ship midstream, pick up their merchandise and sail back to Cross Island; he had coordinated—through the Victoria Docks—with his contacts at Southampton port. It would take three trips. Willie had worked out the how much each load should be. From stevedores to the ship's captain, it had all been taken care of. Willie was assigning chores to each of his men with military efficiency when Dona Maria said, 'What if someone decides to hijack the boat?' Thommo smiled; Charlie smiled. 'We have three Lee-Enfield rifles on board,' Charlie informed her. 'We have that covered. The local coast guard has been fixed, even the police and the politicians. So darling, don't you worry. Remember, this is official work of the Victoria Docks.' The men guffawed and patted each other's shoulders. Charlie was pleased to see that they were building camaraderie. He walked to *Sea Princess Maya*. She was anchored alongside the oak jetty that had been constructed. He looked at her and thought about his daughter.

CHAPTER 2

The Making of Maya

Charlie had been twenty-one-years-old then, working as a stevedore at the Victoria Docks. One evening he had accepted an invitation to an 'English bash'. At the party he had met Caitlin Rafferty, a perky Irish girl. She was easy on the eye and gentle; unlike the prostitutes who were cold professional vessels for his lust. Things went downhill fast. They smiled, drank Irish whisky, laughed, held hands, kissed, slipped into a vacant room...a month later Caitlin told Charlie that she had missed her period. Charlie's heart had missed a couple of beats when he heard that. He suggested an abortionist that he knew. She refused. Caitlin moved away from her parent's home and shacked up with Charlie and his stevedore friend. It was uncomfortable, unhappy and impractical. The baby was born. They named her Maya Strongbow. By this time, the bond of raw passion that Charlie and Caitlin had shared was crawling with maggots of dissatisfaction and disillusionment. They handed the baby to an English adoption agency in Bombay. Maya was two months old when they abandoned her. Charlie talked to an Indian nurse at the adoption centre. Her name was Victoria Fernandes. Charlie told her that he would like to keep in touch with Maya through her. She refused, but Charlie was persistent, and in the end she agreed on one condition. Charlie would not be able to ascertain where Maya was, ever. Charlie agreed. He signed the necessary papers. Charlie and Caitlin looked at the baby. Caitlin wept, touched the child's forehead, turned and moved out of the room. Charlie looked into the baby's deep blue eyes, bowed his head and followed Caitlin out. Caitlin moved back in with her parents. Charlie got drunk every night for a week and cried. This was the second daughter he had abandoned.

A month later, Charlie went back to the adoption centre. He met Victoria who said, 'Maya's gone. Adopted.' When it looked like Charlie wanted to ask her a question Victoria held up her hand and said sternly. 'It is an end for you, a beginning for the child. Let it go.' Through the years, Charlie would often turn up at the adoption centre. They became friends but Victoria would not talk about where Maya was. Charlie stated that he respected her decision, but he hoped that one day, she would, in a moment of emotional weakness, reveal where his daughter was.

Charlie stared at *Sea Princess Maya* gently swaying in the water, like a cradle being rocked, ever so gently. He recalled Maya's deep blue eyes, innocent and unaffected as he had forsaken her in that room at the adoption centre, a long, long time ago. He wondered if she would ever forgive him and absolve Caitlin, of cutting that parental umbilical cord with cold selfish practicality that only benefitted their fractured relationship. A few years after they had abandoned Maya, when Charlie heard that Caitlin had gone back to Ireland, his emotions performed an elaborate Gallic shrug. Caitlin had been dead to him as they had emerged from the adoption centre. Dodo had painted a stark picture of Charlie's emotional bankruptcy and moral wasteland. And Charlie in the depth of his guarded silence knew that Dodo was right. Now all he really had as family was Maya...out there somewhere. He knew that his first daughter, Doris, had been adopted and taken back to England. She was lost to him forever. Did they also take Maya to England? Or Ireland? Or Scotland? Or was she still here in India? The last time he had talked with Victoria, he thought he had detected a look on her face that confirmed that Maya was still in India. 'I hope she is happy,' Charlie thought, 'wherever she may be.' He turned from the boat and walked away.

Back in her home, Victoria sat in her living room reading a letter from Maya that had arrived that morning.

Dear Victoria,

I apologize for not writing for so long. There have been a few troubling incidents. First, I decided to tell Burt about Charlie and Caitlin. He seemed alright with Charlie's life but found it insurmountable to tell his parents that I was born out of wedlock. He was also very angry that I 'had hidden these facts' about myself for so long. I tried to explain that I was afraid, that I had wanted to tell him. He said that he could not trust me anymore. I tried to defend myself, tried to make him understand. I tried, Victoria, God I tried, but we seemed to be going around a circle, coming back to the same mistrust. And that was that. It is over.

I had hoped that one day we could have a family. That will not happen.

There are changes happening to me, inside me. Maybe some day I will explain. I never mentioned this to you before, but I have been questioning the reality of a supreme power for a long time. This experience with Burt was the nail that pierced through and touched an answer, however painful it may sound. I feel that I no longer believe in a God anymore and I am well on my way to becoming an atheist. I had prayed for a normal domestic life and then this happened. I know you will disapprove, Victoria, but this is the truth that I feel inside me. I no longer believe. I asked the question: 'Why me, God? After all that has happened to me? Why me? Am I asking for too much?' It was like talking to a brick wall. I have no Christian guilt about abandoning my belief. My faith decided that. There is really nothing more to add. I will be alright, Victoria; I just need some time to recover. Like Charlie, I am a survivor. My secret horror is that I will become like him. But I have a few good things in life to hold on to. I have some new friends at my place of work. The job is going well and I am happy there.

I know that I talked about meeting Charlie, to try and turn him away from the madness that he is involved with; I am not too sure about it. I don't know him and I am not sure that he will listen to what I have to say. And for selfish reasons, I do not want to deal with Charlie's problems right now. Maybe a meeting will happen sometime in the future.

Please do write.

Sincerely,

Maya

CHAPTER 3

The Coconut Monkey Trap

Willie had worked out exactly how much time it would take for *Sea Princess Maya* to meet the ship anchored midstream. He had calculated the hours it would take for the unloading and the journey back and also the time it would take to unload the cargo on Cross Island and move it to the warehouses. The men knew exactly what each one's role was. Now it was time to go. It was ten p.m. A crescent moon hung in the sky and somewhere, a ship's horn blared, long and lonely.

They powered *Sea Princess Maya* towards the waiting vessel, the *R.F. Scott*. For the first trip, Charlie and Willie were in charge. It was easy sailing. Charlie wondered if the agents at Victoria Docks had explained the plan clearly to the agents at Southampton, the port of discharge. As they pulled up alongside, a sailor flashed a light and Charlie knew that all was going to be well. The ship's winches were ready with the loaded cargo. The sailors on board the *R.F. Scott* had their instructions from the captain and the first officer. The transfer went without a hitch. When the load was all set, Willie checked the number of cases. He flashed a sign with his powerful flashlight. The sailors answered in the affirmative. *Sea Princess Maya* would be back for the second load. When the third and final load was transferred, the captain appeared on deck. He and Charlie would meet once the *R.F. Scott* berthed at the Victoria Docks. Charlie flashed a 'Thank You'. They turned *Sea Princess Maya* and pointed her prow in the direction of home. It was five in the morning when they finished storing the merchandise in the warehouses. That day, the men of Cross Island slept through till late afternoon. Dona Maria and the girls worked while the men slept. They had a detailed sheet supplied by Willie. It documented who got what, how much and where the parcels should be delivered to. They set about packaging the goods, pasting addresses on each parcel, and writing the cost of each packet. Some of the parcels had no cost attached. These were goodwill bribes. This collateral damage was expected; it was common business practice in Bombay. Corruption meant no accountability.

When Charlie awoke, the girls were still hard at work. Eventually the men sauntered into the warehouses and began helping. Willie stopped all work at eight p.m. Charlie had ordered six cases of Scotch for Cross Island. Everybody gathered at The Rot Gut Café. Somebody had a guitar and soon the place was howling with hysteria and laughter. They had had their first business run; and it had been successful. The Irish girls danced and shouted coarse limericks: 'There was once a plumber from Lee / Who was plumbing his girl by the sea / She said stop your plumbing / There's somebody coming! / Said the plumber still plumbing...It's me!' 'Another one,' the men shouted. 'Give us another one, love!' And the girls sang...

The Rot Gut Café was alive and rocking. Men were telling stories about the good old days. Dona Maria was dancing with Charlie, Thommo and Willie. She pleaded for one more, her hands waving frantically in the air. The girls obliged, and as the guitar thundered, her body snaked and slithered into a passionate undulating rhythm. The guitar player upped the tempo. The men stopped talking as they watched her, clapping furiously to the guitar chords; and the girls swayed and screamed. More drinks were downed, good beef was eaten and still more alcohol consumed. The islanders were getting to know each other. They traded personal stories and told each other how pleased they were to be on Cross Island. The party lasted for five hours. Men were beginning to stagger; the songs grew nonsensical: 'I-Ya-Ya-Yo; in India they do it with chillies. / Here comes another one, just like the other one, / In India they do it with chillies.'

Willie put a stop to the rambunctious revelry a little after four in the morning. The girls refused offers 'for a quick one' and Thommo watched for trouble, but the men politely accepted their refusal and sauntered off carrying their corked midnight passions. As people dispersed, Charlie knew that Willie was right. The next day was going to be a long hard slog. They needed them all well rested and sober.

Charlie went to bed thinking about Dona Maria's lush body, and how it undulated beneath the supple silk fabric of her flowing yellow and green dress.

The next day, the packaging continued. Willie had decided on a Monday to Friday work week, nine to five. He sent out runners to the clients in Bombay to inform them of the date and time of the drop off. To every runner he said, 'If those bloody Indians say, "I will give you the money tomorrow." Say NO. Tell them, we do not believe in reincarnation. For us, there is no tomorrow.' It took three weeks for all the packages to be ready. Finally, the time had arrived. Charlie had hired four Leyland pick-up trucks. They were parked off Ferry Wharf. Willie had mapped out the routes, dividing the city into segments. Charlie watched it all with immense satisfaction. Thommo came up to him as he was talking to Dona Maria. He looked at Charlie silently, saying nothing. 'What?' protested Charlie, 'What is bothering you?' 'What happens if some of them do not make it back to Cross Island? Don't you think we ought to tell them, so they might be ready for any trouble?' Charlie rubbed the back of his neck grimacing. His brow furrowed as Johnson's dead face came floating into his mind. 'Hell no,' he said in a whisper. 'What happened to Johnson had nothing to do with what we are doing here. If we tell our people about this; a panic will set in. We do not need that, not now.' Thommo nodded and walked away. Behind his retreating back, Dona Maria placed her arm on Charlie's shoulder and squeezed gently, her fingers moving to his neck and caressing it. Charlie looked into her eyes with yearning. 'Some day,' Dona Maria said. She turned abruptly and walked to where Willie was sitting, adding numbers in a ledger.

Willie had decided that Charlie and Thommo would stay behind on the Island. 'You never know,' Willie explained, 'some idiot might want to come ashore, to find out what is going on. Could be the coast guard, could be a fisherman. Charlie, you have all the necessary papers that state this is the business of Victoria Docks and it is sanctioned by the government, right?' Charlie nodded. 'How many drop offs?' Charlie inquired. 'And how many days will it all take?' 'Sixty-six drop offs,' Willie said. 'It will take six days; and on the seventh day we rest.' Charlie laughed. 'Ahaaa...the good Old Testament.'

Charlie and Thommo watched Willie and the men as they boarded *Sea Princess Maya* with the first consignment. They were going to dock at Ferry Wharf, load the pick-up trucks and deliver the goods. Charlie and Thommo walked to the communal kitchen where the girls were getting dinner ready.

Many of the deliveries proved to be excruciatingly painful. When Joseph Cumberland, one of the Cross Island people, knocked on a door on his list, it was opened by a servant who informed Cumberland, 'Sir not home. Come later.' 'What time?' Cumberland asked. 'Three, four hours, maybe...better you come tomorrow evening, five-six o'clock maybe, but Sunday morning is best time.'

On another drop, a woman opened the door. 'Yes, yes,' she said, 'we are expecting a package. But you will have to wait. Master is doing puja, then has to take food. Will not take long. You wait. Want tea?'

At another location, there was the classic scrutiny of goods. 'Ahaaa...come in, come in, take your shoes out sir. What we have here. Good. Good. Now let us see. Whisky...cigarettes...milk powder...and what is this? I did not ask for this tin cheese and fish. You will have to take this back. Purnima, did you put this on the list...Purnima where are you? Come here and see this. What is this? Oh! You asked for this. Alright, alright. Fine. Next time tell me what extra you are putting on list. It is all good, sir. Now how much did you say I have to pay? Oh! I have just half that money at home. I will need to go to bank. You take half now and come tomorrow for other half, okay?' When the Cross Island man insisted that he would have to take the package back, the client said. 'Now don't get angry for nothing, what is the hurry? Wait...Purnima, go look in cupboard see if there is any money.' The client followed his wife to their bedroom and came back with the full amount. 'Lucky, we had this money at home, for emergencies. Here take it.'

Then there was suspicion and the predictable haggling. 'How do I know this is all genuine? Lot of fake stuff around today. The other day, I bought Rose's Marmalade from black market. You know my son likes marmalade. And I did not check label properly. Arre...it was made in Aden. What do those Arabs know about making marmalade? And what would happen if my son ate the marmalade and became sick? He is my only son, you know. And who knows what else could happen? Maybe we would have to go to hospital all because of marmalade. I wanted English Marmalade. And when I went to give it back, they were fighting with me, saying very bad words and wanting to beat me. Waste of money and useless headache for nothing. Let me taste whisky, just to make sure and the label, what does it say, hmmmm...And this cheese is not stale, is it? The tin is damaged, see here and then here. How much is all this? Yes, yes, now I remember the price that I was told. Can you give discount? You people must be making lot of money. I am going to be good customer. Just one time, come on, give small discount.'

Dona Maria had been helping the girls in the kitchen. It was late afternoon. She set aside her apron and joined Thommo who was having a drink at the Rot Gut Café. They were talking about how Cross Island was all coming together, when Dona Maria saw Thommo staring at Kelly, one of the girls who had come to ask Dona Maria where the meat cleaver was. She smiled and touched his arm after Kelly had left. 'If you want her, I have no problem with that,' she said. Thommo protested, 'I have you. I don't need another woman.' 'You will still have me, Thommo,' she explained, 'I can handle this. I am a practical woman.' Thommo's eyes gleamed as he mulled her proposition. He grabbed her hand and hissed, 'Does this mean that you can also...?' He left the sentence dangling dangerously in mid-air. The line was a potent, unexploded ordinance that had a propensity to do serious damage. Dona Maria instinctively threaded lightly around him. 'No,' she swore, 'You will be the only one, I promise.' Thommo relaxed and flexed his hands. He said nothing. She kissed him on his lips and walked back to the communal kitchen.

What Thommo did not know was that Dona Maria had just set forth her plan to be with Charlie one day. It had been slowly dawning on her, over the months, that Charlie was the one she wanted to be with, to grow old with, after this was all over. Thommo was a wild animal who operated at a gut instinct. He was rough, dangerous and unpredictable. She knew that she could not sustain living on his knife's edge for long. Somewhere, at some time, something bad was going to happen. Charlie was solid, logical, smart and kind. He had depth. He had soul and a great big heart. With Charlie, she could talk, and walk in lockstep. With Thommo, it was always the satisfying physical encounters that really mattered to both of them now. She knew, this would not, could not last. She knew it could result in her slashed body floating in the Arabian Sea. But she would, she told herself, live or die with the consequences.

Darkness arrived. Charlie looked at his wristwatch. Nine p.m., *Sea Princess Maya* would be back soon. Willie's careful calculations had ensured that. But as the full moon crept along the dark sky there was no sign of the boat. Charlie kept looking at his watch. Thommo was pacing the perimeter of Cross Island. Dona Maria and the girls were talking in animated whispers. Midnight slipped into a new morning. Charlie had joined Thommo who was speaking of imagined disasters. 'Something has gone wrong,' Charlie said quietly. 'They should have been here hours ago.' They retreated to the café. There was nothing left to do but torture themselves with thoughts of death, and the destruction of all that they had worked so hard for. Then at three in the morning they spied the silhouette of *Sea Princess Maya* in the distance. She was heading for Cross Island. When she finally docked, a harrowed Willie hopped off. 'Engine trouble,' he hissed cryptically as he headed to the cafe.

Later, they learnt from Willie that after the last drop offs had been made, money collected and everybody was back in the boat, the engine had failed to respond. Fortunately, two of the men had been engineers at the docks and they had managed to fix the problem; but it had taken time. An agitated Willie told Charlie, 'I want that goddamned boat to be inspected, before and after every trip. I am not going through this again.' Charlie assured him that it would be done. That morning, Charlie, Willie and the engineer journeyed to Ferry Wharf and stole what they needed from Victoria Docks. They replaced the malfunctioning parts, gunned the engine and went back to Cross Island. Sitting at The Rot Gut Café, Willie poked Charlie in the arm playfully, 'Bet you thought we were all dead, huh?' What would you have done if that had happened?' 'Packed up and gone home,' Charlie replied sardonically. 'But you are not dead and everything is going to be alright.' Willie looked at Charlie and said, 'When I was sitting there on the dead boat, like a duck exposed to a hunter, I thought of the Cross Island curse. I thought, maybe, this is it. This is a sign.' Charlie held up his hand, shook his head, 'You're an educated man, Willie,' he explained, 'please, let's not hear this superstitious clap-trap. You know better, Willie, come on.'

There were incessant obstacles and problems, but finally the delivery was over. They held a success party at The Rot Gut Café, where the men joked, complained and cursed the problems that they had had with their customers. Willie paid Dona Maria, the girls and each of the men. The profits were shared by Charlie, Thommo and Willie who maintained a careful tabulation of all the money. They stacked the profits in a sturdy old cast-iron 'A to Z' alphabet safe that they had stolen from the docks. Only Willie and Charlie were privy to the security code that Charlie had created. It started off with turning the dial to the numbers 4 and 20 anticlockwise and some other numbers clockwise. The numbers to be turned clockwise were: *2,12,1,3,11,2,9,18,4,19.* Willie laughed when Charlie explained the combination code to him.

It read 4 and 20 BLACKBIRDS.

Chapter 4

Games People Play

Outside their island domain, Charlie noticed that despite the discord and upheavals, the country was beginning to put on a semblance of normalcy by participating in international events. There was good news for Indians from England. At the 1948 Summer Olympics in London, seventy-nine Indian men had participated in thirty-nine events in ten sports. It was the first time that India had competed as an independent nation at the Olympic Games that had started on July 29th and ended on August 14th. The Indian field hockey team had defeated the British team, four-zero to win the country's first Olympic Gold medal. This was great national news in India after the Indian cricket team, on its maiden voyage to Australia, was thrashed by Don Bradman and his boys.

The Indians were ecstatic that Pakistan had been humiliated four-one by the Netherlands in a fight for third place and returned home empty-handed. Out on the streets, people lit fire-crackers to celebrate, danced to raucous music and thumped their chests proclaiming superiority over Muslim Pakistan. Muslims were insulted and accosted on streets and if they protested or retaliated, the familiar communal riots occurred.

Bombay had more reason to celebrate than the rest of India.

Eight players on the victorious team were Bombayites. Dona Maria sneered at her islanders when she read the news in the papers. 'The next thing they will do is win at cricket against the English team,' she announced. Thommo who had been drinking growled at her, 'Shet up woman, watch yer tounge! What do you know about cricket? You need cork balls wrapped in leather and a stiff willow; you don't have either! What did Portugal do at the games, drink dodgy wine and fok' Englishmen? I read they got a complimentary bronze and silver for that!' Dona Maria looked into his eyes and the liquid malice glittering in his pupils. She decided to hold her tongue and retreat beyond the boundary line. 'Let it go,' Charlie counselled, 'I am happy that the Indians won. This is their Jesse Owens moment. They bloody deserve it.'

The girls at the House of Tarts had been busy. Business was good and steady. The party was wild. The singing and dancing, predictably joyous and loud. Dona Maria was sitting on a log, sipping black rum when Kelly sidled up to her. Dona Maria raised her eyebrow as she looked at Kelly. She knew what was coming. 'Thommo wants to...' Dona Maria cut her sentence off. 'I know,' she said softly. 'It is alright. He has my permission.' Kelly looked worried. She had heard about Thommo's violent ways. If something went wrong, she did not want to be with her back against a wall, pleading with Thommo. 'I can't do this!' she exclaimed and walked away in a huff.

Dona Maria smiled. The theatre of passion had just opened. Act One: Scene One. For some strange reason, she could not explain to herself why she was savouring this real-life thirller. She watched Thommo from the corner of her eye talking to Kelly. She saw him shrug and turn away. Kelly walked up to Willie, motioned that she wanted to talk. Dona Maria watched and waited. This was going to be an interesting development.

Willie walked up to Charlie's shack the next day. He recounted what Kelly had said to him. Charlie instantly knew what Dona Maria was trying to accomplish. He told Willie that he would talk to her. Alone with his thoughts, Charlie decided that if the choice arrived where he had to choose between the success of Cross Island and Dona Maria, the Portuguese lady would lose. It was too early for her to start this game. If Thommo even whiffed a connection of passion between Dona Maria and Charlie, blood would flow, plans would be disrupted, and the future would sink into the fiery maw of hell. They had all worked too hard, given up too much; his passion and her bleeding heart would have to wait. Thommo had journeyed with Willie to the mainland to set up the parametres of the next consignment. Charlie summoned Kelly. 'Ask Dona Maria to come here,' he ordered. Kelly began protesting, 'Why me? Let somebody else go tell her.' Charlie pointed his forefinger to his door. 'Go,' he said very quietly. Kelly hurried out to Thommo's shack. Dona Maria took her time arriving. Charlie knew she was playing her usual game. He decided to humour her instead of displaying the irritation he felt inside.

Finally, after an hour, she walked in. Charlie smiled. Dona Maria smiled. 'Sit,' he ordered. 'My, my,' she cooed, 'the general is upset.' Charlie ignored her. Charlie had never been one for perfunctory conversation. He sliced to the bone with his first sentence. 'Dona Maria,' he said, almost formal in his address. 'Right now, at this moment, at this time, if I have to choose between you and Thommo, I will choose him. I need him more than I need you. Your foolish actions could put Cross Island in jeopardy. I will not let that happen. You understand. Our time will come, of that I give you my word. You need to stay with him till Cross Island is stable. It will take time, it will happen. Let me think, let me plan. If you try and set Thommo against me for whatever twisted reasons, you will go down with this ship that will surely burn. Lives will be lost. I do not want that, and I am sure that you don't want that to happen either. Do not put yourself in a position where your dreams clash with our reality here. Do you understand? Tell Thommo that you have reconsidered your generous offer, that you are *not* okay with him sleeping with other women. Warm his bed until the time is right. I will always be here for you.' Dona Maria was looking straight into Charlie's eyes as he talked. 'Are you finished?' she asked in fury. 'May I leave now?' Without waiting for his dismissal, she stood up, kicked her chair back and walked out.

Charlie sat still, deep in thought. Had he said the right things to her? Was he too abrupt and harsh? He knew that he had got through to her, still...He recalled reading about a woman scorned, in a play he had read a long time ago. Was it Shakespeare? Charlie went to where his books were and found *The Mourning Bride*, a 1697 play by William Congreve. He read the lines out loud: 'Heav'n has no rage like love to hatred turn'd. Nor Hell a fury, like a woman scorn'd.'

That night, Dona Maria mauled Thommo in bed. She bit, clawed and scratched her frustration on his sinewy body. When it was over, Thommo's animal instinct sensed trouble. 'What's wrong with you, woman?' He queried. She laughed as she licked a spot of blood on his lower lip. 'You don't like?' she pouted. 'I love you, Thommo,' she lied looking into his eyes. 'I was just trying to show you how much.' Thommo laughed. She kissed him, deep and long. 'I do not want to share you with another woman,' she said, 'that was just a test.' Thommo protested, 'I thought that we were not going to do that again. Remember? We had agreed...' 'Yes,' she consented, 'I made a mistake. Forgive me, Thommo, please.' 'No more tests,' Thommo cautioned, 'no more, do you understand?' She glimpsed the glint of madness in his eyes and held him close, thinking of Charlie. The next day Dona Maria talked to Kelly. She told her that she was relieved that Kelly had turned down Thommo. 'I promise you,' she reassured Kelly, 'there will be no trouble. I have talked with Thommo.' Kelly sighed with relief. The two women embraced and walked to the communal kitchen to start cooking breakfast.

Charlie and Willie were sitting at a corner table deep in discussion. It was decided that Willie would send a telegram to his contact in Southampton. They expected the next consignment to be large. News of the impending prohibition was going to be great for business. Liquor was going to be their cash crop. Payment would be made after the consignment was sold. It would be sent in hard cash, with a ship's captain. Charlie shot down Willie's idea that they increase the number of the orders. 'We are not ready yet,' Charlie advised. 'We don't need that extra pressure right now. Let's not get greedy with the smuggling, boy!' Willie laughed.

Chapter 5

The Insanity of Madness

They sent out runners to meet with their 'clients' to ascertain what they wanted, how much, and how large the next consignment should be. They were shocked by the sheer numbers of the orders, they were huge, almost daunting. Friends and relatives of their clients now wanted in on the black-market finery. When Willie tallied the orders, they were looking at an amazing three hundred and sixteen drops! Many of the rich women socialites wanted Cow & Gate baby milk, exotic French perfumes and European gourmet chocolates. Orders for Scotch, canned cheese and ham, State Express 555, Benson and Hedges and Rothman cigarettes had quadrupled. 'You still want to do this twice a month?' Charlie said to Willie with mock horror.

The schizophrenic attack came in the dead of night. Charlie began hearing storm sounds, thunder crashed and the crack of lightning whiplashed his body. Then all was calm. Distorted faces began appearing. They jeered and spat at him. Told him they were going to half, quarter and dice him. Charlie rushed into the kitchen, grabbed a knife and began waving it in the blackness. Sister Rosemary was standing naked in front of him. Then she smiled and her teeth were jagged. It seemed to go on for hours. When it was over, he found himself in a fetal position on the floor lying in the foul wetness of his urine.

Another storm came the next afternoon as he was discussing business with Willie, who recoiled in horror as Charlie's sentences fragmented and exploded into gibberish. He watched, alarmed. He shook Charlie by his shoulders. Charlie attacked him, swinging wildly. Willie fled from the shack and came back with Thommo. Charlie lunged at the two men. Thommo hit him, once in the stomach and once on the jaw. Charlie reeled backward and fell heavily against his table. His eyes rolled in his head. He was unconscious as he fell to the floor. Willie and Thommo looked at one another. This, they could not comprehend. 'Is he drunk?' Thommo asked. 'No,' said Willie. 'Something is very wrong here.' Together they hauled his lifeless body from the floor and placed Charlie in his easy chair.

They sat around in silence waiting for him to come back to reality. It took Charlie half an hour to awaken. He did so slowly. Finally he sat upright, massaged his stomach, then his jaw. He winced as he stared at Thommo and Willie. 'Something happened to you,' Willie explained in a halting voice. 'You attacked us. You were talking nonsense.' Charlie's body slumped. His head hung low. He knew he had to tell them. Let them in on the secret of his disease. 'I have schizophrenia,' he confessed. Thommo did not really understand what schizophrenia was all about, but Willie did. He, said, 'Are you taking medicine for this?' Charlie shook his head slowly. 'Why not?' Willie shot back. 'This is dangerous, you know that. You have to get this treated. At least it can help contain it. You have to see a doctor, otherwise Charlie, this whole Cross Island dream land will crumble.' Charlie knew that what Willie was describing was true. He promised that he would see his ayurvedic doctor the next day. Thommo patted Charlie on his shoulder, 'Sorry I had to hit you,' he apologized, 'You went crazy.' Charlie smiled, 'I had heard that you packed a steel punch, now I know. I hope,' he continued, 'we will keep this between us. Thommo, keep this away from Dona Maria, it could get around, you understand, and that will be bad.' Thommo promised that he would say nothing. Willie did the same. Thommo said 'Cross Island is more important than any two-bit woman, you don't have to worry.' Charlie was not surprised that Thommo had no real feelings for Dona Maria. That was the way the sub-human called Thommo had been created, Charlie understood his soulless existence better than anyone alive.

Their pledge of *Omertà* was violently shattered the next morning even as Charlie got ready to go see the doctor. In the communal kitchen, with everybody having breakfast, the chemicals in Charlie's brain exploded. The Charlie that they all knew disintegrated and distorted into an ugly, sneering, frightening thing. At one point he just stood amongst them, silent, his eyes rolling, his mouth dribbling saliva, a big tremble in his arms. 'He's gone mad,' was the whisper that went around the staring and frightened people. The girls from the House Of Tarts were weeping. Dona Maria was talking animatedly with Willie, while Thommo looked on laconically. It took two elongated hours and fifteen minutes for Charlie to emerge from his schizophrenic cage. Like a wounded animal, he crawled out of the trap, disoriented and humiliated. He looked at Willie with imploring eyes. Willie stood on a chair and told everybody what Charlie suffered from. He painted his affliction with hope, this could be handled and managed, he explained. He was going to take Charlie to a doctor and all would be well. Nobody spoke to Charlie as he sat there transfixed. He looked through them at a horizon only he could see. Willie turned to Charlie. 'Let's go. Doctor,' he barked. Charlie meekly followed him to *Sea Princess Maya.*

Back on the mainland, they took a taxi to the ayurvedic

doctor's dispensary. 'Why don't you go to a real doctor?' Willie asked. 'This Eastern mumbo jumbo is rural village medicine Charlie!' By this time Charlie's confidence had returned. 'Ayurvedic medicine has a track record that goes back thousands of years. If you read, like I do, you would know that.' Willie decided to let the insult fade. This was a wrong time to start an intellectual argument on the merits and demerits of medicine. The doctor was pleased to see Charlie. 'Where have you been?' he inquired. 'You know if you stop taking the medicine bad things can happen.' 'Bad things are happening,' Charlie replied. The doctor nodded. He asked Willie to describe the episodes. 'This is not good,' was his diagnosis. 'I am going to give you a more powerful mixture. Let's see how it helps. But, Mr Charlie, you have to come here every three weeks so I can monitor your progress and change your medication according to your needs. And remember, no liquor.' Willie promised the doctor that he would guarantee that Charlie would stay off the sauce and he would visit the doctor with regularity. When they were leaving with the prescribed powders, the doctor said, 'I heard that Victoria Docks has started a new project on Cross Island,' he turned to Charlie and continued, 'I also heard that you are in charge of this project. Good luck, I say.' Charlie grimaced. Willie looked at the doctor poker faced. So everybody knew, he thought. This was not good.

When they got back, Dona Maria arrived at Willie's shack. 'How is he?' she inquired. 'He's fine,' Willie answered. He hoped she would leave. He was tired. 'Can what he has be cured completely?' she wanted to know. 'No,' said Willie, 'It can be contained, but his schizophrenia will only end when Charlie is in a coffin.'

That night Dona Maria dropped Charlie Strongbow from her future. She sat by her window all night, thinking, scheming and planning. By the time the first rays of the sun appeared, she had a basic plan in place. She was going to take over the operations of Cross Island. Using Thommo as her bulwark, she was going to anchor the business on the island. It was a mission that had suicide scrawled all over it. She joined Thommo in bed. She planned to get rid of him in the future; but now, she was willing to gamble in a house of ill repute, knowing that the cards were in all probability marked. The deck was stacked against her, but the game was on. As sleep washed over her drooping eyelids, she thought of Willie Watson and his clever calculating mind. She turned lethargically, half asleep, and cradled the muscled back of a snoring Thommo.

Three weeks passed without a major incident. At a meeting, Dona Maria turned to Willie, 'The next drop is big. Maybe I can help you. I am good with numbers. I can help you with all the paperwork and planning, this will help take a big load off Charlie's shoulders.' Willie deferred to Charlie. He raised an eyebrow in question. Charlie thought for a long minute and nodded his consent. Unknown to them, Charlie had now begun to feel a massive insecurity. It had started to erode the confidence that he had once considered infallible. As a dark depression enveloped him, he walked out silently and headed back to his shack. Dona Maria was about to say something when Willie interrupted. 'Give him time,' he explained. 'He is worried about this madness that he has to deal with.' Dona Maria placed her palm on Willie's shoulder. She squeezed it gently and said, 'I understand.' Her affection had not gone unnoticed; her lingering fingers had transmitted a message. Willie smiled at her and looked into her eyes. 'He will be alright,' he assured her, 'let's leave him alone for some time.'

Later, alone in his shack, Willie thought about Dona Maria. Maybe, some day in the future, when this is all over, he thought.

The pragmatist in him set forth a warning that cautioned Willie. But, thinking of her, his heart seemed to be beating faster. He knew that he would have to leave her alone; but that could be a problem since they were now going to spend long hours together getting ready for the next drop. Willie promised himself that he would keep his hands and heart far from Dona Maria. She was not worth the destruction of their lives and business on Cross Island, and he was petrified of Thommo's murderous wrath. Willie poured himself a whisky and sipped it, savouring the malted barley. He had another drink and wondered why he had never had a permanent relationship with a woman. There had been more than a few, but when the physical attraction had diminished, Willie had moved on. He knew instinctively that Dona Maria would offer him a short future of togetherness before she moved away. That was the way she was; but again, maybe she wanted to settle down...'Who the hell knows,' Willie mumbled. When the liquor had warmed his insides, he strolled out of his shack and headed for the House of Tarts.

Sitting in his easy chair, Charlie was battling Dodo. The bottle of whisky, perched on his table was a dangerous invitation. He wisely ignored its liquid message of compassion and sympathy.

Dodo: *Where are we going to go from here, Charlie?*

Charlie: *I am a stronger man than you think. I am going to contain and beat this animal that is trying to tear me apart. This is my family. They will be there for me no matter what!*

Dodo: *Give me one name that will stand beside you once your power disintegrates. Of them all, maybe Willie, maybe...but don't count on it. Nobody wants to be shackled to a burden, Charlie. There is a power game coming. How can you manipulate and* *scheme when the demons turn you into an irrational bumbling idiot? That is what I was trying to explain*

Charlie: What do you want me to do?

There was no answer. Dodo had retreated into the ether beyond the darkness. Charlie sat there, immobile in his cloud of doom; his mind alone and vacant. Finally, he grunted like a wounded animal. The crippling mental anguish showed on his countenance as his cornered mind looked for a way to survive in the future. Charlie eased himself out of the chair and shuffled to the bottle.

And then, suddenly there it was, in the newspapers and on the radio. The Bombay Prohibition Act of 1949 was now the law. Now orders for alcohol flowed fast and furious. 'This is our Golden Age,' Willie crowed. 'God bless Bombay and its prohibition.' 'Now, we are in business,' Charlie said, 'We are going to be millionaires.'

As the weeks rolled on, they worked in overdrive getting ready for the next consignment. Their clientele now included the A-list glitterati from the Hindi-film industry, leading industrialists, politicians and top brass police personnel. Charlie and Willie made frequent trips to the mainland. On the surface, everything looked calm and manageable; but something was wrong. People on the island noticed a perceptible change coming over Charlie. He was growing dictatorial and suspicious of mundane things. He asked unnecessary rude questions, searching for motives and imagined conspiracies against him; like a sodden drunk looking for a provocation, he riled everyone he came across. Charlie was not entirely conscious of his disquieting obnoxious behaviour. And in the morning, when he awoke, like a drunk, he remembered nothing. But there were days, when he behaved rationally, like the old Charlie, soft spoken, logical, direct and firm. His oscillating behaviour grew into a sad whispered joke on the island. 'Let's see, which Charlie shows up tomorrow?' His myriad, complex characteristics were abrasive entities that seared and abused everyone on the island, and slowly a mild resentment began to surface against a man who had once been universally respected and loved.

Willie knew what was happening; the disease was getting progressively worse. Charlie still visited the doctor, swallowed the powders, but his alcohol intake had grown. Willie was nobody's fool; he could hear a major breakdown rumbling in the distance. He would never plan to intentionally hurt Charlie, but he had to have something in place, just in case Charlie drove himself to incapacitation. That's when the secret meetings began. Dona Maria, Willie and Thommo began talking. At one of these meetings, Thommo placed his finger on a question that no one had thought about. 'Who will look after him when he breaks down? Do we throw him into the sea?' Dona Maria looked away. Willie gripped Thommo's arm forcefully, his fingers biting into muscle. 'Charlie is family,' he said, 'we will cross that bridge when it comes. If something happens to him, if I find out that it was you who stuck a knife in his back, I will leave Cross Island. You and your woman can take over. Do what you want with it. We'll see how that goes.' Thommo grinned, 'You don't have to get huffy about it mate, I was just asking,' he said defensively.

Dona Maria proved to be an invaluable asset. She studied and dissected Willie's sheets and sheets of paper, spotting mistakes, offering suggestions and solutions. Charlie watched her work; and was impressed. Willie, whose philosophy was 'the proof is in the pudding', was amazed that she could handle the complexity with ease and dexterity. When she suggested that they raise their price, Charlie disagreed. Her eyes flashed but she held her tongue. 'It is too late now,' he counselled gently. 'We have to give our clients a heads up. But it is a good idea. Let's inform them that we will be increasing our costs the next time onwards.' He looked at Dona Maria. 'That is fair, don't you think?' She smiled now. 'Yes, sir,' she chimed, 'I agree.' Dona Maria asked the girls from the House of Tarts to prepare three hundred and sixteen notes. Each package would include a note thanking their clients for their business and explaining briefly why the 'Blackbird Pie Company' had to regretfully raise the price. That was Charlie's idea. Willie read the cryptic reason for the hike that Charlie had written: *Limey Christian bastards at English ports demanding bigger bribes. We regret a price increase on the next consignment on all goods. Please Note: The price for all alcohol will be increased on the current consignment because of the risk factor of the recent prohibition.*

May the good Lord bless you all.

They laughed at his humour as they worked towards three hundred and sixteen drop offs. The waiting list for future alcohol orders was now eight hundred names long. Willie had to work out the logistics of transferring tons of merchandise from a ship anchored in mid-stream. A small misinterpretation could be disastrous. If a member of the coast guard said, 'Okay, we will see.' What did he mean? Indians usually said things like this. Both Charlie and Willie knew that it could mean anything. Yes, no, maybe. They set out to meet with the coast guard. Once again, as he had done so many times in the past, Charlie used the Victoria Docks as a backdrop for the meeting. The office of the assistant commandant had asked them to meet a junior subordinate who was in charge of local maritime activities around Ferry Wharf. 'That's good news,' Willie said, 'the lower the rank of the coast guard, the better for us.' The junior subordinate, a harried, overworked man, was having a tough day. Charlie presented him with the necessary papers and then slid the case of Scotch whisky under his desk. He explained that they might have to do a mid-sea transfer of the merchandise. 'If this is Victoria Dock work, why don't you unload at the docks?' He wanted to know. Charlie began explaining, 'Sir,' he said, 'it would be easier for us to offload the merchandise mid-sea near Cross Island. The cost of transport from the docks is expensive and...' The junior subordinate, looked at Charlie, who seemed to be stumbling for words. 'Sir,' Willie chimed in, 'beside our usual cargo, we are getting medicines for Saint George hospital. We forgot to include it in the cargo manifest and the bill of lading. The hospital badly needs this medicine to treat tuberculosis. We volunteered to get these medicines to them for free. It is very difficult to get them in India. I am sure you understand. Because of these small items that are not included in the manifest, unloading at the docks could be a problem. We are willing to compensate for this. Please help us. Please help the hospital.' 'How do I know,' the junior subordinate stated, 'that you are not bringing in arms? This consignment has to be inspected. If it has only commercial stuff, then it is alright. But the coast guard will have to inspect it. I am going to authorize a mid-sea transfer just this one time. If there is anything out of the ordinary then the consignment will be confiscated. I will get my secretary to call Saint George Hospital to confirm.' Charlie and Willie thanked him and assured him that his compensation would be delivered to his home.

When they emerged from the junior subordinate's office Charlie exploded, 'What's the matter with you, Willie? Saint George Hospital? Medicines? Have you lost your bloody mind?' 'Let me handle this,' Willie said calmly. 'I had to bluff; otherwise there was no way in hell he was going to authorize a mid-sea transfer.' 'Now what?' Charlie asked. Willie smiled and said,

'We pay a visit to Saint George Hospital near Victoria railway terminus.'

After being told that the dean of the hospital was busy, they cajoled and argued with hospital staff, and finally managed to meet with him, telling his assistant that it was a matter of life and death. After introducing themselves, they told the dean that they owned an import-export corporation and were involved with many charities across India. 'We have a big consignment of antibiotics to treat tuberculosis coming in, that has been donated from the people of Great Britain,' Willie told him. 'We will personally hand over this consignment to you once it lands. We are having some problems with the customs. Oh! You know the usual bureaucratic nonsense, about papers and manifests...All they want to know is that the medicines are for Saint George Hospital.' The dean who was extremely busy said that he was happy to assist them, if it meant a free donation to his hospital. He assured them that he would take care of the customs if and when they called.

When Charlie and Willie left the hospital and were on the street, Charlie shook his head. 'This is insane. I cannot believe this!' Willie laughed. 'That's how you do it ol' chap, with a wide smile and a small lie.' 'And what are you going to tell the dean? He will be waiting for his medicines.' 'Oh!' said Willie, 'I will tell him that the consignment was pilfered at the docks. You know how they are there. Heartless thieves, every one of them; and I will offer him monetary compensation with the appropriate humble apologies.' Charlie smiled and joked, 'What would my life be without you,' and added, 'Willie you're the best bluffmaster I have ever seen.'

There was more work to be done. Gift packages were offered to police personnel, bribes set in place, promises made. Telegrams flew between Bombay and Southampton port. The man in charge of the port at Southampton was a big link. He was the one responsible for buying, storing and transferring the goods into the store houses, bribing port officials and then getting the goods transferred to a hold on the delivery vessel while he made sure that the forged paperwork was in order. The whole consignment, to save costs, was jettisoned to a legit company in England who were transferring goods. Paperwork was juggled, books cooked and insurance companies hoodwinked as the consignment made its way to the 'Blackbird Pie Company'. It was a colossal complicated illegal international operation, run under the blue-blooded nose of His Royal Majesty, King George VI.

CHAPTER 6

High Tide and Black Waters

It was common knowledge that a ship's crew stole from holds. Charlie's point man at Southampton had checked the locks on the hold personally before the vessel set sail. He made sure that only the captain had the keys to the hold where the illegal merchandise was stored. A hundred loose ends were knotted and secured. It was a mammoth operation; one slip and the whole operation would sink into the sea.

Sunday morning, *HRM Wave Runner* would anchor near Cross Island as she awaited her berth at Alexandra, Victoria or Princes's Docks. Victoria Docks was a semi-tidal dock with vessels docking and departing at high tide. The *HRM Wave Runner* was scheduled to arrive at low tide so she would have to wait for the tide to turn before she entered the docks. It would be twelve hours and twenty-four minutes before high tide. In that window of time, Willie would have to get all his merchandise cleared in mid-stream. Once the *HRM Wave Runner* entered Victoria Docks, the operation would get complicated and expensive. 'We need another two boats,' Willie told Charlie. 'I am not going to take a chance with twelve hours. Make sure...tell them that we want our own men running the vessels.' Charlie knew owners of sturdy sand trawlers. He was confident that he could hire them for a day. They had tough sea dogs on the island that had the expertise to run any vessel. It was Thursday; Sunday morning loomed like an albatross; the shadow of twelve feet of wingspan, magnified a hundred times hovered over the minds of the people on Cross Island. They were nervous, which way would the wind from the wings blow come Sunday morning? It was mid-July; the middle of the monsoon season, and this would make a mid-stream transfer even more dangerous. The heaving sea and whipping winds could jeopardize the drop off, and if it started raining while the operation was in progress, anything could happen. They could lose the cargo, lives might be lost. If the deluge was too strong, the captain would not be able to get the winches on the ship manned.

Willie knew that the entire consignment was sailing in on a credit line; if something went wrong and they lost the cargo, this would all be over in under a week. The crew at Southampton had big connections with their Bombay counterparts. If they could not honour the pay back in time, blood would flow, lives would be lost. He would probably be the first to be murdered. They knew it was Willie who controlled the finances of Cross Island. Cross Island itself would no doubt be torched and burnt with the fires of vengeance. No one would survive. That was the accepted brutality with which international laws of illegality worked.

Sunday morning arrived. There was news from the docks. The *HRM Wave Runner* had been delayed, bad weather. It would be a week before she came into the Bombay harbour. She could arrive at high tide and sail into Victoria Docks. Now the sailor's knot loomed over their heads, threatening to slip down on their necks. Charlie, Willie and Thommo spent days at the docks trying to surreptitiously organize ways to move their merchandise from Victoria Docks. The load was too much, they were told; there were inspections going on; government informers, masquerading as dock workers were lurking in the shadows, no one wanted to risk an illegal operation. Dock bosses blamed it on the new red tape being laid out. It will all be over in a month or so, they assured Charlie.

Charlie, Willie and Thommo now knew that if the *HRM Wave Runner* did not arrive at low tide they were dead in the water. But there was nothing they could do but return to Cross Island, and wait in agony. Thommo began talking of an escape strategy on the way back, 'I know a place where we can hide for months, if it all goes wrong,' he confided. 'We can then slip through and leave for a European country.' 'And what happens to the rest of our people?' Charlie wanted to know. Thommo shrugged. Charlie and Willie looked at him with open contempt. 'No, thank you,' Charlie snarled, 'I will die here, with my people. They are all good men and women. You and your woman can leave.' Willie nodded, 'I will stay,' he promised Charlie, 'No matter what happens, we will try and work it out.' Thommo looked away and stared at the black horizon as *Sea Princess Maya* cut through the darkening late evening sea and headed for home.

They waited in anticipation, making frequent trips to Victoria Docks to try and mitigate the problem. Nothing changed. Finally the *HRM Wave Runner* arrived. She flowed in at high tide and powered straight into Victoria Docks. Charlie had a meeting with the captain who had already talked to the dock bosses. There was no way to pull this off. And then, he added a further problem, his chief engineer was being difficult, he did not want to take a risk, but even if he did, the captain explained, there was no way to get around the dock supervisors. The place, they had told the captain, was crawling with government spies. They could not stop on the way out because the coast guard was patrolling the area heavily. 'We have taken care of the coast guard,' Charlie assured him, but the captain was still wary. And, he cautioned, it was the middle of the monsoons, even if they stopped in mid-stream, it would be impossible to make the transfer safely. The best thing to do, the captain advised, was to let the merchandise stay on board and ship it back to Southampton. It seemed like the end.

The mood on Cross Island turned sombre and dark. A hundred 'What ifs' circulated. Thommo called a meeting with Willie and Charlie. He told them that he had a plan. The *HMS Wave Runner* had sat in the docks for two weeks. After she had been unloaded and the usual maintenance was administered, she was cleared to set sail in two days. Thommo slipped into the docks the night she was scheduled to leave. He boarded the *HMS Wave Runner*, donning the official overalls that the dock's deck workers wore and hid in the engine room. Charlie had talked to him about the estimated time it would take the ship to reach the vicinity of Cross Island once she left the docks. Thommo materialized before the chief engineer like an evil apparition. He placed his knife near the chief engineer's groin. 'Stop the fokkin' ship,' he commanded. 'Radio the docks; tell them you have a minor problem. Tell whoever you have to tell that you have engine problems. We have taken care of the coast guard.' The chief engineer trembled as Thommo's carving knife pressured his groin. He radioed the captain. The captain called the docks. It was a safety routine that had to be followed. A tugboat soon arrived to offer assistance if they needed it, but returned to the docks when the captain told them that the problem was minor; and was being taken care of.

The driving rain had ceased, but the sky was heavy with

dark grey clouds. In five minutes, three boats from Cross Island arrived. The sea was choppy and wicked; tons of heaving water constantly bobbed the boats that were now fastened to the ship. They bucked and listed, like wild animals straining to be set free. The captain wanted to call off this madness. He looked desperately into the dead eyes of Thommo standing beside the chief engineer and pleaded, 'You see the sea; this is extremely dangerous! You could lose your cargo. Worse, you are risking the lives of my men and yours.' Thommo nodded, barely blinking, saying nothing. The captain sighed, ordered the winches to be activated. Thommo stood close to the chief engineer; he eyed the sturdy English seamen who were getting ready to start winching the loads. 'If you order your men to attack me, your chief engineer dies,' he warned the captain. So intense was the chief engineer's terror, that he soiled his underwear. Thommo, smelling his fecal fear, snorted a contemptuous spotted hyena laugh; 'Now see what you've done, mate,' he chortled, 'bet you six pence the Missus wouldn't like to see you like that, eh!'

The unloading process began. It took six tortuous hours. A winch snapped; the swinging loads on their way down to the boats swayed murderously in the ripping winds. A number of crates nearly landed in the sea. The wet ropes cut deeply into the men's hands as they guided the lowered crates to a safe landing. One was struck in the head as a load came crashing down; he lost consciousness and had a broad gash on his skull. Finally the last load landed on *Sea Princess Maya.* Thommo shook the captain's hand. He apologized to the chief engineer. 'There will be no problem,' Thommo assured the captain. You can make up for the lost time. Fix the logbooks to show that you had a problem.' 'Thank you for telling me how to do my job,' the captain replied dryly. Thommo ignored the jibe. 'You will both be compensated very well for this, I promise you, so it is in your interest to stay silent.' He scampered down the ship's ladder and boarded *Sea Princess Maya.* The coast guard arrived, and began inspecting the merchandise. They were following orders, looking for arms and ammunition. When they finally finished their search, Thommo thanked them and slipped a thick wad of notes to the coast guard supervisor.

The people on Cross Island erupted with joy as the loaded boats pulled up alongside and anchored. Willie and Charlie were still slumped in dazed relief that Thommo had actually pulled off this suicide mission. The women tended to the crew's injuries. They looked like severely wounded soldiers who had been ambushed and had barely managed to escape, dragging their bleeding lives to safety. The unconscious man had come alive; he would be taken to a doctor the next day. Dona Maria embraced Thommo who smiled sheepishly. He headed for the Rot Gut Café, to 'water the dryness in my throat'.

The next day the packing began. But instead of euphoria, Charlie felt a great and surprising sadness come upon him. He tried to rationalize it; the depression grew worse. He began spending time alone, holed up in his shack, drinking. Willie came in, talked to him. Charlie insisted that he was alright and wanted to be alone. When Willie left, Charlie went to bed. He dreamt that he was with Maya, now grown and beautiful. Long flowing blonde hair and deep blue eyes that twinkled as she spoke. He looked at her in admiration. Then she began to turn grey; a sickness had come upon her. He held her in his arms, the deep blue eyes closed as she died.

Victoria had been waiting for a letter from Maya. Finally it arrived.

Dear Victoria,

Thank you for writing and giving me the moral support that I so badly needed. It has been almost nine months since my last letter. I am doing well and have got over the disaster that was Burt. I have begun writing a children's book and have found a talented young man who is a great illustrator who is going to be working with me. Who knows, I could be a published author soon.

Victoria, I have a new best friend. Her name is Neelam Chopra. She is an architect. Her parents are doctors who have retired, and now live in Madras. We have gotten very close. We go out shopping and take walks in the park and spend a lot of time together. There are many nights when we just talk and if it is too late for her to go home, she spends the night at my place. We talk of love and life and religion and God and so many things. When I am with her, I can laugh and be silly. It is a simple thing but it makes me happy. I am no longer afraid to be honest. She is a beautiful, pleasant person and we get along well, and she is a great cook who can create exotic Indian dishes. I am extremely happy that she has come into my life. I have told her about my past...Charlie and Caitlin, and you...she understands, without being judgmental or critical. The past, she said the other day, is a river that has flowed into the sea. I think that is a wonderful statement, so wise, so true.

Victoria, it would be so great to see you. I wish you could travel and come and see me. I know that your age and health do not permit you to do so, but in many ways, you are part of my family and my friend, and I would be overjoyed to see you. One day, we will meet, I promise you. Thank you for staying on in my life. I hope that Charlie is safe and well.

Victoria, I am very happy now. I am excited that I am creating the children's book. It is about a wild parrot who visits a young girl's garden every day. And the girl and bird talk...silly innocent things; childlike enchanted fantasies and flying free and so many other good things. The child's parents have bought her an exotic talking parrot that is in an ornamental cage on the verandah. The wild parrot convinces the girl that it is wrong to cage a bird, and the beautifully designed cage is a horrible jail. And one day, when her parents were not at home, the young girl opens the door of the cage and sets the parrot free. She is momentarily very sad to see her pet and best friend go, but the girl smiles and claps her hands in glee, as the two parrots fly off into a beautiful forest nearby to live their lives, free and happy.

Hope you like my little story.

I will write again.

Sincerely,

Maya

CHAPTER 7

Speaking in Tongues

The next morning Charlie woke up with a head banging hangover. He poured himself a drink, gulped down the raw liquor. His eyes watered as he filled the glass again. He heard a knock on the door. Willie, Thommo and Dona Maria entered. 'How is the packing going?' Charlie asked. 'Never mind the packing,' Willie growled, 'You need to stop drinking.' Charlie looked down at the floor. He was ashamed that they were seeing him in the state that he was in. 'I dreamed of Maya last night...' he began. Dona Maria cut in rudely, 'No excuses anymore, Charlie. Have a bath, change your clothes. I can smell your stink. Get out there. There is work to be done.' No one had spoken to Charlie like this. He looked hard at Dona Maria, ready to tell her to go to hell. Willie could see the beginning of an argument. 'Charlie,' he said gently, 'we need you out there. Decisions have to be made. Only you can do this. Come on, my friend. Get ready and let's go.' Charlie nodded slowly. He turned towards Thommo, smiled and said, 'You going to hit me again?' Thommo laughed. They left Charlie who took a long bath, changed into clean clothes and walked out to join the bustle of packing. In the weeks that followed, the pace and frenzy of sorting, packing and labelling grew intense. Charlie managed to stay off the sauce. He was back in command as he issued directions. He felt good. He started visiting the House of Tarts, again, sometimes twice a day. The islanders heaved a collective sigh of relief. Old Charlie was back.

Willie insisted that Charlie go to the mainland and deliver packages. He did not want him hanging around the island doing nothing. Willie knew that left alone for too long, he would turn to the bottle again. They started delivering packages the next day. Willie stayed with *Sea Princess Maya* as the men went about their assignments. They would all return to Ferry Wharf in the evening around six p.m. and then head home. By six-thirty p.m. all the men were back. Charlie was missing. They waited till eight p.m., then turned the boat around and headed back to Cross Island. Now panic set in. Early the next morning, as they continued to deliver packages, Thommo and Willie contacted people they knew around Bombay. Nobody seemed to have seen Charlie. They inquired at the docks, the bars and smuggling dens. Charlie had disappeared.

After delivering his package, Charlie had decided he had time to go see his old friend Victoria. He had wanted to describe his dream to her, to see if she could interpret the sadness. She had been pleased to see Charlie. They talked about Cross Island and her daughters who were now in England. 'So, how goes it with you, my friend?' Victoria asked. Charlie told her that he had dreamed of Maya. In the middle of his narration, he asked for a drink. 'You know where the bottle is,' she said, 'go ahead.' Charlie began drinking. The attack came, brutal. Victoria watched in horror and fright as Charlie's rational speech disintegrated as he entered the tower of Babble.

When the episode passed, Charlie woke up to the reality that he was still in Victoria's house. 'What is wrong with you, Charlie?' she asked, concern in her shaking voice. He had to tell her.

'Have you seen a doctor?' she inquired. 'Yes,' said Charlie, 'it does not seem to be helping.' What he failed to mention was the ban on alcohol. Charlie started drinking again, till he grew woozy. Victoria led him to the guest bedroom where he passed out.

Back on the island Charlie's disappearance had a profound effect on everyone. It was all they talked about as they worked. On the mainland they continued to search, with hope fading as the weeks dragged on. Willie and Dona Maria took control. Willie missed the steady hand of Charlie on the helm. Fortunately, the drop offs were going well; one more day and the last of the three hundred and sixteen packages would be delivered. Charlie had now been missing for four weeks. They were sure he was dead.

Back at Victoria's, home, Charlie had been drifting in and out of his stupor. He was paralyzed in bed most of the time. Victoria looked after him. She wanted to know how to contact his friends on Cross Island. Charlie refused to help her; they had moved, he lied, to another small island. Charlie did not want his friends to see what had happened to him. With some of the money that had been handed to him for the packages he had delivered, he bought a case of whisky from the local liquor store and wallowed in its liquid sympathy. The little food that he ate, he vomited. The attacks now came with devastating regularity. Charlie refused to bathe. He stank; Victoria began fearing that he might die. In desperation she decided to take a chance. She contacted a local fisherman she knew and paid him to ferry her to Cross Island. The fisherman did not want to go. He claimed that the island was haunted and anyone going there would not return. She promised to double the fee. He could stay on the boat while she visited her English friends on the island. It would be a short visit she promised him. Finally he consented.

They saw her boat chugging to the island. Thommo was sent to investigate. As it pulled up alongside, Victoria said, 'Your friend Charlie is in my home. I think he is going to die.' Astounded, Thommo yelled loud and hard for Willie, who came running to where the boat was. Victoria refused Willie's invitation to come ashore. She had her address scrawled on a piece of paper. She handed it to Willie and said, 'You had better hurry, he is in terrible shape. He is my friend. I don't want him to suffer.' Willie thanked her profusely. Victoria nodded to the frightened boatman who turned the boat around and headed back to Ferry Wharf.

News that Charlie was alive was greeted with shouts of joy. Thommo, Willie and Dona Maria jumped into *Sea Princess Maya* and gunned her towards the mainland; from the Wharf, they took a taxi to Victoria's home. The sight of Charlie curled in bed shocked them. His body was emancipated, his clothes smelled of rot. The room stank of sour alcohol, vomit and urine. They picked him up, cradled his limp body and walked to the waiting taxi. Willie thanked Victoria again and promised that he would keep her informed of Charlie's progress. She looked sad and devastated. 'I did not know what to do,' she explained, 'he told me that you were no longer on Cross Island. I am sorry that I could not come sooner.' 'It is not your fault,' Willie assured her, 'I don't think he told you this, but liquor only makes his disease worse. Don't ever offer him liquor again.'

They got Charlie back to Cross Island, still unconscious. Dona Maria suggested that they admit him to a hospital. Willie disagreed saying, 'Charlie would not want that. He would not stay there. They might stick him in a nut house where he will die. We'll take care of him. All he needs to do is stop drinking and take his medicine regularly. I don't know if that will help, but it certainly won't hurt him.' Thommo and Willie stripped

Charlie of his clothes and bathed him. He began waking up as they splashed water on his body. He made a feeble attempt to stop them but they could see recognition come into his eyes. 'What happened?' he slurred. Willie replied, 'You are home, safe on Cross Island. Your friend Victoria helped us find you.' Charlie looked at them helplessly; he did not have the ability to say anything more. They moved his bed into Willie's shack. One of the girls fed him beef soup.

The next afternoon as he sat up in bed, weak and disoriented, Willie explained it all. Charlie listened, ashamed and scared. He swore that he was going to stop drinking alcohol. 'If you don't,' Willie said without emotion, 'You are going to die a horrible death. If that is what you want, nobody can stop you.' Charlie looked down at the sheet covering his shrunken stomach and legs. 'I don't want to die, Willie,' he said in the voice of a lost frightened child.

Charlie had no recollection where the rest of the money for the packages that he had delivered was. He did not remember buying whisky. Willie told him it did not matter. They were all rich now. Slowly, painfully, Charlie came back to his original life. He began eating again and going for long walks around the island. Soon he started jogging. He stayed far from the bottle and his medication seemed to be working. The attacks had stopped. He knew they would return but he hoped the intensity would be diminished. He hoped...

It was not long before Charlie was back in command again. He moved back to his own shack. Dona Maria secretly wished that Charlie would slip into the matrix of his madness again. She wanted Willie; she wanted to rule the island with him, but first Charlie had to be incapacitated, and then, Thommo had to go. Willie had been meeting with Charlie's contacts in the docks and on the mainland. Charlie had consented to this, knowing that if his schizophrenia came roaring back, he would be helpless and dysfunctional. He did not want Cross Island to suffer with him.

There would come a time soon, Dona Maria told herself, when Charlie would not be needed. She waited with the patience of a scavenger, circling quietly, sniffing for death, never taking her eye off the victim.

Willie kept his promise to Victoria. He journeyed to her home and told her that Charlie had pulled through. She was happy, invited him in and offered him a drink. Willie told her that he was in a hurry. She held up her hand, 'Just a minute,' she said, 'I have something for you.' Willie wondered what it was. She walked slowly into the room where they had found Charlie and came back with a brown paper bag. She handed it to him. Opening it, Willie looked at her with astonishment. Inside were the remnants of the money that Charlie had left behind. 'It's a lot of money,' he said, 'You could have kept it. You can keep it; payment for helping Charlie.' She smiled, 'I don't need to be paid to help Charlie. We go back a long way. Besides, I can't accept money that is soiled. I have heard of what goes on there. I may be old, but I know people who know people. Ask Charlie to drop in when he has the time. Good day, sir.' Willie left without saying a word.

Back on the Island, Willie told Charlie what had transpired at Victoria's place. Charlie frowned, 'You made a big mistake offering her money. She is my friend. A good woman. I will go see her one of these days and apologize.' 'How do you know her?' Willie asked casually. Charlie grew pensive, 'It's a long story,' he said, 'someday I will tell you. In more ways than one, she's family to me. Willie, everything I have, all that is important to me, is here in India. That's one of the reasons why I never wanted to go to England. And I know, I will never really belong here, but England is a foreign country to me.'

Charlie recalled a conversation with an Anglo-Indian from Calcutta, Bobby Peters, who was visiting Bombay. Peters had sauntered into The Mulberry Bush and had sat at the bar next to Charlie. They had started talking when Peters had asked Tom the bartender where he could find a restaurant that served good Railway Lamb Curry. Charlie had looked at him, smiled and asked, 'You are Anglo-Indian?' Peters nodded. 'Are you planning on leaving and going to England?' Peters' answer surprised Charlie. 'People like me are stuck in a no man's land,' he explained. 'The Indians, most of them, don't like us because we openly opposed the British leaving. We have a confused loyalty to the British. England is a place that most of us have never seen, and we are sure that we will never gain a social acceptance there, even with our western upbringing and rather fair skin...but we pledge our allegiance to that far away country. It makes no sense. Here in India, we are now known as kutcha-butcha—half-baked bread—not a flattering description of our mixed heritage! But it is what it is.' 'So what do you think is the lesser of the two evils?' Charlie asked. 'I don't know,' Peters had said, 'but, I have decided to stay. India, I know. England, I don't. I will never be accepted as an Englishman, and I will never be embraced by the Indians as one of them. Indians know what we Anglo-Indians think about them. I think that is one of the many reasons why they don't like us. We don't have any connection to Indian music, art or culture. These Indians, their hygiene is appalling: spitting, urinating and defecating in public. Their idols and their loud festivals, their customs and their superstitions. It is an insult to how I was raised.' 'You say, "these Indians",' Charlie observed, 'but, if you don't mind me saying so, you are one of them.' 'No, I am not,' Peters said with conviction, 'Half my heritage is English, I honour and cherish that, and at the same time, I do not totally disregard my Indian half. The Indians despise us; they say we try to "act white", and the British patronize us for the same thing.' But if you put me on a scale, it will tip on the side of my English half.' Charlie laughed, 'Boy, you have a bloody problem. I had no idea it was this complicated.' 'And what about you?' Peters asked, 'Will you be packing up your polo sticks and double barrel guns and going home to Blighty with your Indian trophies?' Charlie smiled, 'I have decided to stay. I've never seen England. This is home. I have nowhere to get back to.' Charlie ordered another round of drinks and they continued talking. Charlie told Peters the story of his birth and life in India. It was getting late, they were the only two people left at the bar. Charlie tapped Peters on the shoulder, wished him luck and said, 'There is a restaurant, around the corner here called The Waiting Room, you will find the best jalfrezi, country captain chicken and railway lamb curry there.' They shook hands, and Charlie told Peters, 'In many ways, I am like you. I will never be totally accepted here, and England is a foreign country for me. So my friend, we both sail against the same wind, rain or shine. I accepted my reality and stopped trying to make sailboats out of sawdust a long, long time ago.'

September arrived, the monsoons began to fade. It was hot and sweaty. The men, now flush with money, were busy contacting people on the mainland and documenting their orders. Back on the island, Charlie had another episode but it was mild compared to the demons of the past and he managed to avoid alcohol.

Dona Maria decided the time had arrived to put Thommo on the back burner. One night, in bed with him, she pulled out one of the oldest tricks in the world from under her cotton night gown. She curtailed his unlimited access to her body; said it was a 'woman thing'. Thommo was aware of the cycle of her periods.

It was not that time of the month. He accepted her explanation in silence. Night after night, she rebuffed his hormones. There were times when he tried to set fire to her lust as she lay beside him. All he got for his efforts was a dispassionate response. One evening, frustrated and angry, he tried to rape her. Holding her down with murderous rage, he began ripping off her clothes. He would have succeeded if she had struggled, screamed and tried to twist out from under his writhing hot body. Instead, she just lay there, looking at him calmly, her body emotionally dead, cold. Thommo stopped midway. He was expecting a stiff ferocious resistance that would have fuelled his burning vengeful lust. He longed for her to abuse him, strike him, call him filthy names; then his reflex would jack hammer her face; feel bone crack, see blood, watch her crawl, cry, beg for mercy, naked and defenseless. But she had handed him a dead limp figure that promised an experience that bordered on necrophilia. Her half naked body was absolutely still. She had closed her eyes. Thommo snarled with frustration, rolled off her body, pulled on his trousers, and stormed out into the darkness, bare chested.

Dona Maria began breathing normally again. She stayed in bed, thinking of her next move. She looked at her ripped clothes and smiled. When the clock struck midnight, she slipped on a dress and walked to the House of Tarts. The girls had the wisdom to refrain from asking questions.

The carpenters were requested to construct a shack for Dona Maria. While she waited for the construction to be completed, she stayed at the House of Tarts, and was polite to Thommo when their paths crossed. In three weeks she had her new home, but before she moved in she had a long conversation with Thommo. Charlie had advised her to calm him down. 'If you don't,' he had warned, 'bad things will happen to you.' She told Thommo that she was undergoing a radical change and was not interested in men anymore. By this time he did not care. He had been satiating his lust at the House of Tarts. 'They are more skilled than you will ever be,' he sneered. 'Maybe you should learn something from them, bitch...I know you,' he continued, his words cutting and snarky, 'you have some twisted fokkin' plan. I don't care. Fok' you' She endured his venom in silence, knowing that a retort right now would set off a fire storm. Both Charlie and Willie talked to Thommo. He assured them that he was 'finished with that skanky whore'. He promised them that he would not hurt her.

Working long hours with Willie, Dona Maria now had her chance to forge a relationship with him. It was not easy. Willie was reticent to expose himself. He worried what a physical relationship with her would have on the workings of Cross Island, and more importantly he was anxious on how he would handle a monogamous partnership. He was not used to compromise and petty arguments and having to be responsible for another human being. Willie was a lone ranger, who did not have a mortal fear of being alone. When Dona Maria queried him on his past, Willie balked. He said there was nothing really important about the flat white canvas of his past life and moved to talking about the next assignment. So she waited, doing small things for him. She washed his clothes, stitched a tear in his shirt, polished his shoes and cooked fish delicacies that pleased him. She mothered him, and at the same time had the wisdom to leave all decisions to him. Careful not to contradict him, she became his willing accomplice, ready to bend over and prostrate herself before him if he ordered it. Gradually, Willie began to crawl out from under his inhibitions. The wary armour around his heart began to melt. He jokingly began referring to her as 'Mother'. When Charlie overheard this he laughed and thought, 'Old Dr Sigmund Freud would be amused!' Charlie had read Freud's summary of his treatment of 'Little Hans', titled 'Analysis of a Phobia in a Five-Year-Old Boy'. He was unaware of Willie's past. He had no idea how close he was to the internal fire that burned in the subconscious mind of Willie.

One evening, when Dona Maria and Willie were sharing a bottle of Portuguese wine at The Rot Gut Café, Willie suddenly began talking about his past. Maybe it was the wine, or the soft Arabian Sea breeze, maybe it was what Dona Maria said. The question that possibly triggered this was her wishful thought that one day; maybe she would like to have a child. 'If I cannot have a baby, I will adopt a little girl,' she explained. It took Willie back in time. He grew nostalgic. 'Adoption,' he said softly, 'I know a little bit about that. I was born in Bath, south west England,' he started hesitantly, 'or so I was told, but that's where I grew up. I was an orphan brought up by a lovely couple. My adoptive father worked in a brass foundry; my adoptive mother stayed home and looked after me and the cottage we lived in. They were ordinary humble, God-fearing people, content with what fate and Jesus had offered them. I don't remember when, but my adoptive father started drinking, staying out late and the neighbours whispered that he had a woman on the side. By then, I was eleven years old, I think. I wanted to kill him. I remember my adoptive mother holding me, stroking my head and crying. I had often wondered where my real parents were. My adoptive mother used to insist that the only person in the world who knew this was her husband; and he would not talk about it. One evening, when I insisted that I had the right to know, he slapped me and walked out of the house. He never came home that night. I spent the night in my adoptive mother's bed hugging her. We both cried a lot. Not long after that, my adoptive father moved out of the house after an argument. He still contributed money to keep the home fires burning, but he was gone. I spent a lot of nights in my adoptive mother's bed comforting her. She smelt like the fresh bread she baked to sell in the local market. She despised her husband but we were Catholic; divorce was not an option; and so she stayed alone with her loneliness and bitterness. It was difficult for her, she was relatively young, but the thought of taking on a lover never crossed her mind. It was alright for a man to do it, like her husband had, but in those days if a woman ventured out of her domestic circle she was branded a prostitute. So she overburdened me with her affections. Maybe that's why I turned shy. At school I was often beaten up for being a sissy.

'When I finished school, I got a job as an apprentice to an accountant. I discovered that I had a talent for numbers. I was promoted to head bookkeeper. Now I had money that I could spend and enjoy myself. That was when I began gambling in the shady card dens around Bath. I also discovered prostitutes. When the owner of the accounting firm died, the business was bought by a shady businessman. By this time I was in charge of the company. He taught me how to cook the books for his clients so they did not have to pay the crippling taxes the government demanded. Business boomed. One rainy morning, Her Majesty's Revenue and Customs men barged in. I was arrested, spent five years in jail as an accessory. My adoptive mother, heartbroken, forlorn and ashamed, drank herself into a grave. By the time I was released, I wanted to leave England. I heard through a friend that a firm in Bombay was looking for an experienced bookkeeper. He was working with the British Civil Service and was on his way to Bombay. He offered to put in a good word. I thanked him and in two months his letter arrived. The job was mine if I wanted it. There was no background check. I sold the house and hopped on a ship for good ol' Bombay. Later, after years at Blackie and Sons, the accounting firm, I met Charlie in a bar one night, and we became drinking bum chums, in a non-homosexual way, I must add. One evening, he told me that a position as a junior assistant to the deck supervisor had opened up. No experience was required, you learnt on the job. Work at the docks would make me some real money, I remember him saying. It was corrupt there, smuggling was rampant and there was no accountability. He worked at the docks as a foreman at that time. He could fix this job for me, if I was interested. I did not hesitate. The rest you know.

'I often wondered, growing up, where my real parents were. Why did they abandon me? Was that action justified in their minds? Was I illegitimate? Did they miss me sometimes; wonder what happened to me? After all these years, I miss my adoptive mother. I think my being in jail killed her, I still carry that guilt. This may sound silly and strange, but sometimes, I miss the smell of her warmth.'

Dona Maria did not have the guts to ask if something more than maternal love occurred between Willie and his adoptive mother. After a hasty internal consultation, she decided to bury the question.

She smiled at Willie. 'I am glad that I now know what you went through. We all go through troubles. The important thing is that now, today, you are successful and happy.' She placed her foot near his leg and rubbed gently. Willie smiled. It was the first time she had physically touched him in a sexual way. Willie smiled, 'Oh! Mother,' he whispered, 'not here, not now.'

Chapter 8

Passion Plays and Ecstasy

By mid-May, it had turned hot and humid. Charlie decided that they would refuse all orders once the number reached five hundred. Dona Maria tried to convince Charlie that they could handle another fifty orders but Charlie stood by his number. She was still living alone in her shack. Willie, it seemed, had shown no interest in her moving in with him. He still frequented the House of Tarts; there was nothing she could do but bide her time and wait. She once broached the idea of them living together, casually. He had replied rather curtly that he was not ready. He and Thommo had a fantastic working relationship; maybe, she thought, he did not want to jeopardize the friendship. Or perhaps, Charlie was behind this. She had no idea how this would all play out, and it made her nervous and uncomfortable. If the men conspired and decided that she would have to leave the island, her world would sink in the Arabian Sea. What if they gave Thommo the green light to plunge his knife into her chest? Would they do that? Would he agree? For the first time in her life, naked fear attached itself to her insecurity.

It wasn't the finality of death that bothered her, or the cold pain of Thommo's knife. It was the possibility of being set adrift from Cross Island that terrified Dona Maria. She had an easy familiarity with all the men, they were comrades in piracy and she had grown to love the girls. This was her family here; she had nowhere else to go. She could retire to the farm in Portugal. She had money that her ex-husband had unwillingly parted in exchange for her silence. She also had a substantial sum stashed away from the Cross Island venture. But what would she do at the farm with all that money? Invest in a better pedigree of cows, pigs and goats? Make cheese? Worry if the wine was fermenting well, should she add more yeast, more sugar...? Deal with labour problems; volunteer at the local parish; church on Sundays; get dressed on Feast Days; listen to a grizzled old fadista sing a nostalgic Fado about Saint Anthony; entertain the neighbours; and then as always, life would revert back to the pig pen. She could get a dog, a cat, a man...roll with feisty inexperienced, sex-starved young lovers in the barn, while ruminating animals watched, occasionally reacting, stamping their hooves at the passionate guttural sounds that ricocheted off the cracked old oak timber. It all seemed so mundane, rural, rustic and predictable compared to life on Cross Island. Life here was exciting; anything could happen.

She had to get Willie into her home.

After his suicidal hijack of the ship, Thommo became a minor celebrity on Cross Island. He accepted their fulsome praise and admiring glances with a smile and a shrug. But Charlie was now determined to get back on his seat of power after its sheen had been considerably diminished by his schizophrenic attacks. He held daily meetings with the men as they journeyed to the mainland every morning to document the orders that would make up the next consignment. 'Just one more five hundred-drop before Christmas,' Charlie declared. 'Anything more will be a problem.' Some of the men argued that they could handle a bigger amount, make more money; Willie and Thommo agreed with them, but Charlie stood firm. This was his decision. They argued with his assessment, but in the end Charlie prevailed.

Willie and Dona Maria began drawing up the timetable. They figured they would finish all deliveries a week before Christmas. They were going to be obscenely moneyed people, free to buy the luxuries they had dreamed about. Many of the men were making plans to go home for a while and buy country cottages. One day, when their years reached a grey pensionable age, they would retire to their country mansions, settle down and lead lives of genteel comfort; sip a dram, savour pasties filled with juicy beef steak, onion, potato and swede, with sea salt and white pepper; and talk of the good ol' days on Cross Island. The girls from the House of Tarts were planning a trip to Ireland. Charlie, Willie, Thommo, Dona Maria and a few men decided to stay behind and look after the farm while the men and women were away. Meetings were held, plans were discussed. It was consensually decided that they would all leave after Christmas and be back by the end of March. Travel had now become easier, no more arduous long ship journeys. On 8 June 1948, a Lockheed Constellation L-749A called the 'Malabar Princess' had taken off from Bombay and landed at London's Heathrow airport. This was Air India's first international flight. They could now fly back to London, and back to Bombay via Cairo and Geneva.

Willie was already thinking about Charlie. He wondered how Charlie would react to the inactivity. Would he turn to the bottle again? How would Thommo behave on discovering that he and Dona Maria had a little more than platonic vibrations between them? Thommo had shown no discernible interest in getting back with Dona Maria again, but, if push came to shove, Willie thought, with an animal like Thommo, you never know. He had postponed making a move with Dona Maria; but he knew that he wanted her, and now that they would be closeted on the Island without the distraction of work or people, something was bound to happen.

Maybe I should give it to him straight, Willie thought, *tell him the truth*. He had heard American sailors often use the phrase, 'let the chips fall where they may'. *Perhaps*, thought Willie, *that is how I should handle this. Hopefully this does not turn into one big cock up*.

Charlie in consultation with Willie decided that they would have to try and figure out a way to unload their next assignment at the docks. Mid-sea transfers made captains nervous, there was too much marine traffic in the bay, and anything could happen if some desperado tried to hijack the load. Word had filtered out of the docks that the secret government spies had left; they had been haunting the dock area because the police had been tipped off that a large consignment of guns and ammunition were coming in from the Gulf of Aden, a port in Yemen, to arm the Muslims against rising Hindu oppression and aggression. This proved to be a false tip and the police had retreated.

It was Charlie's job to organize how the contact in Southampton would receive the money to pay back the credit for the last shipment. For a sumptuous fee, a ship and captain—vetted and certified as safe by the contact in Southampton—would carry sealed metal cartons of hard cash in rupees equivalent to the pounds spent on the cargo. A week later, Charlie met the captain of the *HMS Sherwood*. After a hearty meal of beef and potatoes on board, Charlie handed over the crates to the captain; said goodbye and nonchalantly exclaimed, 'If that money disappears, you know what will happen...' He smiled to erase the threat. The captain laughed, 'I know your contact and his crew in Southampton, Charlie.

They are friends of mine. I know what they are capable of, you don't have to worry.' Charlie nodded and walked off, already thinking about the next consignment.

That evening as he sat in his shack reading, Dodo came through. Charlie ignored the voice in his head, but Dodo with his incessant chatter forced Moby Dick out of Charlie's mind. He placed Herman Melville on his lap.

Dodo: *They are all going to be gone soon, Charlie. What are you going to do? Where are you going to go, when they go back to England? This cannot last, you know that. At some point in time, the bribes are going to get larger; local hoodlums will want a share of the action, and the politicians and police will be forced to put an end to your business and possibly your lives. They all have the contacts. It may take time, but eventually they can and will do what you are doing. Why don't you go to England?*

Charlie: *I do not want to. My life is here. England is a foreign country to me. At some point in time, I will establish contact with Maya; I know that in my gut and soul.*

It was at this moment that Willie entered unannounced. He wanted to discuss a few operational problems. He heard Charlie's last line and stopped in his tracks. 'Who are you talking to?' he asked, in a voice that betrayed his concern that Charlie was in the midst of yet another schizophrenic attack. Charlie waved his right hand, 'Oh,' he explained, 'I'm just talking to myself, I get lonely sometimes. I'm alright Willie, you don't have to worry.' 'You should visit the girls,' was Willie's laconic advice, 'it will do you good. Perhaps you should go and visit your friend Victoria.' 'I have been visiting the girls,' Charlie said smiling, 'and yes, Victoria...I need to go see her, especially after she saved my life.' Willie pulled up a chair and they began discussing business.

The next afternoon, Charlie was supervising work on one of the generators. He overhead one of the carpenters talking about a carving he had created. Charlie, in a fit of nostalgia, walked up to him and asked, 'Can you make me a small wooden replica of *Sea Princess Maya*?' 'It will take time to get the details right,' the carpenter said, but yes, he would do it when he had time to spare. Four weeks later, Charlie had his little boat. The carpenter had also painted the boat's name on its starboard, and had carved twenty-four miniature black birds on the port side. It was a work of fine art, detailed and beautiful. The carpenter had refused payment for his work. 'It is my gift to you,' he said, 'I hope someday, you find your daughter.' Charlie was amazed at the man's intuition; he thanked the carpenter for his concern.

He could not have known this then, but the little wooden boat he now held in his hands, would one day follow him to his grave, far, far away from Cross Island.

Work on organizing the next drop was now proceeding in full steam. Five hundred orders had to be streamlined. Dona Maria, Charlie and Willie worked twelve-hour days, while Thommo tied up all the loose ends on the mainland. The rest of the men worked on maintaining the equipment and shacks that the monsoons had played havoc with. Seeing that things were flowing smoothly, Willie was beginning to relax; Charlie did not foresee any problems, and the people who would be going back to England on vacation discussed their plans with mounting fervour and excitement. And then, suddenly one evening, Thommo said he wanted to speak with Willie privately. Willie's body seemed to instantly lose all its heat. He hunched over as if in pain. He knew this was going to be about Dona Maria. 'Let's go to my place,' Thommo said, 'we can talk there.' Willie looked around for Charlie, desperation in his eyes. He could see him talking to one of the girls at the entrance of the House of Tarts.

She was laughing—Charlie must have said something funny. Willie hoped that Charlie would finish his conversation, turn and head his way. Out of the corner of his eye, he saw the girl take Charlie by the hand. They walked into the brothel. *This is it*, thought Willie, *I am a fokkin' dead man.* He wondered where Dona Maria was. Thommo seemed to be looking through him, staring at Willie's spine that had turned into soft, yellow marrow. He could smell the fear emanating from Willie's body and see the naked look of helpless desperation in his enlarged pupils. Thommo smiled. Willie recoiled as if a King Cobra had just spat venom at him. 'What are you waiting for?' Thommo hissed, 'I can come back later if you are busy.' Willie heard his jeering tone. He thought about making a run for the House of Tarts to seek refuge behind Charlie's back, but suddenly the whore house looked too far away. He got out of his chair like a shackled man on his way to a noose and shuffled after Thommo. His mouth was dry, his intestines coiled, and he felt the dull pain of his over-filled bladder.

When they reached Thommo's house, Willie collapsed in a chair. Thommo closed the door, turned and walked into the kitchen. Willie was sure that he would come back with his knife; he sat there waiting, unable to speak. Thommo returned with a knife, cheese, a bottle of black rum and two glasses on a tray. He poured the drinks in silence; sliced the cheese. Willie accepted his glass, eyed the cold metallic glint from the knife with trepidation as it cut through the cheddar cheese block. Thommo watched as Willie's glass shook its way to his mouth. The rum helped. Willie licked the remnants of liquor from his thick moustache. 'I know what is going on,' Thommo said softly. Willie suddenly found his voice; it spewed forth like uncontrollable vomit. 'Nothing, nothing, nothing...' he began blabbering, his voice rising to a pleading tremulous crescendo.

Thommo held up his right hand. It was an order that demanded the immediate cessation of all sound. Willie held out his glass for a refill, and was relieved that his shaking hand had momentarily subsided to a slight but visibly embarrassing tremble. Thommo began talking. 'I am not going to hurt you, Willie,' he said. 'You are too important to Cross Island. I am not stupid, I see the two of you, I see what she is doing, Willie. I want you to know; I don't care. Enjoy it while it lasts. The reason why we are talking in private...well I want to warn you. She will manipulate you, and then she will leave on her own sadistic terms. If you fall in love with her, she will destroy you. What she really wants, I don't know, but I know that she is willing to go to great lengths to get what she needs. You understand?' Willie nodded his head in affirmation. 'She wants power. She wants to be in total control; she wants to be a goddess that men crawl to for favours. Maybe I am wrong, but this I know, she is dangerous. I have seen men with her kind of attitude when I was in prison, and god knows, I learnt a thing or two in those places. There is something wrong with her mind, so she uses her body; know what I am saying...'

Willie was relieved that he was not going to die. He asked to use the lavatory, told Thommo that he had nearly pissed in his pants. Thommo laughed. Willie remembered the time when they had moved to Cross Island. Thommo had walked to his assigned shack and urinated around it. When Charlie, perplexed and faintly amused, had asked him what he was doing, Thommo had stated that he was 'marking his territory', and anyone venturing near his home uninvited would be attacked. When Charlie called him a wild animal, Thommo laughed with glee.

After Willie came back, Thommo continued, 'If she begins to plot against Charlie and me, I want you to let me know.' Willie looked into his friend's expressionless eyes. He knew that

Thommo was confessing that he would murder her if she moved in that direction. Thommo talked for half an hour. Willie drank. Finally Thommo said, 'There is an old Portuguese saying: "It is a sad house where the cock lays the eggs and the hen crows at sunrise." That is what your life will be like if you decide to make her a partner in your life. Yes, she may even decide to marry you, if she has no other option. I hope that you will have the good sense to run away from her. That's all I wanted to say.' Willie, now drunk, patted Thommo on his back and swore eternal allegiance to him. His spine, that had turned to marrow, had reverted to its original bone structure; and his heart was beating normally again as his legs wobbled out of Thommo's house and led him to the House of Tarts.

Chapter 9

An Underground Warning

The next assignment was scheduled to arrive at the end of November on the *Ocean Queen*, a big cargo carrier. The three docks—Alexandra, Victoria and Prince's—were interconnected. It was important for Charlie and Willie to know where she was going to berth. They had contacts at each dock and would need time to grease the wheels. For unexplained reasons, they could not get information from Southampton where the *Ocean Queen* was going to berth. They realized that by the time they received the status of her berth it might be too late. Again, Charlie's leadership proved invaluable as he made a crucial decision. He told Willie that, according to his calculations, the *Ocean Queen* would head into Alexandra Docks. He had studied her cargo weight, fresh water, ballast water, fuel, provisions and crew. He knew her deadweight tonnage from information he had received from Southampton. As employees of the docks, Charlie, Willie, Thommo and some of the men, had open access to all three docking facilities, but each dock had its own black-market modus operandi. They decided, on Charlie's assumptions, to bribe personnel at Alexandra Docks. If the *Ocean Queen* docked at Victoria or Prince's docks, they would not have the time to redirect the operation; the huge bribe money would be lost and their cargo confiscated.

As the day of the *Ocean Queen*'s arrival drew closer, Willie, in sheer desperation, decided that they would take the risk of meeting her mid-stream. His plans were rebuffed by their contacts at Southampton. The captain and chief engineer were refusing a mid-stream transfer. Finally an explanation arrived by telegram from Southampton. The ship was carrying hardware for the Indian army; she would have army boats escorting her into the bay. If the captain stopped mid-stream, a storm would follow and the captain and chief engineer would be interrogated. Faking an engine problem was dangerous; protocol would demand that army engineers board the ship and inspect the engine room. They would have to unload their consignment at the docks once the army had retrieved their cargo. There appeared to be no other way to do it. They still did not know which of the three docks the *Ocean Queen* would berth at. Its destination was a governmental defence secret that a bribe could not unlock.

As the date of her arrival drew near, Charlie began to unravel. The entire operation hinged on the accuracy of his prediction.

He had assured everybody that she would dock at Alexandra. If she docked at Victoria or Prince's docks, all eyes would turn to Charlie's miscalculations. They would blame his schizophrenia for the disaster and question a leadership he was desperately striving to sustain.

Charlie began to secretly drink again. Whisky fortified his insecurity and justified his decision. He told himself he would stop after the consignment was safe on Cross Island. Willie smelt the liquor on his breath; he understood the pressure that was wringing Charlie's gut. Charlie sheepishly assured him that he would get back on the wagon as soon as the consignment was safe. Willie had his doubts, but he too was also feeling the mounting pressure and did not have the energy to explain to

Charlie once again, the danger that alcohol posed to his sanity. Willie was worried. If they lost this colossal load that was floating in on credit, retribution would be instantaneous. They would have to leave Cross Island in a hurry. Payback would be brutal and swift.

And then, four days before her arrival, word arrived from a contact at the docks. *Ocean Queen* would berth at Alexandra Docks. Charlie and Willie celebrated at The Rot Gut Café where Charlie assured Willie again that he would stop drinking when their assignment was safe on Cross Island. Willie was too happy and relieved to argue. Once again, Charlie's leadership had survived a near catastrophe.

Thommo, as usual, was in charge of security for the next drop. He surprised Willie and Charlie when he came up with the number of outside helpers he needed. Dona Maria was there at the meeting when Thommo said, 'I need fifteen men armed with knives. Five at the docks, three on each truck, and seven at Ferry Wharf when we unload our goods. A lot of underground people know about this operation. They might try and snatch it all. Once the assignment disappears into Bombay's underbelly, we will never find it. I know how they function.' Dona Maria stated that the number of thugs Thommo thought he needed was excessive and too expensive. She tried to get Willie to bolster her argument. Thommo ignored her. Willie started to talk, 'I don't think...' Charlie raised an authoritative hand and overrode their objections. Thommo thanked him. With a satisfied smirk his dead eyes momentarily moved to Willie's face, then shifted to a space between the heads of Dona Maria and Willie. He added a causal comment: 'You are a good man Charlie, you understand,' he drawled, 'I might have to kill for you in the future.' Thommo then lowered his gaze and bit into a sandwich. The last ten words of his sentence were unnecessary to the discussion they were having. Charlie and Dona Maria looked at him quizzically. Thommo's eyes were focused on his sandwich. Willie looked down at the ground; he knew that Thommo had flashed his first warning; a rapid blinking message of murder directed at the unsuspecting life of Dona Maria.

Willie now spent a lot of time on the mainland. He sent word out that his consignment was going to be heavily guarded. Word snaked out, and down into the filthy feral by-lanes of the underground. Charlie took care of the police and dock personnel; Willie had the logistics ready.

Tuesday morning, Cross Island moved into top gear. This was the day. A cold wind blew across the island. Late November was wintertime in Bombay. When they docked at Ferry Wharf at five in the morning, locals who started work on the first shift in nearby factories were huddled around small wood fires, sipping sweet tea. The army had moved fast. The docks had confirmed that they had unloaded their hardware on priority basis, cutting through the red tape and usual bureaucratic delays that were precursors to bribes. Thommo's little army of 'Hindu hoodlums' was there. Charlie, Thommo and Willie drove the three trucks into the docks. In the back of each vehicle was a gangster with a long knife. They stationed the trucks near the *Ocean Queen* and the transfer began. By ten a.m. they were done; the loaded trucks moved out and rumbled to Ferry Wharf, where five rented boats, including *Sea Princess Maya*, were docked. Thommo looked around, all seemed calm and normal. A man walked up to Charlie and said 'hello'. Charlie was supervising the loading and barely heard him. The man repeated the greeting. Charlie turned to look at him; he had seen him somewhere...Then his heart seemed to stop. It was Detective D.H. Desai, the official whose transfer Charlie had facilitated because he had been investigating the work on Cross

Island. Desai looked at Charlie. 'Someone killed my German Shepherd,' he said and walked away. Charlie stood still. Desai was supposed to be in Calcutta. What was he doing back in Bombay? Thommo had been watching the strange encounter from the corner of his eye. He walked to where Charlie was. 'Who was that?' He inquired. 'Oh, just some curious man with nothing to do,' Charlie mumbled as he turned his attention to the loading.

It was late afternoon by the time they finished transferring the consignment from the trucks to the boats. Thommo paid his hired help; he let them keep the long knives as souvenirs. It was time to go home. The men were jubilant. Willie and Thommo congratulated each other and talked of the money they had coming to them. Charlie sat alone on the ride back. Thoughts of Desai, the subtle threat that he made, the German shepherd, and Calcutta, darkened his mind. Thommo watched Charlie, deep in thought, repeatedly running his fingers through his beard. He was well-aware of Charlie's nervous beard-stroking when plans began to disintegrate. He knew that trouble and danger were ahead. Willie followed Thommo's gaze. 'Something bad has happened,' he whispered to Thommo, 'this is not good.'

There was no time for a meeting with Charlie once they landed on Cross Island. The consignment had to be sorted and stored. Dona Maria had devised a system. All liquor was stored together, scotch in one pile, rum in another; the cigarettes were stacked by brand names; canned goods and cheese were placed in another section of the storage shacks. They worked through the night and into the early hours of the morning till the last bottle of Johnny Walker was stored and locked. Thommo posted a guard at the storage facility; and two men on the periphery of Cross Island. They were now protected night and day. He did not know what Charlie had heard or seen but had decided this was no time to take chances. The armed men worked in five-hour shifts, armed with Lee-Enfield rifles bought from the Bombay underground. The Lee-Enfield rifle fired .303 rimmed cartridges and could be fixed with a ten round box magazine. 'Let the fokkin' bastards try something now,' Thommo told Willie, 'this is something they will not dare fok' with.'

On the way to his shack, Charlie told Willie and Thommo that they had to have a meeting later that day. Back home, he poured himself what the Indians called 'a Parsi Peg', half a glass of Scotch, diluted with a little water and a cube of ice. He gulped it down, sucking the cube till it melted in his mouth. The liquor swirled in his empty stomach, seeped into his bloodstream and exploded in his brain. Charlie relaxed, poured himself another one, which he sipped gingerly as he sat in his easy chair. Perhaps it was the sleep deprivation, the fallout of meeting the detective, the Scotch, or a combination of all three factors that led him to a trance.

Charlie emerged from his reverie, hoping that this was not a prelude to another cacophonic attack. Eventually he began to doze off in his easy chair, thinking of the hatred that he had seen on the face of detective Desai. Charlie knew that Desai, if given a chance, could throw a vicious spanner in the works. Was Desai's appearance in Bombay a coincidence? Was he back to take revenge for what they had done to him? Charlie's thoughts unravelled: *Where will I go? What will I do, if my home on Cross Island and all that I have worked so hard for came to an end? I have no family. Doris and Maya are lost and even if I knew where they were, perhaps they would not want me. Maybe I can live with Victoria.* Fortunately, sleep arrived and transported him to merciful oblivion.

Victoria was getting ready to go to the market when she noticed the letter the post man had slipped underneath her door.

Dear Victoria,

How are you? Your last letter set me thinking about the past again. It is not always pleasant to do so, but I fear I must, there seems to be no choice, because thoughts of years gone by, come to me, whether I like it or not. You mentioned my elder sister Doris. I have known of her existence for some time now through your letters. I don't know where she is and have no urgent desire to find her.

I have discussed this with Neelam for months now. Victoria, I feel nothing as far as Doris is concerned. Yes, we are half-sisters, if that is what we want to call it, but I feel no emotional connection here. For all I know, she is a bitter woman who will not stop talking about Charlie. I don't think I want to discuss betrayal and bitterness with anyone; and with Doris, if I had to meet with her, I suspect the conversation will turn rancid and accusatory. I don't need that in my life right now. Wherever Doris is, I hope she is happy. Meeting Doris will open a can of slimy worms. I think it is better if we let that can stay sealed and preferably, I would like to bury that can of worms and hope they all die. I do not want to deal with this.

Real sisters have a bond: of love and petty fights, of changes together, of maturing together, of finding different ways, having different philosophies and opinions, and still keeping in touch wherever they may be. Would Doris want a sister who is a sister because of the fleeting lust of their father? That's all that binds us now, because I do not know the woman! And she does not know me! The common denominator that binds us is that we were both abandoned. Is that emotional rope sturdy enough to tie us together for the rest of our lives? I don't know.

Do I feel bitterness? Anger? Shortchanged by life and Charlie? Of course, I do...from time to time that bitter bile rises in my throat. But, I have learnt to manage that and live with it. I have learnt to leave the emotionally crippled things in my life alone. Has Doris done the same? I am afraid to find out.

I do not have the mental ability or strength to deal with a sister, for who I have no answers, only questions. I can be of no help to her and I fear that we could end up hurting each other; because Charlie still stands between us, for better or worse, until death do us apart. I will have to tell her, if we do meet, that I am still concerned about Charlie and through you, I know what is happening to him. Doris could see this as a betrayal.

I could be wrong. I could meet Doris, and we may both agree to let Charlie go and we both can live happily ever after. But Victoria, I have learnt the hard way, in life, things do not work out like that. Again, I could be wrong; but am I willing to take a chance? Right now, I don't know, so I would like to leave it alone. The bridge that we have to cross to be reunited as loving siblings has crumbled; the time has passed for us to be sisters. Maybe, I say these things because I am afraid for myself and need to stay away from an influence that will not be good for me.

Victoria, I am not angry that you mentioned Doris. I am just trying to explain. I know you will understand.

I hope that you are well.

Sincerely,

Maya

It was early evening when Charlie emerged from his shack. He walked to Willie's place and asked him to fetch Thommo. Dona Maria was not invited to the meeting. When Thommo arrived, Charlie began to explain. 'The man I met at Ferry Wharf as we were loading our boats was Detective Desai.' Thommo and Willie had both forgotten about him. Charlie looked at Thommo and said, 'Remember that German Shepherd you poisoned?' Thommo nodded. 'That was his dog, remember?' Now it all came back to Thommo. Willie who had not been directly involved with Desai was filled in on the details. Charlie continued, 'He has either come back on his own accord or he is now working with the detective department. We need to find out what happened in Calcutta. Did he leave? Was he sacked? If he has pulled political strings and has been reinstated in Bombay, we are in deep trouble. That means that a powerful political figure, possibly in New Delhi, has been briefed, and the word has gone out secretly that we should be destroyed. This could be the beginning of the end if we let it get out of hand.' Thommo interrupted rudely, 'Why don't we just put a fokkin' knife into the bastard. End of the hero detective story.' Charlie looked at him the way a curmudgeon old scholar would look at a student who had the gall to offer an inadequate answer. There was a slight irritation at Thommo's stupidity and also a degree of sympathy for the limitations he was born with. 'You kill him now,' Charlie said sternly, 'and we all go to hell. If he has connections, they will all come after us. It is a question of who has more power. Remember, we are British; this now, is their country. There may be people out there who may be purely nationalistic, possibly out of the range of a big fat bribe. Another bloody Gandhi, I don't know, I'm just guessing here. All we poor bastards have is a lot of money. Suddenly that may not be enough.' It was decided that they would tap all their above and underground contacts. 'We need to know, where he is living, is his wife with him, does he have parents in Bombay; is he back with the police force and who are his godfathers,' explained Willie. 'If he decides to move against us, I guarantee he will do so with big powers behind him.' Thommo added, 'And find out if he has a dog.' Both Willie and Charlie looked at him, daggers in their eyes. 'I was only joking,' Thommo protested when he perceived their genuine disgust and rage. 'If you see him,' Charlie warned Thommo, 'ignore him, leave him alone no matter what he says or does, at least for now. Do you understand?' Thommo nodded. Before Willie and Thommo left, Charlie added, 'Maybe this was a coincidence, maybe...we will find out. Nobody else here needs to know about this. It will set off a panic which we will not be able to deal with. Add two more men to the security detail; tell them it's just normal precautionary measures.'

Charlie walked back to his house deep in thought. *To hell with the schizophrenia* he thought when he was home. He walked to the shelf in his kitchen, took down a bottle of whisky and opened it. *Five hundred drops to be made*, he thought despondently as he headed for his easy chair. *People are going to die.*

Dona Maria was now in charge of all sorting and packing. She documented each package meticulously and passed the information to Willie who rechecked the amounts, addresses and names. The men and girls talked of nothing but their coming vacation as they got the consignment ready for delivery. Charlie, Willie and Thommo now spent most of the day out on the mainland, trying to determine Detective Desai's location and intention. Charlie and Willie talked to the police, politicians and local social heavy weights. Thommo quizzed the pimps, police informers and hoodlums who usually kept an alert ear to changes in police personnel that would affect their business. Thommo cajoled, pleaded and threatened. Willie and Charlie pledged huge monetary bribes, free whisky and cigarettes. When they talked to top guns from police and political circles who they knew had a penchant for prostitutes, they offered the girls from the House of Tarts in exchange for information on Detective Desai. For two weeks they gumshoed through every contact they had. Nobody seemed to know where Detective Desai was. He had resigned his post in Calcutta and disappeared. The whereabouts of his family were unknown. Charlie contacted his sources in Delhi and Calcutta, who tried to get information from the precinct that Detective Desai had worked in; but an opaque screen seemed to have come down between Detective Desai and the world. He was a ghost that people had heard of and no one had seen. The few leads they thought they had led them to a winding trail that evaporated into smoke. A woman said that she knew where Detective Desai's parents lived. When Thommo got there, the door to the house was locked, the neighbours said that they had moved; nobody seemed to know where.

Back on the island, Dona Maria knew that something bad was happening. Charlie, Thommo and Willie had meetings from which she was excluded. When she asked Willie what was going on, his answers were vague and confusing. The men who were going to make the drops were told they needed to carry knives for protection, 'in case some nutter tried to steal the packages'. Thommo purchased knives and a dozen brass knuckle dusters from an underground contact. Charlie's contacts at the police station assured him that it was business as usual. 'If someone up high was cooperating with detective Desai, why are the police still willing to work with us?' Charlie asked Willie, who replied, 'Wish I knew, Charlie, it's a puzzle, I don't know. Maybe, he is setting things up, biding his time. Maybe he will make a move when he thinks the time is right.' 'Why not hit us right now?' Charlie argued, 'What difference will it make to them?' Willie shrugged in resignation.

Dona Maria interrupted one of their many meetings to tell them that all the packages were ready. The drop offs would start the next day. Charlie informed them that he would not be delivering packages this time; he needed to get to the source of Detective Desai's disappearance. Thommo accepted the added chore of Charlie's packages.

The next morning, Charlie rode with the rest of the men to Ferry Wharf armed with a short, serrated stabbing knife and a vicious knuckle duster, the ends of which he had filed to cause maximum damage. After the men had dispersed, Charlie headed for the home of Victoria Fernandes. She was overjoyed to see him. 'You look well!' she exclaimed, 'Better than the last time I saw you.' Charlie thanked her profusely for saving his life and apologized on Willie's behalf for offering her the money that Charlie had left behind. When they were seated, Charlie told her what was happening. She listened in silence. 'I can make an uneducated guess here,' she said, 'a confrontation on Cross Island with English people could start a fire. Again, this man Desai could just be a man you destroyed, prowling about waiting for revenge. If that is the case, you do not have a problem. I am sure you can deal with him, but Charlie, is all this necessary? You have your money, why don't you all just leave? Go to England or leave Bombay and live in one of the many hill stations in India. You all can retire without all this humbug.' 'You don't understand, Victoria,' he argued, 'Cross Island is home.' 'You are a grown man, Charlie,' she retorted, 'you make your bed, and then you lie in it, however uncomfortable it may be. You may not get much sleep, but it is your bed, my friend.'

As they talked, Maya's letter lay in its envelope on the coffee table a foot from where Charlie sat. Victoria smiled. If only Charlie knew, she thought.

Dear Victoria,

Your letter telling me that Charlie has schizophrenia came as a shock. I cried. I don't know what to say. There is nothing I can do about this deadly unfortunate disease that has afflicted him. Please do write and tell me if he gets worse or is in some hospital. I thank you for looking after him. Maybe someone from Cross Island will take care of him. I hope he does not suffer and die.

I had thought that maybe, sometime, somewhere we would meet, Charlie and I, now it does not seem that that possibility will ever become a reality. I still sometimes wish that we could meet and at other times, I don't want to. I guess I am just sad and confused right now. In the end, he is my father. Please do keep me informed of what happens to him.

Sincerely,
Maya

This was the first time that Charlie had heard a near-rational explanation to the problem that was Detective Desai. And then Victoria added, 'This man Desai, he is the ghost of Cross Island. Remember people have always talked of Cross Island as being haunted. In a strange way, Desai is that ghost. There are many ways, in which disturbed spirits manifest themselves. Maybe this man Desai...the ghosts of Cross Island have possessed him. He is their medium. In reality, Cross Island will destroy you, not the politicians and police.' Charlie looked at her in amazement. 'Now, you are talking like an ignorant Indian,' he said, 'this is complete bloody nonsense.' Victoria looked at Charlie silently and shrugged.

Charlie said his goodbyes and left. He turned and headed for the main road where he hailed a taxi and rode back to *Sea Princess Maya.*

By late evening they were all back on Cross Island. The drop offs continued, day after day. Nothing was guaranteed anymore. Anything could happen.

Delivering packages, the men discovered, was like walking on the edge of a dangerous canyon. At a private bungalow whose owners had ordered a large package, the Cross Island courier knocked on the door. He was invited into what he realized too late, was an empty abandoned house. He was confronted by four men armed with knives. They stole the merchandise, stripped the courier naked. 'Don't bother to come back and look for us,' they told him. 'We will not be here.' They then kicked him out of the door. Around his neck, they hung his knife and knuckle duster on a cheap jute thread necklace. He could hear them laughing as he ran out, naked, scared and embarrassed.

The men on Cross Island now began to have second thoughts about the whole operation. They talked amongst themselves, and many of them felt that given the violence and uncertainty, it would not be long before one or more of them would be permanently crippled, grotesquely disfigured, or dead. Suddenly all the money in the world could not justify their participation in a dream that was turning dark.

Meanwhile, Charlie's search for Desai had intensified, but every trail led to a dead end. He felt he was looking for a man whose existence had been torched on a pyre and reduced to ashes and smoke. In the evenings, when the men came back home after delivering their packages, Charlie waited to hear that someone was missing. He heard the stories of how they were being robbed. The anticipation of the occurrence of deaths turned Charlie into a wreck. His drinking intensified as he left the management of the five hundred drop offs entirely to Willie and Dona Maria. Charlie was obsessed with finding Detective Desai. He spent days scouring the mainland, harassing his contacts, and sometimes, much to the consternation of the people on Cross Island, failed to come back at night. Charlie was going to break soon. Willie tried talking to him; only to be brushed aside with obscene language and rude gestures.

And then one night, as Charlie trolled the cheap bars and whore houses in the gullies and by lanes of Ferry Wharf, he found the first clue. A clerk who worked at the police department was drinking at the bar with his friends. Charlie had occasionally slipped him small amounts of cash for his help in moving Cross Island's paperwork through the bureaucratic mess at the police station. Charlie walked up and said hello. The clerk said that he wished to speak to Charlie alone, so they left the bar they were at and walked to the Raja Bar, further up the street. The place had tiny wooden cubicles with curtains for privacy. It served as a temporary lovers retreat for poor young couples who wished to have a drink, talk and fondle one another. A small cover charge was added to the bill for this illicit luxury. Charlie ordered whisky and a plate of boiled eggs. When the waiter placed the drinks and plate of eggs on the rickety table, Charlie pulled the cubicle's tattered grimy curtain shut. They had half an hour before the waiter would return to inform them that if they needed more time, they would have to pay another cover charge. Charlie had used this place to have secret meetings with contacts in the past. He knew the drill. He was also aware that the waiters all thought he was homosexual, because the only companions that Charlie brought there were men.

The clerk began tapping the tips of his fingers on the table. Charlie smiled, he knew what that meant, he got out his wallet and handed the clerk some money. Now the clerk was ready to talk. He had been crafting secret dossiers of dirt on senior personnel for a long time and would use it if they tried to get rid of him. 'Other day I hear,' he whispered, 'I hear big boss saying. He was talking, don't know to who? I think big boss was talking to small boss that big message coming from Delhi to have report on Cross Island ready. I hear them saying this is very, very top secret. I was outside door, so I heard.' Charlie heaved a sigh of relief. He tried getting some more information from the clerk who insisted that that was all he had heard. Charlie asked for the name of the big boss and slipped the clerk some more money. 'Char-lee Sahib,' the clerk pleaded, 'please don't mention that I am telling you all these things, otherwise I will be on footpath, no job, no home, no nothing. I have wife and two children, please sir, not to be mentioning.' Charlie repeatedly assured the clerk that he would not implicate him, and left. He stayed in a hotel and met *Sea Princess Maya* the next morning at the dock.

'Where the hell were you?' Willie growled, 'Why can't you inform us when you are going to be spending the night away from Cross Island?' Charlie smiled and patted Willie on the back. 'I will deliver some of the packages today,' he said, 'I have news, good news.' Thommo was relieved that he did not have to shoulder the burden of delivering Charlie's packages anymore. 'It's about that fokker' Desai, I hope,' he asked, 'is it...?' Charlie was exuberant, 'Better than that,' he exclaimed, 'this could be the solution to our problems.' It was late evening when they all set off for Cross Island. Charlie sat alone, a look of accomplishment on his face, much like a marathon runner who had taken part in the race, not to win but test his endurance, and had managed against all odds, to finish running the gruelling distance. His, grit and tenacity had paid off. That is how Charlie felt.

That night, Charlie triumphantly detailed his encounter with the clerk to Willie and Thommo. 'I was lucky,' he said, 'I just happened to be at the right place at the right time, that's all.' 'So what do we do now?' Willie wanted to know. 'We find out what his weaknesses are,' Charlie said, 'we need to know everything about him. I have a contact in the police canteen, a cleaner. He is an incurable gossip. He would know the dirty details, if there are any; of this officer whose name is Raghav Modi. Through him, we will get to the source that is in New Delhi. Maybe all these attacks on us have nothing to do with Desai, maybe they are being orchestrated from New Delhi.'

Charlie contacted 'the sweeper' after he had finished his shift at the police headquarters. They decided to meet at the nearby Crawford market which was situated close to the Victoria Train Terminus. After settling in a tea shop, Charlie paid the ritualistic bribe. They then began conversing in Hindi because the sweeper's grasp of English did not go beyond, 'You wel-com saaaar.' Charlie was astounded by the wealth of information the sweeper had assimilated in his dirty mental dossier. He was a disgruntled employee who felt he was overworked, underpaid and constantly abused on a job that was far below his mental capacity. He had wanted to join the police force as a constable. He had worked hard and had a High School certificate. This made him academically qualified for the job; but he did not have the necessary contacts and bribe money to get to first base. To add to it, he was a social cripple, born an untouchable, a fact he repeatedly stated was the underlying factor for all the misfortunes he had had to endure. And so he compensated the inferiority brought on by society and the establishment by gathering information on the vices and faults of his superiors. They had blackballed him; this was his payback. It partially lowered the heat from the flame of prejudice he had to constantly live with.

The sweeper told Charlie that Raghav Modi was a gambler, who lived beyond his means. He liked to drink expensive whisky and visit houses in red-light areas. His peers at police headquarters all knew this; he had frequently overheard them talk in the canteen. But the man was good at his job, at least that's what the other officers and constables said, and more importantly, he had contacts with powerful politicians in New Delhi. The sweeper stated that Modi was married with three daughters; he knew his wife's name and which village in India she originally hailed from. He hated the man, because here he was...a hardworking, morally upstanding untouchable and then there was Modi, a corrupted Hindu greaseball respected by society. When the sweeper had once begged for an appointment, through Modi's secretary, to plead his case for a job as a constable, Modi had scolded his secretary and told her not to waste his time. The sweeper had been incensed and humiliated when he heard this. There was nothing he could do about his station in life but mop the floors, hoping that some incurable sexually transmitted disease would make Modi's life as miserable as his was.

Charlie now had all the information needed, but he sat there, offering tea and sympathy to the sweeper who was grateful that a white man had consented to associate with him and treat him kindly. Charlie did not mention the fact that he considered himself a Brahmin. As the sweeper continued his vitriolic angst against the Hindu-controlled establishment, Charlie slipped him some extra cash and told him he had to leave. The sweeper thanked him, and hoped that Charlie would need further information on personnel who worked at the police headquarters. Charlie was almost euphoric. He knew that he was the only one who had the ability and contacts to unravel this problem. To safeguard against another schizophrenic attack, he knew that he would have to give up alcohol, for now at least, he told himself.

To Willie's surprise, Charlie stopped drinking and started taking the powders that the ayurvedic doctor had prescribed with regularity. Through Willie, they started tracking the source of Modi's whisky supply. Willie knew it would be a problem if Modi was obtaining his whisky through one of their competitors. Willie had studied all their clients who lived near Modi's home, and finally discovered the connection. Modi had no clue that he was indirectly buying Cross Island smuggled whisky.

Charlie checked the prostitute parlours that the sweeper had mentioned. The women at all five places confirmed that Modi was a frequent client. Willie did a fact check on the sweeper's allegations that Modi was a gambler. Willie knew every slick, slimy card house that the sweeper had mentioned. Again the allegations proved to be true. Modi had an impressive and dangerous credit line in the gambling houses that was tolerated because he was a high roller who was employed in a position of awesome legal power. He was the hammer of the law that could destroy their lives and businesses. Charlie now had a file that could hang, draw and quarter Modi. The next move, Charlie decided, was to have an informal meeting with him, far away from police headquarters.

Meanwhile, the business on Cross Island continued. The five hundred drop offs would end in a week. The men were in a state of paranoia and revolt. There had been violent incidents. One of the Cross Island couriers had to use his knuckle duster to fight off two assailants who tried to grab his packages. He managed to save the merchandise but suffered a slashed arm in the process. A vicious blow to his forehead had nearly made him lose consciousness, but he fought them off and delivered his package to a client who was aghast at the sight of him bleeding. Back on the island, the men collectively said that they did not want to have any part in the deliveries and there was open talk of them leaving Cross Island. Charlie and Willie, after a hasty meeting, informed the men that they understood the dangers and that now all the men would share in the profits. Just one more assignment, Willie lied to them, and then they could all take their riches and retire.

Dona Maria worked alone, directing all traffic to and from Cross Island, much to the admiration of Charlie, Willie and Thommo. She maintained the books, ironed out problems and at the same time ran the domestic chores on Cross Island with an impeccable work ethic that called for applause. She wisely apologized that she could not wait to consult them because she knew they were busy trying to solve bigger problems. They had excluded her from what was going on, but Dona Maria knew that something bad was happening and knew that in time, they would have to consult with her. She worked and waited to be let back into the inner sanctum.

Charlie, Willie and Thommo argued fiercely about the place where they would corner Modi. Thommo came up with the solution. 'The whore house,' he said, 'is the best place. He will not have his police protection. We can bribe the Madam, tell her we want to meet him to ask for a favour. We present him a bottle of our finest Scotch, invite him to have a drink and then gently place the hook into his mouth.' They agreed, and Charlie set about finding out when Modi would be making his next nocturnal rendezvous. It was decided that Willie and Charlie would represent Cross Island; Thommo hated cops too much. It would not be prudent to include him, in case he flew off the handle.

The night of the meeting, Charlie and Willie dressed in their Sunday best. Willie had Dona Maria assemble a generous 'family pack' of cheese and chocolates for Modi's family. Charlie carried three bottles of Scotch. They were ready for the whore-house encounter. At a private luxurious bungalow, the Madam who had been bribed by Charlie welcomed them. Modi was in a bedroom; they would have to wait. The Madam had informed him that a few businessmen wanted to meet with him for five minutes. Modi had never had a 'meeting' in a whore house. He had been reluctant and had initially refused, but the Madam who had been bribed with a large sum of money had vouched persuasively for Charlie's credentials. She assured Modi that this meeting would stay underground. She argued with him that her 'friends' already knew that Modi used the services that her girls provided. They wanted to talk business. They were not interested in his private life. Finally Modi had consented to only listen.

When he emerged from the bedroom, Charlie and Willie introduced themselves. They were ushered into a comfortable back room. 'How did you find out that I come here?' Modi wanted to know. 'Oh! I come here too, all the time,' Charlie lied. 'You don't have to worry, Mr Modi, we are not interested in using this against you.' Willie offered Modi the gift package for his family. He accepted it and said, 'Talk, you have five minutes.' Charlie had rehearsed his speech. He delivered it with the finesse of a professional orator. Modi listened in silence, his chin on his clenched fist. When Charlie had finished, Modi said, 'I am going to talk. I want no interruptions. This order has come down from New Delhi. Someone alerted the Ministry of Industry and Supply; I don't know who. I have no interest in what goes on at Cross Island as long as there is no trouble. I am aware of what goes on there. I am also aware that various police personnel have been bribed by you to ignore Cross Island. If you want to put an end to this you will have to get through to someone from the office of Shyama Prasad Mukherjee, who you know is the Minister for Industry and Supply. I have been asked to supply a report by his office. I have heard that it was a former detective from Bombay who contacted them. I don't know his name. I have been told that this detective is standing by, awaiting orders from New Delhi. I am telling you all this because I am sure that if you do not get this information you will resort to blackmail. I have dealt with dogs like you before. If you know this about me, I am sure you know the rest. I can destroy you all, but I don't want an inquiry into the deaths of English people which I am sure your government will initiate. We have trade and other relations with Great Britain which might get affected if your government hears of a massacre of its citizens. I do not want questions asked over your deaths, and I do not want to get into a political mess over this. So this is what I am going to do. I will hold and delay my report for three months. If New Delhi eventually clears this detective to come to us and work against you, I will have to allow him. You will now supply me with whisky and whatever my family requires whenever your shipment comes in. Inform the person who supplies me that from now there will be no exchange of money for these products. I will also require you to make a small donation, every month to a police fund that I am setting up. Instructions will be sent to you on Cross Island. If you can go to Delhi and kill this at its source, well then, this will all be over. If you, at any time, try and use what I do in my private life against me, I will destroy that leper's colony you have constructed on Cross Island, regardless of the consequences. Do I make myself clear?' Having said that, Modi abruptly got out of his chair, grabbed the whisky and gift package and stomped out of the room. They could hear his angry voice screaming at the Madam.

Charlie and Willie walked out of the room, found the back door and slipped out. The next day they heard that the private brothel had burnt down. The papers reported that five women had perished in the fire. The local fire department attributed the fire to a kerosene stove that had exploded in the kitchen. The police, one of the newspaper reports said, were trying to determine who the owner of the house was. Unconfirmed sources stated that the bungalow may have been a house of ill repute.

Modi had sent them a searing message written in fire. Charlie and Willie were shocked and appalled by what they thought was a hysterical overreaction. The only one impressed with Modi's brutality was Thommo. 'We have three months, before we walk the plank,' Willie said. 'How the hell are we going to handle New Delhi?' Thommo asked. Charlie stayed silent, he was thinking about New Delhi and the Ministry of Industry and Supply; he did not know a living soul who could get through to the politicians there. New Delhi was as foreign to him as England. There has to be a way out of this, he thought in desperation. Charlie did not doubt the veracity of the threat from Modi. In three months it would be hang time for Cross Island. Meeting Modi in the brothel had been a bad idea; they should have met him in a restaurant or park. They had caught him with his pants down, humiliated and scared him. The man had a wife, relatives, children, and a respectable polished veneer that society saluted, but it was too late for regrets now. Modi would kill them all and burn their world on Cross Island to cinders if he was slammed against the wall again. Charlie was sure that Modi was already preparing alibis if he had to destroy Cross Island. Charlie went into a tailspin of dark depression. He felt trapped, alone and lonely. The whisky beckoned and Charlie drowned his desperation in its amber soothing comfort.

Chapter 10

The Language of Lust

Dona Maria was passing by Charlie's home the next morning. She heard an animal snarl and pushed the door open. She found him, beady-eyed, conducting a heated dialogue with the devil. She screamed and fled calling for Willie and Thommo. By the time they got there, Charlie had risen to his feet; he was flailing his arms like a windmill in a storm and rushed forward in attack mode. Thommo tackled him, brought him to the ground as Willie and another man held his body down. They took him back to Willie's house, kicking, screaming and spitting and tied him to the bed as Charlie raved, ranted and howled in the throes of pain, as Satan's sizzling hot pitchfork, sliced the skin and soft flesh of his stomach, entered his intestines and twisted his guts. The explosive sound that shot out of Charlie's mouth was a true reflection of the hell his mind was in. They all looked at him, helpless, not really understanding the scale and intensity of the attack. Only an exorcist would be able to deal with this satanic body, Dona Maria thought. This is not schizophrenia; he has been possessed by the devil. She tried to explain this to Willie, said that she had seen similar incidents in her village in Portugal when she was a young girl. She suggested they get a Catholic priest. Willie coldly disregarded her country-bumpkin analysis, insulted her Catholicism and called her an idiot. 'This is his sickness,' he explained in a voice one would use on a witch doctor who said she could perform open-heart surgery. 'This is because the fokker' continues to drink and take his medicine at the same time. God knows what it is doing to him. The devil has nothing to do with this. Johnny Walker is the bloody fokkin' problem.' Willie was furious that Charlie had done this to himself and endangered Cross Island at this crucial time. All he could hope for now was that Charlie returned from the fires he was in. Willie had never seen Charlie attacked like this before, it was frightening. What if he did not recover fully? What if was never the same again? Willie walked to The Rot Gut Café and sat alone, drinking black rum, feeling scared and insecure. Thommo and Dona Maria joined him. He looked at Dona Maria, 'I did not mean to...' he began. She interrupted him with a voice that was kind and sympathetic, 'I understand, Willie,' she said softly. 'We are all confused, I am not angry that you talked like that. You still have Thommo; and I am always here for you. We can run Cross Island and take care of this problem.' 'So what the fok' are we going to do now?' Thommo asked. Willie raised his arms up to the sky and brought them down on the table with a thump. 'Fok' alone knows,' was all he said. Dona Maria who was ignorant of the reasons for all the consternation asked what had happened. Willie felt that there was no point in holding out anymore, so he narrated the entire sordid story of Detective Desai, the meeting with Modi and the looming death knell sound from New Delhi that was clanging in their ears. 'I know,' Willie said, 'Charlie has absolutely no political contacts in New Delhi, which is what drove him back to the bottle. The poor bastard is suffering for us all. Maybe it is time to shut this whole thing down.'

Dona Maria was silent. She smiled. Willie's hackles began

rising again. *What the hell is she smiling about?* he thought. *This is serious business. We could all be dead in three months.* 'We don't need to shut this down, Willie,' Dona Maria said. 'Maybe we can work it all out. My ex-lover, who is still in Goa, knows people,' Dona Maria continued. 'What?' asked Willie who was preoccupied with his thoughts of doom. 'What did you say?' 'My ex-lover knows people who are connected to the Minister of Defense, Baldev Singh. I know that he is secretly helping them to try and understand the Portuguese position on Goa, which as you know is still ruled by the Portuguese.' 'Your ex-lover is a spy?' Willie exclaimed. Dona Maria was silent. 'Oh my God,' Willie moaned, 'this is turning into one of those lousy mystery books that Charlie reads.' 'He is helping the Indian government now,' Dona Maria confirmed. 'That is why we came to India. The Indians do not like the Portuguese. They have been working behind the scenes, before their independence from the British, to one day throw the Portuguese out of Goa. My ex-lover is helping them. He used to work for the Portuguese government as a diplomat. He has contacts. I can get him to help us.' Willie wished that Charlie was here to hear this. This all seemed so far-fetched, complicated and unattainable. 'And why would he help you?' Thommo asked contemptuously. 'He likes to take little boys into his bed,' she said without emotion. 'If the Indian government finds that out, his game is over. He has these boys working as servants for him, the parents are happy, the boys are well paid, and he...you know...his official role is working with the Indian government for which he gets a lot of money. I am the only one, apart from his young lovers, who knows his dirty little secret. He will help me, I can guarantee that.' 'What is your ex-lovers name?' Willie asked. 'Faustino Eduardo Christo,' she said. 'Oh, sweet mother of God!' Willie exclaimed laughing. 'Doesn't Christo mean "follower of Christ"?' Dona

Maria nodded and lowered her eyes, 'I am ashamed that he is the way he is. Homem doente, homem doente,' she repeated. 'That is what we Portuguese call a very sick man; my ex-husband is a molestador de crianças, a child molester, that is the reason I left him.'

The next day the final packages were scheduled to be delivered. Dona Maria had efficiently taken care of the five hundred drops. Willie designated a twenty-four-hour watch that monitored Charlie who was still submerged in a deep dark well of depression. He stared at nothing, said nothing, and accepted food with a defeated resignation.

Dodo arrived, watched, tried to say something, received no response, shook his head in dismay and disappeared. The people of the island now viewed Charlie as an acquired family burden with an incurable disease who was slowly slipping into oblivion. Here was a brilliant man who had shown great promise; he had got them this far, now they would have to function without the light of his fire. There was no choice it seemed, unless he came back from whatever dark place he was in. Willie and Dona Maria took charge, with Thommo serving as assistant commander.

While Charlie lay in a near-vegetative state, the islanders got ready to depart for their vacation. It was December, a week before Christmas and the mood was festive. They planned a party on Christmas Eve. Willie hoped that Charlie would get through his fog and see the light of day soon. He had contacted Charlie's ayurvedic doctor who had to be persuaded to visit the island. He examined Charlie, who did not recognize him, charged a hefty 'house call' fee and notified Willie that if Charlie's symptoms persisted, he would have to be admitted to a psychiatric hospital. Charlie was now being fed his medicine regularly as Willie watched his slow progress with anxiety.

Christmas Eve arrived. The girls had cooked a traditional British Christmas dinner that included plump roast ducks, Brussels sprouts, browned roast potatoes, stuffing made of nuts, tiny sausages wrapped in bacon and lots of rich gravy. For dessert there was Christmas pudding which had been liberally doused in flaming cognac. Thommo set up the bar and a guitar player sang merry Christmas songs of gliding reindeer, snowflakes and baby Jesus in a manger. Dona Maria dressed Willie as Santa Clause, and after Willie had a few drinks under his broad Santa belt, he stumbled around in his fake white beard yelling, 'Ho, ho, ho, ho…' People exchanged presents and talked excitedly about their coming vacations. Dona Maria told stories of her childhood and how she had once run away with some gypsies to get away from her dominating mother. She also described the strange sexual requests she had got from some of her past lovers. The men howled with laughter and the girls nodded knowingly as people applauded. They gathered around her as she regaled them with rambunctious episodes from her colourful past. The celebration was subdued compared to the last party on Cross Island; the spectre of Charlie's disintegration covered the sky above Cross Island like a dark cloud.

They had dressed Charlie and sat him down by the bonfire. He watched the festivities with suspicion in his eyes. For Charlie, it was an unholy night. Demons bounced off his brain and played with the bright sparks that the crackling angry bonfire was spitting into the darkness.

Christmas day, the people of Cross Island packed for their vacation. Dona Maria had contacted Cox and Kings, a travel agency in Bombay and had made all the necessary ticket arrangements. The next day, sixteen Cross Island residents left for their long-awaited holiday. Each one went up to Charlie at different times to wish him well and say goodbye. Charlie looked back with a vacant, hollow-eyed stare. Dona Maria grew tearful as the moment of their departure arrived, and hoped that they would all be back at the end of March. Willie and Thommo dropped them off at Ferry Wharf, from where they took taxis to the Royal Air Force Santacruz Airport.

When they returned to Cross Island, the place seemed lonely and deserted. Charlie was asleep. Willie, Thommo, Dona Maria and the four men who had stayed, sat at The Rot Gut Café, drinking whisky and talking about the future. When the men left for their shacks to sleep, Willie asked Dona Maria how she was going to handle her ex-lover.

'I plan to leave for Panjim next month,' she confided, 'I have booked my train ticket.' 'Do you want one of the men to come with you?' Willie asked. 'I need Thommo here to take care of business.' Dona Maria shook her head decisively, 'I have to do this alone.' 'What we need,' Willie explained, 'is a contact at the office of Industry and Supply in New Delhi. We need to get to the man who is handling the Cross Island file for the minister. It is through this man, that we can get the minister to drop the investigation into Cross Island, and get Detective Desai off our backs. I don't know if, or how it will work, but we have to try. The minister has bigger problems to take care of. If the point man at his office can be convinced to advise the minister that Cross Island is not a threat, maybe the minister will decide to drop the investigation. Right now I don't know how we are going to handle it. Maybe by the time this happens, Charlie will have regained his bloody senses.'

Dona Maria secretly hoped that Charlie would reside in his vegetative state and eventually die. This is what she had wanted: to rule and run Cross Island with Willie. Thommo had no choice, now that Charlie was a basket case. Harming her or Willie would not be practical. Thommo had been forced by circumstances to help her get what she wanted. Dona Maria did not bring up a future romantic alliance with Willie. The time was not right. She would wait till Cross Island settled down to make that move.

The next day they began the work of paying back the credit line on the consignment and seeing that all the numbers tallied. Thommo and the four men carried out maintenance work on the Island and *Sea Princess Maya.* Through the weeks they often journeyed to the mainland to dine in one of the many restaurants. They were rich now, so they ate at posh places and drank the best liquor that money could buy. Occasionally the men visited exclusive whore houses which charged a fortune for an hour. Meanwhile back on the Island, Charlie had a constant 'nurse guard'. One of the four men looked after him in shifts. They now knew that Detective Desai would not make a move until word came down from New Delhi, so Thommo was not overtly concerned of an attack at night.

CHAPTER 11

Of Masters and Boys

Dona Maria planned to surprise her ex-lover. She could have sent a telegram to his home in Panjim, but if he refused to see her, or left Goa on the day of her arrival, she would have made the trip in vain. If her plan to blackmail him were to succeed, she would need the uncomfortable element of an unannounced, unwelcome visit on her side.

Early January, Dona Maria left for Portuguese ruled Goa with the promise that she would have something positive when she returned.

Much to Willie's delight, Charlie slowly began emerging from his tunnel of troubled solitude. It was the middle of January, when Charlie began speaking. His depression had abated to a manageable level, but the paranoia that schizophrenia brings tainted his perception. Willie could not hold a normal conversation with him, but Charlie was now aware of his surroundings and requested for food when he was hungry. He was still suspicious of everything. He asked where everybody was. As Willie began explaining, Charlie lapsed into a now familiar silence. From the look on his face, Willie knew that another attack was taking place. At least, Willie thought with relief, this time it was a non-violent assault.

Dodo had returned and was preaching the gospel of Judas Iscariot inside Charlie's fevered brain. Suddenly, Dodo stopped talking. Willie was staring at Charlie whose face now grew contorted. Willie was wondering what was going through his tortured brain when Charlie's eyes slowly opened and grew wide with fury as he glared at Willie. Charlie lunged at him with the little strength he could summon, screaming, 'The art of war, the art of war...' Willie yelled for Thommo and together they tied Charlie to the bed. 'How long is this fokkin' nonsense going to go on?' Thommo complained, 'Maybe he will be better off in a nut house.'

Dona Maria got off the train at Margao and took a taxi to Panjim and directed the driver to the Fontainhas Latin Quarter. That's where her ex-lover lived amid splendid, elegant luxury, in a mid-18th century double-storeyed green, pale yellow and blue bungalow with red Mangalore tiles. The house was a proud exhibit of the grandeur of Portuguese architectural finesse. The garden was immaculate; as it had been the day she left. She got out of the taxi and stood looking at the house, remembering the good times. Two teenaged gardeners were inspecting the fountain which had stopped working. One of them recognized her. 'Hello Anthony,' she said, 'Is Master Faustino at home?' 'No madam,' he replied in halting English, 'Master go Delhi. We not know when he be back.' 'That's fine,' she replied, 'I will wait for him. I have some urgent work with Master Faustino. Can you please take my luggage into the house?' The boy was flabbergasted. He also felt threatened that she was back. They looked at each other; he knew that she knew of the illicit, illegal relationship that the 'Master' had been having with his help. He lowered his eyes in embarrassment and proceeded to unload her luggage from the taxi and take it into a guest room. The maid who cooked and cleaned had finished her chores for the day. Dona Maria liked her. She called out to her as she was leaving, 'Oh, madam,' the cook exclaimed, 'Nice to see you. Are you coming back to stay?' 'No, no,' Dona Maria exclaimed, 'I have to talk with Master Faustino about some business. They told me that he was in Delhi. I will wait till he returns.' The cook wanted to know where she was living, what she was doing, was she married...? Dona Maria laughed and conjured up some half-truths which seemed to satisfy her. Two young house servants appeared. She did not know who they were. The Cook told them that Dona Maria was a close friend of the 'Master' and asked them to take care of all her needs. She told Dona Maria that she would be back the next morning and would be delighted to cook her anything she wanted. Dona Maria thanked her and asked one of the boys to get her a bottle of red wine and a plate of cheese. After he had placed a bottle of wine, a cut-glass chalice and a plate of assorted cheese on the carved table in her room, she closed the door, walked into the luxurious attached bathroom and filled the large tub with water. As she undressed and lay in the tepid water sipping sweet wine, she began thinking of what she was going to say to her ex-lover when he arrived. She looked at the label on the bottle of wine. It was vintage *Quinta Do Noval*. 'You must admit,' she chuckled to herself, 'the man has good taste.'

The next day, Dona Maria wandered through the Fontainhas Latin Quarter. She had walked these narrow winding roads before and began feeling nostalgic. The simple sights, the sounds, the smells, they all seemed so familiar. The houses were well kept, almost immaculate. It was a law in the Fontainhas that residents had to paint their homes after every monsoon. This law was enforced with military strictness. A shoddy unpainted peeling house received a hefty fine. She found herself at the southern end of the Fontainhas outside the gleaming whitewashed church of Saint Sebastian. She walked in and headed for the hanging Christ which had originally been housed in the dreaded Palace of the Inquisition in Old Goa. Dona Maria knelt before the cross. The eyes of Jesus were open. Perhaps this is the only crucifix in the world, she thought, where the eyes of Christ are wide open. Staring into his eyes, she began feeling cold and guilty. She had looked into those eyes before and pleaded for forgiveness, succour and minor miracles. Today, they spooked her. Dona Maria looked down, made the sign of the cross and left without genuflecting. Outside the church, she wondered when her ex-lover would be back and what kind of reception she would receive. She wondered; did she really know him...? Dona Maria had read disturbing stories about him in the newspapers.

The Portuguese government was aware of the subterranean rumours that the Indian government had secretly employed the expertise of Portuguese turncoats, like Faustino Eduardo Christo, to bring an end to Portuguese rule in Goa, Daman, Diu, Dadra and Nagar Haveli, collectively known as the *Estado da Índia.* They sensed that he might be secretly working with revolutionary groups like Azad Gomantak Dal (The Free Goa party). The Portuguese newspaper *Expresso* had constantly printed stories about this alleged collaboration, without being specific or naming names. Unknown to Faustino Eduardo Christo, or the Indian government, Agente Casimiro Monteiro, a Portuguese secret service gunslinger working with PIDE (*Policia International de Defense do Estada*), had been tracking Christo's covert movements, hoping to prove that the underground whispers were true. The Governor-General of Goa, Fernando de Quintanilha e Mendonca Dias, had decided that if the rumours proved to be right, Christo would be nailed for treason, and crucified to aid the ascension of Roman Catholicism and the continuance of Portuguese dominance.

Back on the Island, Charlie meandered between blackness and light. In desperation, Willie visited the Thana Mental Hospital located off Bombay and met with an English missionary doctor who treated schizophrenia. Willie described Charlie's symptoms in detail. The doctor was silent. After Willie finished explaining, the doctor said, 'I have to examine your friend to make a diagnosis.' 'He will not come here,' Willie confessed. 'Well then I cannot help him. But there may be hope for people like him down the line,' the doctor explained. He looked at Willie and said in a low conspiratorial voice, 'A French pharmaceutical company, Labouratoires Rhône-Poulenc, has been researching a new drug they say will revolutionize the treatment of schizophrenia. I know that human trials are being carried out in London. The name of the drug is Chlorpromazine. The team of French scientists Pierre Deniker, Henri Leborit and Jean Delay who have discovered this antipsychotic drug are working with doctors at Saint Bernard's Hospital in Southall. I am in regular touch with the doctors at Saint Bernard's where human trials are underway. From what I have heard, it is a modern miracle. Unfortunately it is not available right now. Maybe, in the coming years, we could have a drug that will treat and control the symptoms of schizophrenia, so that people affected with this devastating neurological malfunction, can perhaps lead almost normal lives.' 'My friend does not have years to live doctor,' 'Willie explained, 'he needs help right now.' The doctor spread his hands in a gesture of resignation. Willie requested for paper and a pen and wrote down the exact spelling of the drug. He then got off the padded chair he was sitting in, paid the doctor's appointment fee and thanked him. He decided to try a quick exit line as he headed for the door, 'Dr Youngblood,' he inquired casually, 'do you have any good contacts at this hospital?' The doctor smiled, he knew what Willie was asking. 'Yes, I do,' he confessed, 'but I cannot reveal the names of the doctors who are involved with this experiment. Let me add a cautionary note here, if I may,' the doctor continued, 'this new drug is still at an experimental stage. It is a cocktail of chemicals that laboratory scientists in France are still working on. They are trying to make the recipe palatable for schizophrenia. Like any medical concoction, the measures that go into the final product are carefully calibrated and then added to the mix. Addition and subtraction happen as researchers watch what happens when the chemicals interact with human chemistry. Add less salt, a little more Gin, maybe a teaspoon of orange juice, a twist of this, a dash of that...I hope you understand what I am trying to say...but as a doctor I must warn you that there is always a possibility that the side effects, if there are any, might lead to permanent disability or even death. There might be side effects that the doctors might be unwilling to mention till they fix the problem. I don't know, I am not privileged to receive that kind of information. Be careful of what you do. The doctors right now are 'reasonably sure' that Chlorpromazine can help schizophrenics, but reasonably sure in my profession has often led to disaster. Please remember, the drug is still at a human-trial stage; the clinical researchers have still not announced their final verdict.' Willie knew that it would be futile to try and argue, beg or plead for more information. He walked out of the room and hospital smiling. He would get this drug Chlorpromazine for Charlie through his underground contacts in Southampton.

It had been five days; her ex-lover had failed to materialize. Dona Maria hoped that he had not taken off for Portugal.

It was a warm, beautiful afternoon. She was sitting in the garden listening to the melodious sounds of a kingfisher having an animated conversation with its mate. Somewhere, hidden in a mango tree, a cuckoo called. It would be so wonderful, she thought, if I knew what they were saying. A car pulled up at the gate. And there he was. Faustino Eduardo Christo dressed in a three-piece English tweed suit, with a Swiss gold pocket watch. His hair was longer but the arrogance of someone who is absolutely sure of himself still dominated his suave features. As he was walking towards the mansion, Dona Maria emerged from behind his yellow rose bushes. His striding gait faltered and then came to an abrupt halt. 'Dona Maria!' he exclaimed, visibly shocked and alarmed, 'What are you doing here?' 'Is that any way to greet an ex amante?' she asked her ex-lover, smiling. 'What brings you to Goa?' he insisted. His forehead furrowed, his brows inched closer to each other and his lips beneath his luxurious moustache formed a thin line. It was a stark portrait of disapproval and abject loathing; Dona Maria got the silent message, loud and clear. The servants had heard his voice and rushed to the car to attend to his luggage. 'We will talk later,' he added in a hostile voice that implied that she was not welcome. She waited in the living room while he bathed, preparing for his antagonism, but when he walked into the living room, Faustino's emotions were masked by a diplomat's veneer. He had defanged his shark-toothed demeanour and his voice was placatory. 'I am sure,' he said, 'you have good reason for coming here. The matter must be of some importance. I apologize for my harshness.' Dona Maria nodded. 'I should have sent you a telegram, but there was no time. I need your help.' Faustino reached for a silk cord and tugged at it. A bell tinkled in the kitchen, the teenaged servant boy appeared. Faustino asked her what she would like to drink. The servant came back with a bottle of gin, tonic water, ice, wedges of lemon and slices of cucumber. Faustino fixed the drinks, raised his glass and exclaimed 'Brinde!' 'I would prefer that we speak in English,' he said, 'I don't want the servants to understand what we have to discuss. 'Eu entendo,' she said she understood. Dona Maria explained that she had started an import-export business in Bombay and they were running into problems from people in Delhi. She needed to talk to somebody at the Ministry of Industry and Supplies to get it all sorted out. She needed to get to the person who was handling her file. 'Why don't you bribe their branch office in Bombay?' he asked, 'That is the way everybody does things.' 'It is a little more complicated than that,' she replied. 'I know that you have good political connections. I am asking for your help.' Faustino smiled, 'This story that you are reciting, this nice fairy tale, is not true; still I don't want to know, it is really none of my business. But why should I help you? What do I gain from this?' The teenaged servant had entered the living room with a small silver plate on which were his expensive cigars. Dona Maria glanced at him, waited until he had left, and whispered, 'My life depends on this. I did not come here to beg. I will do what I have to do to get your help, even if I have to force you to do this.' 'Ahaaa...meu deus...eu não acredito que isso...My god, I can't believe this...blackmail,' he hissed. 'How charming!' 'I thought we were only going to speak in English,' she joked, hoping to ease the tension. He glared at her. She averted his eyes, looked down at his Persian carpet and the texture of her voice changed to a quiet pious confessional tone, 'Faustino look,' she explained, 'I have never uttered a word of what goes on here, I want you to believe that, and I never will. I don't care what you do with your life, but right now my body is to the wall...' He was silent. She made herself another drink. He lit his cigar, left the living room and walked into the garden. She could hear him pacing on the grass. It was a long five minutes before he returned to the living room. Puffing his cigar furiously, he consented. 'I know the person you are looking for at the Ministry of Industries and Supply. She is the supervisor of the typing pool. She monitors the work of fifteen typists who type all the reports for the Ministry of Industry and Supply. She will know which officer is handling your case because she is the one who catalogues all the files. After that, it is up to you.' 'What is her name?' she asked. 'I cannot tell you that,' he replied. 'I will have to contact and bribe her personally. I will need to know the name of the business that is being investigated so that she can locate the file and the officer who is handling the case. Now, why don't you tell me the truth of what this whole business is all about? Through her, I will find out anyway, so...' 'I cannot do that,' she argued, 'I have to discuss this with my associates.' 'You don't understand,' he snapped, 'I am not suggesting that you tell me the name of the business. I am demanding, because the typing supervisor will only deal with me and no one else. That is the way these things work. If I give you her name and you approach her, she will not cooperate, or she might say "yes" if you bribe her, and then tip off the officer who is handling the case, then things can get extremely complicated. Anything can happen. I am sorry. I cannot help you if you plan to be stubborn and stupid.'

Dona Maria gulped her drink down and told him the story

of Cross Island. He sat there, puffing his cigar, sipping his gin, and listened to every word she said. When she had finished, he shook his head in dismay, 'This is so estúpido,' he observed, 'I thought that you would have better sense than to...anyway I am no one to judge you. What you do with your life is no longer a concern of mine. There is danger and death here...' Dona Maria deliberately moved her head sideward; she stared at a pile of *Expresso* newspapers on a small table. Faustino exploded, 'Don't believe everything these prostitutas print. I am well protected. There is no truth to anything they write, and anyway it is no business of yours.'

She could read the jagged lines of contempt in his blazing eyes. Faustino lapsed into a stubborn fuming unnerving silence. If he refused, despite the threat of blackmail, there was nothing she could do. In desperation, he could have her killed. He had shady social contacts, political power, and the monetary wherewithal to get away with murder. When Faustino spoke again, his voice had lost its contempt. 'Dona Maria,' he said, 'you and me, we have had some good times. You were a perfect host when I had my parties. The four years we spent here, you ran this house well, and you were always loyal to me. You did not trouble me when you decided to leave Goa, except for the large amount of money that you demanded and got. You kept your promise that you would not talk about why you left, and for that I am grateful. Now you come here, and blackmail me. That is not nice. Bad things can happen to people who do things like this.' He paused, got out of his Louis XV armchair, walked up to her, stared into her eyes and confessed, 'I did think about slitting your wrists to make it look like suicide. I think the officials would understand why you killed yourself. A spurned lover returns to find that she is still not wanted; she has nowhere to go, so she gets into the bathtub with a bottle of champagne, and drowns her miserable life. It has happened before. If there were any problems, the local police would believe my story after I greased their palms. But, I don't want to complicate my life. I have more important things to do. I promise you that I will get the information you need in a week. I will send you a telegram. You can collect it from the post office near the Ferry Wharf area. I want you to leave tomorrow evening, I will make your train reservations, and...if you try this merda again...eu prometo que você vai se arrepender.' He warned her she would regret it if she ever tried to blackmail him again. He then tugged at the silken rope, a bell tinkled in the kitchen, a young boy servant appeared and Faustino ordered the table be set for dinner. Dona Maria requested that her food be served on the balcony overlooking the garden. She dined alone and wondered if he would fulfil his promise to her. When she was finished, she walked past the palatial dining room. The boy was clearing dishes from the antique rose wood table. Faustino had retired to his bedroom.

The next afternoon, while Dona Maria was having lunch in the garden, Faustino handed her the first-class train ticket a contact of his had dropped off at the house. He was impeccably dressed and ready to leave. 'I may be many things that you despise,' he said in a voice laced with anger, 'but I am not a hypocrite and a dirty chantagista, a blackmailer, so I shall not wish you adeus.' Faustino pulled out his gold watch and checked the time. He appeared to be in a hurry. His eyes moved from the watch to her face, he started to say something. But he turned away, quickly aborting his thought process. He bent, picked up his leather briefcase and turned back to her with a glare of naked fury. She stared directly into his angry eyes as he adjusted the knot on his blood-red silk necktie. He hissed like a pressure cooker letting out a short burst of steam and whispered, 'Nunca mais volte aqui.' Never come back here again, he had said.

Chapter 12

Capital Punishment

Dona Maria got off at the Victoria Terminus railway station in Bombay, took a taxi to Ferry Wharf and paid a local fisherman to ferry her to Cross Island. 'I thought you were never coming back,' Willie joked as he helped her unload her luggage. 'Oh,' she replied, 'these things are delicate, they take time, you know.' 'So, what happened?' Willie asked. 'Did you get some information?' As they walked to The Rot Gut Café, they were joined by Thommo who welcomed her back with a snarky comment about child molesters. She ignored him. Dona Maria explained in detail what had transpired in Goa. Willie looked worried. 'What happens if he doesn't come up with the information... we're running out of time.' 'I don't know,' she said, 'I have tried. I hope he has better sense than that. He knows what he stands to lose.' Later, as Dona Maria was walking to her shack, she visited Charlie, who was sitting in his easy chair staring at eternity. His eyes moved to her face as she greeted him and there was a glint of recognition. 'Hello, Dona Maria,' he said, 'they tell me you were away in Goa.' 'Yes,' she replied, 'I had to meet a man there. Some important family matter.' Charlie looked away, disinterested. His acute depression now made normal conversation impossible. As Charlie retreated to his tower of silence, Dona Maria sighed and walked out.

Willie began visiting the post office every day hoping that Faustino would honour his promise to Dona Maria. Blackmail, he thought, was a dicey bargaining tool. There was no guarantee that the telegram would arrive. At the end of the week as he entered the post office, the clerk told him that a telegram had arrived for his friend Dona Maria; would he be willing to sign for it? 'Hell, yes,' Willie answered. The telegram stated: DONA MARIA STOP NAME OF MAN SANJAY TANDON STOP FAUSTINO.

Willie rushed back to Cross Island. He wished that Charlie was present as they discussed ways and means to get to Sanjay Tandon, who was handling the Cross Island file at the Ministry of Industry and Supply in New Delhi. The next day Willie was back at the post office. He placed a long-distance call to his contact in Southampton. Willie carefully spelt out the word 'Chlorpromazine'. He explained why he needed a month's supply and emphasized that it had to be done urgently. Money was not an issue he stated; he had to have this drug to save a life. He threatened that if this could not be done, there was a high possibility that all business between them would come to an abrupt halt. His contact in Southampton was unsure; getting a drug meant to treat schizophrenia was not a normal order. 'Look,' he said his voice crackling and tinny over the long distance, 'this is not like getting hold of whisky and you tell me that it is not even on the market. This is going to be difficult.' Willie spelt out the name of the French company making the drug. 'Please try and find out,' he urged, 'how they move this drug from France to Saint Bernard's Hospital in Southall. Maybe you can hijack the vehicle as it makes its way to the hospital; I don't care how you bloody do it. It is a matter of life and death for us all. I will call you again in a week.'

Willie's contact in Southampton knew exactly who he

would have to talk to. If this did not work, it would be the end. He bribed the man in charge of the warehouse where the consignments were stored. The next day, the storage manager informed him that a shipment from France belonging to a French pharmaceutical company 'Labouratoires Rhône-Poulenc' was scheduled to arrive in four days. It would be stored in the maximum-security section till the director of Saint Bernard's Hospital in Southall arrived and signed for it. Willie's contact gained access to the section. All he wanted at this stage was one pill. He was aware of the security that surrounded medical supplies. The storage manager was an expert at breaking and resealing containers. Willie's contact now had one sample of Chlorpromazine. He took it to the local market and managed to find a pill in the exact size, shape, texture and colour. He purchased thirty-five pills of this fever medication, telling the pharmacist that the pills were for an orphanage where fever had afflicted the little children. When night fell, he was back in the security section with the storage manager. They extracted thirty-five pills of Chlorpromazine from seven sturdy plastic boxes, substituted and mixed five fever pills in each container and carefully resealed the lids. As they worked, the storage manager said, 'Why the hell do you want these pills, there is no money in this. Nobody from the black market has asked for them?' Willie's contact sighed. 'It's a long story. I was told that it is a matter of life and death. That's all I know mate.' A wad of folded money changed hands in the dim light of the security section. Later the storage manager informed Willie that this shipment had been arriving at the docks regularly for nearly seven months. It comes in, shipped from Paris, every month. He could now have access to a regular supply.

The same week, a telegram came in from Southampton to the Ferry Wharf post office. Charlie's medication was on its way to

Bombay. Four weeks later, Charlie had his illegal experimental drug that could possibly save his deteriorating mind, or destroy his life with its still to be determined side effects. Back on Cross Island, Willie followed the instructions that Charlie's contact had managed to get from a nurse at Saint Bernard's Hospital in Southall: half a pill after breakfast, and the other half after supper every day. Willie dissolved the dose in a quarter glass of milk and told Charlie that it was his ayurvedic medicine. Charlie swallowed it. Willie smiled and exclaimed jovially, 'Now, there's a good boy!' Charlie ignored him and returned to the solemn darkness of his suspicion and gloom.

The month of March had begun with trepidation. The Cross Island residents would be returning home at the end of the month. Officer Raghav Modi would be sending his report to the government, and detective Desai would make his move if he was not stopped by New Delhi. They had thirty-one days to cut the noose that was hanging over their heads. They had to meet with and convince Sanjay Tandon from the Ministry of Industries and Supply in New Delhi that Cross Island was not worth an investigation. For days, Willie, Dona Maria and Thommo discussed, argued and debated the best approach to get Cross Island off the hook. Finally it was decided that Dona Maria and Willie would travel to New Delhi and try and meet with Sanjay Tandon. They tried making an appointment by phone. All they got was 'He is busy. Call next week.' They were running out of time.

Sitting in the first-class compartment of the train to New Delhi, Dona Maria proved that she had learnt something from her ex-lover. 'We tell everyone that I am a representative of a

European firm that wants to invest in India. We cannot have you represent us because unfortunately you are English, I hope you understand. Once we are in the building, we will head for Sanjay Tandon's office and talk to the doorman who will get us to Tandon's secretary. We then convince the secretary to give us an appointment. We want to talk business. We need half an hour. We have money, lots of it. That is what his secretary has to tell him. Once we are before him, let me start talking, you come in later. I have seen how Faustino used to operate; he is a great diplomat. I know exactly what to say to Tandon in case he gets nasty and tough.' 'Why did I come along?' Willie protested. Dona Maria smiled, 'Indians,' she said, 'do not like to deal directly with a lone woman who thinks she is "the boss". India has always been a male-dominated society. You will be my strong silent partner. The *man*, who will be actually running everything behind the scene, the real boss. I am just a mere mouthpiece. That is the impression we have to project, that is how I will introduce you.' Willie looked at Dona Maria with new respect. She caressed his hand lightly, Willie smiled. After a light supper, they got into their respective bunks to sleep. In the morning they would be in New Delhi. Dona Maria and Willie had booked separate single rooms at the hotel. He was tempted to fall into her arms and surrender, but Thommo's warning flashed in his brain. Now was not the time, he told himself, for love, lust, infatuation or plain old stupidity.

After a quick lunch at the hotel, they walked to the Ministry. Dona Maria's initial plan worked like Swiss clockwork. However, when they were finally sitting in front of Sanjay Tandon in his office, it all turned into a block of Swiss cheese with holes everywhere. Tandon was curt, cold and authoritarian. He did not even offer them tea, and demanded that Dona Maria stop talking. He then called for the Cross Island file. Willie noted with some satisfaction that it was slim. The minister thumbed through the few pages, looked up at them and said, 'We have reason to believe that you people are smugglers, the confidential reports say that.' The way he said 'you people' made Willie cringe. 'I am expecting a report from Bombay at the end of March. It will then be decided how we act.' Dona Maria began talking, 'Sir,' she said, 'We are an export-import firm that operates from Cross Island in Bombay...' Tandon cut her off with brutal rudeness. 'Madam,' he said quietly, 'Don't sit there and tell me a fairy tale, I have heard enough of that wonderful fiction when I was a child. We know what is going on. We have reports. I believe the source where it is coming from. We have also heard stories, and it's here in the file that you are involved in a little more than smuggling. Do you know what I mean, madam?' Willie had heard enough. 'Mr Tandon,' he said, 'with all due respect. I am not denying that we get foreign goods into India. But we do not harm anyone. It is a question of supply and demand. We are willing to pay our dues in the form of any donation that you may desire. Sir, we just want to be left alone to do our business.' 'Your business is illegal,' Tandon barked. 'What do you have to say about that?' Turning his head away from Dona Maria, Tandon eyeballed Willie, 'You are British,' he snarled. 'Your people have stolen from us for hundreds of years. I am shocked that you still continue to do so and now you have the audacity to come here.' Willie was rendered speechless. Dona Maria decided that it was time to sink or swim. 'Sir,' she said, 'we know that your boss, Mr Syama Prasad Mukherjee is thinking of forming his own party. My contacts with the Portuguese government have confirmed this. We are willing to make a large donation to his new party.' For the first time, Tandon was silent. If his boss heard that he had turned down a large donation, he would have to answer a few uncomfortable questions. He decided to test Dona Maria. 'If you are so informed, can you tell me the name of the new party…very few people know this.' Dona Maria smiled, 'The Bharatiya Jana Sangh party,' she said coyly, and added, 'I too have good solid sources that I can trust.'

Now Tandon seemed to lose his bravado, he hesitated…*This woman*, he thought, *does have connections*. Dona Maria pounced for the kill. 'If you cannot work with us, we will approach your boss with our offer,' she said, and added quickly, 'But, we would rather deal with you. Make us a reasonable offer and we will honour your request. All we ask is that we be left alone to conduct our business. We do not pose a threat to the new Indian government, or to any Indian organization. We are just providing a service. And may I add this with all due respect, if we would not be doing what we do, there are many Indians who will do so. There are Indians in Bombay who are already smuggling goods in from Europe in their own small way, but I guess, you already know that. Like I said before, we are willing to make a donation towards your boss's new party. He is going to leave the Indian National Congress party. It is going to happen at some point in time, you know that and I know that…so…' Tandon looked down at a writing pad on his table. He then looked up, his eyes shifted to Willie. 'How much of a donation are you willing to make?' he asked softly. 'We don't know…as long as your demand is reasonable,' Dona Maria said. Ignoring her, still looking at Willie, Tandon said, 'Give me two days. I cannot promise you anything, we will see. Make an appointment for Friday, nine a.m. I will have an answer. If nothing can be worked out, you will need to close your operation on Cross Island. Do I make myself clear?'

They thanked him for making the time to see them and walked out. Willie looked at Dona Maria with admiration. 'That was amazing...how did you know all that?' 'I know people, who know people,' she said with a condescending smile. 'You never go to an important meeting without bartering tools. I did my research. You don't think I spent all that time with Faustino without learning a thing or two, and making contacts, did you? Willie, I am more than...' she pointed to her breasts, 'this...' and then brushed her groin, 'and this...' Willie raised his eyebrows, opened his mouth in mock shock and laughed.

Willie and Dona Maria spent the next two days rambling through Delhi. They visited the Red Fort, Qutub Minar and the Cathedral Church of the Redemption. They also travelled to see the Taj Mahal and walked in the Mehtab Bagh in Agra, known as the moonlight garden. Here Dona Maria, overwhelmed by the serenity, confessed to Willie that she would like to spend the rest of her life with him. Willie nodded and mumbled, 'Maybe...we will see.'

Friday morning they were back in Tandon's office. 'Hundred thousand rupees,' he said. His face was expressionless as he folded his hands in his lap and sat back. Willie was shocked at the figure. 'We cannot do that, sir,' he exclaimed. 'We do not have that kind of money. We have a lot of overheads. If we have to, we will shut down our operation.' Tandon watched him silently. Willie stood up, for him the meeting was over. 'Sit down,' Tandon ordered. 'How about fifty per cent now, and twenty per cent in the near future,' he suggested. 'Sir,' Willie explained, 'in all honesty we do not know how long this Cross Island business is going to last. We have big problems, but they are not your concern. We can afford to make a donation of twenty-five thousand rupees; and if we are still there, a year from now, I promise you that we will pay an extra twenty thousand. You have my word on that.' Tandon fell silent again. Finally, he stood up. 'Okay,' was all he said. 'How are we going to do this?'

Dona Maria asked. Tandon pretended that he had not heard her. He looked at Willie and informed him that he needed to telephone his office in a week. He would be given the name of a contact in Bombay who would be authorized to accept 'the donation'.

Once they were outside the building, Willie said, 'All that money is not going to fund his boss's new party. Tandon is going to pocket the full amount. Sure, he will call off the investigation and inform his boss that Cross Island is an insignificant problem; he has the power and authority to do that, but make no mistake, the twenty-five thousand is going to line his greasy pockets.' 'What do we care?' Dona Maria answered wearily, 'Our problem is taken care of. Let's go home.' She turned to look at Willie, 'Did you notice how the fat greaseball ignored me? I told you about them being a male-dominated society.' Willie nodded. They walked to their hotel in silence, relieved that the problem had been sorted out. In the foyer of the hotel, she held his arm and said in a congratulatory voice filled with admiration. 'I never knew that you could negotiate so well.' Willie laughed, 'I used to be, and still am a cardsharp. I know when to hold my cards, call a bluff, or pack it in. I knew exactly what I was doing when I stood up to leave his office. I could see the wheels turning in his greasy mind. I remember my mother used to tell me all the time, "half a loaf is better than none". If he had let us walk out of his office without making a deal, he would have lost his chance to get that half a loaf. And you, my dear, you were magnificent; without your knowledge of that new party and Tandon's boss, we could not have pulled this off.'

Chapter 13

Cross Currents on Cross Island

The end of March arrived and Cross Island's people returned. Charlie's progress was slow and unsteady; he still resided in his temple of doom. Dona Maria, Willie and Thommo were in charge. She hoped that the new drug would bring devastating side effects that would put an end to Charlie's misery. She needed him dead to make her next move.

After the euphoria of being back on Cross Island had diminished, work on the next drop began in earnest. Willie had done a fine-comb review of the numbers and decided to raise the drops to a thousand. They needed money to compensate for all the bribes and operating costs. The twenty-five thousand to Tandon's contact had been paid and the money for Charlie's pills had been dispatched to Southampton. The investigation had been killed, but Willie was uncomfortable. He calculated that they were living beyond their means, and if they were to survive, they needed more income. Willie had decided to levy a hike of fifteen per cent on each item. He wondered if this would work. Would they start losing clients? Would his clients now approach the small-time smugglers?

By the middle of June, Charlie slowly began emerging from his darkness. The new drug seemed to be working. Willie watched him with skeptical anticipation, looking for side effects, and hoping that he could once again discuss Cross Island's problems with him, but more than anything, Willie just wanted his friend back. Thommo felt the absence of Charlie's steady hand and hoped that he would recover enough to take part in the decision-making process. Thommo had disagreed with the fifteen per cent hike. He thought it was too steep, but he had stayed silent, not wanting to put any extra pressure on Willie.

By August end, Charlie began showing signs of normalcy. Willie decided that the time was right to tell him about the Chlorpromazine pill. Charlie listened in silence. Willie thought that he was going to get a stern lecture on the miracles of ayurvedic medicine. He expected Charlie to reprimand him, but Charlie smiled, 'It seems to be working,' he said, 'So, I guess, I will continue taking it till some nasty side effect shows up. Thank you for going through all that trouble.' The two men looked at each other in silence; words were not necessary to vocalize the bond that existed between them. Willie stood up, playfully swatted Charlie on his back and walked away.

The next day, Charlie wanted to know what had been happening on Cross Island. From Goa to New Delhi, Southampton to Bombay they detailed it all. Willie had his ledgers with him. He showed Charlie figures, explained the arithmetic of the expansion he had worked out and waited for Charlie to absorb the information and make an analysis. 'We need to have a solid political force on our side,' Charlie explained. 'I need to think about this. If we are to survive, we need political protection from the Centre. That is the only way we are going to survive. This man Tandon is going to come back for more. We need one source, a powerhouse in New Delhi who we can bribe. All the protection we need will trickle down from this man. He will take care of all his subordinates from

New Delhi to Bombay. If we continue to bribe Tom, Dick and Harry we are going to go broke and we will be attacked, I can guarantee that. We need to get someone powerful from the governing Congress party who will keep the dogs away. We also need our local police cooperation so that they keep the small smugglers from encroaching into our business, and inform us of any danger. We need to have one man in Bombay we can bribe; someone high up in the police department. Once his cronies know that we are operating under his authority they will back away. Again, we cannot keep on bribing a long list of people in Bombay, the same goes for New Delhi. If we can get these two things in place, we will survive.' Willie smiled, 'Welcome back,' he said with relief. Dona Maria looked away.

The next day, two of the men who were out on the mainland contacting new customers did not return. Willie was sure that they were being double crossed by New Delhi. He called Tandon, who swore that the investigation had been called off. He talked to Officer Modi at the Bombay police station who assured him that Detective Desai had been contacted and told that the case was now considered closed. After a meeting, Charlie, Willie and Thommo came to one simple conclusion. Detective Desai had to die. The problem of course was that nobody knew where he was. Dona Maria agreed to go to the mainland twice a week to try and find the whereabouts of the elusive detective. The men on the Island were growing increasingly restive. They were now demanding a bigger cut of the profits. In a week there was a full-scale revolt on the Island. Work came to a halt, fights broke out, and one of the girls from The House of Tarts was assaulted by a drunk. Thommo had broken the man's jaw and resentment kept on rising. Charlie, Willie and Thommo held a meeting. Dona Maria was excluded from the discussion. She was visibly annoyed. Charlie took her aside and explained that they needed her to concentrate on coordinating the efforts to get new clients. 'Planning a killing is man's work,' he joked. The common consensus was that Detective Desai was now operating on his own. Willie told Officer Modi that he would have the detective killed if they found him. The officer shrugged, choosing his words carefully. 'We received a message from Delhi, the case is closed, we are not working with him, and we do not know where he is living. He is not our responsibility.'

Charlie called a meeting. He informed the men that their pay packets would be increased and would they now please go back to work. Charlie had described in detail what Detective Desai looked like. He warned them that he was dangerous. Now every man who went to the mainland carried a knife and a knuckle duster with instructions to kill Desai or his hired assassins if they were attacked. They needed to find Desai fast and put an end to his vendetta. He was operating at will, daring them to find him. Charlie instinctively felt that Desai was an arm's length away, probably living in the Ferry Wharf area, watching them and laughing at their ineptitude.

Chapter 14

To Kill a Mockingbird

When he had been transferred to Calcutta, Desai had managed to maintain the pressure on Cross Island through his contacts in Bombay. But now he felt that his existence had been bludgeoned into a groveling submissiveness that would not survive the humiliation of the transfer. His colleagues viewed him with suspicion and he was assigned the ignobility of a desk job. His professional woes were exacerbated by his wife who complained incessantly about cultural differences and standoffish neighbours. She goaded him to right the wrong that had been placed upon his neck. There were discussions that morphed into arguments which invariably flamed into violent screaming as bitterness gnawed at the foundations of his marriage. He slapped her once with savage intent, when she insinuated that he had lost his manhood.

Desai hated the mustard-oiled Bengali culture of pseudo-intellectualism; and their gluttony for the hilsa fish sickened his vegetarian stomach. The city was filthy, the people dirty and everything he touched appeared wrapped in the silent process of helpless disintegration. Circled by squalour, he talked constantly to the locals hoping to achieve a rudimentary insight into the social structure. The occasional optimism he thought he would encounter never materialized; all he heard were stories of hopelessness and despair. This was a city of we wish...we hope...and who cares. The streets, it seemed, were afflicted with a communicable disease that spread like ringworm on the filthy skin of the city, and the contaminated flesh and vital organs underneath appeared to seep out of the potholes in a pulpy oozing rot. Out on the streets, remnants of the Babu culture still wagged its obscene behind. Local politicians and social workers during the British Raj and after, had preached *ad nauseam* about social upliftment projects and jobs, and helping the poor to try and get out of the gutter of human degradation. After the customary initial speeches and handshakes, they had all disappeared into the grime with the allocated project funds. And now, another name had appeared on the do-gooder list. The locals talked of a gora nun, Mary Teresa, who had appeared like a white apparition and was now teaching unschooled children from the slums, soothing the dying, and offering medical aid to lepers. 'Why some gora lady coming here to get dirty disease and die, I not understanding? Why she not going back to her Ingland?' a homeless man wondered, and then perhaps to explain it all he growled in Bengali, 'Se abashyai pugle.' After hearing his analysis on her mental stability Desai had to admit, 'Yes, this woman must truly be mad to come here alone and try to save this place. Why was she here? To do what?'

Desai had no idea that in the filthy disease-racked slum settlement, Moti Jheel near the centre of the city inhabited mostly by destitute Muslims, Mary Teresa was questioning her decision to venture into the blackhole. Like Desai, her faith had been infected, weakened and shattered by the leprous environment. She had heard the whispered allegations of misuse of funds, poor medical treatments and religious evangelism. In her letters to friends, she admitted that deep down in her soul she had lost her faith. She wrote of the stark empty darkness inside her. She told them that now, here in Calcutta, nothing touched her soul and that her smile was a cover that cloaked everything she did. She wrote that she was a hypocrite who had surely made a mistake when she answered what she thought was a call from the sacred heart of Jesus to come to Calcutta. Desai and Teresa shared a spiritual common denominator; they had lost faith in their respective Gods.

A Communist skeptic Desai muttered to himself, 'There is nothing anybody can do here where Marxist philosophy mingles with Tagore and fish curry.' An 'intellectual' teacher pontificated, 'Calcutta is a Tower Of Silence waiting for the vultures.' Her reference to the carrion birds made Desai think of the photographs of Calcutta shot by American photographer Margaret Bourke-White for *Life* magazine showing the aftermath of the Hindu-Muslim 1946 riots. 'The vultures are still picking this rotting city to the bone,' he thought with disgust. 'I have to get out from this pyre forsaken by the Gods.'

Unable to cope with this deluge he had resigned from his job, sent his wife and daughter back to his wife's village and returned to home ground, Bombay. Desai then met with a businessman he knew. The man was looking for land to start a garment factory. Desai persuaded him to fund his Cross Island enterprise. In return he promised the businessman the use of the island after he had got rid of Charlie and his associates. Desai then bought four burqas and practiced speaking in a low-pitched husky female voice. For a week he lived on a footpath in the Colaba area, testing his new covered burqa persona, and then moved to a Muslim tenement near Ferry Wharf. He told people who asked that his name was Fatima. He circulated a story that she was a widow whose husband had been murdered by the Hindus. Fatima talked to no one, and no one talked to her. People left her alone; she was the grieving widow, dressed in black, dealing with her bereavement and hatred for the Hindus.

Desai knew that by now Charlie's people would be looking for him, and in all possibility, the Bombay police too. Using the burqa as a cloak of anonymity, Desai could move about freely. His extensive contacts with the underworld now paid off. He had managed to torture the Cross Island residents. Now he planned a full-scale war. He knew he could rely on knives for hire if and when he needed them. Desai's next plan was to cut off the Cross Island water supply. But he was in no hurry, time was on his side. He had started with a slow burn; now he was going to incinerate them in a roaring pyre. They had killed his dog, destroyed his career and fragmented his family; now the animals were going to pay.

As Desai sat on the floor of his tin-roofed rented tenement eating rice and dal from an aluminum plate, he shook his head and laughed in bitterness. When he was in high school he had been chosen to play a detective in a play; acting had always fascinated him. Now here he was, a real-life detective, playing a woman. Life can be strange sometimes he thought. His daughter and wife had not been happy with his decision to go after Charlie, but he had promised them that he would be back once he had settled the case. He had explained that if he let this humiliation pass him by and succumbed to defeat; it would haunt him all his life and day to day existence would cease to matter. He had to do this; he hoped that his wife understood his need to close this chapter of his life. She had looked at him in silence, as she and their young daughter got on the train. In her heart she was sure that she would not see him again. She remembered their dog. He was going to end up dead. But as his wife, she had to obey his dictates. She was going to wait for him in the home of her parents. She did not know, and he did not say, how long this would all take. Madness, she thought, does not have a timetable; it just happens.

Back on Cross Island, Charlie, Willie and Thommo were trying to figure out ways to ferret Desai out from his hole and into the open.

Thommo had come up with the idea of staging a hunting expedition. They were going to use live bait, just as big game hunters in India had for centuries. They were going to load *Sea Princes Maya* with empty boxes; hire a low-life Englishman to guard the boat at night, and wait for Desai to make a move. Thommo would be there, in the shadows at Ferry Wharf, waiting with his long knife. 'Yes,' Charlie said, 'that is an excellent idea. It could work.'

On the evening of the set-up, one of Desai's contacts alerted him. Concealed behind a steamroller at an abandoned water transport hub project on Ferry Wharf, Desai could see *Sea Princess Maya.* He knew that it was the Cross Island boat. Why would they have precious cargo sitting on a boat at night, guarded by one man, he asked himself? The next morning the boat went back to Cross Island. The next night it was docked in the darkness again, loaded and waiting. Desai smiled. 'It is the old shikar trick,' he told himself. 'They must think I am stupid.'

Charlie waited a week before he called off the hunting expedition.

Victoria received a letter from Maya.

Dear Victoria,

The news of Charlie's illness has affected me badly. I can't stop thinking of him. From what I have read about the illness, it is incurable and usually ends badly.

I go to work in a trance sometimes trying to picture him. It's like trying to put a face on a ghost. I cry at nights, thinking of the many ways our lives could have been different; it is wishful thinking at this stage, but it is all I have got. I feel like a bird suddenly afraid of heights, paralyzed, cowering in its nest, wing tied and very quiet. Neelam has been a great help. She soothes and holds me night after night when this sadness engulfs me.

I guess now, I will never see Charlie again. I have tried to rationalize this, look at the facts, of how I was abandoned, just two-months-old, and Charlie and my mother went about doing what they did in their lives; but something will not let me close this door completely. I am not smart enough to figure this all out. All I know is that this grief has possessed me. I don't know why I am miserable and crying for a man I have never really known.

I could abandon everything that I am doing, come and meet him and take him away. Maybe we could live the remainder of his life together. Would he give up everything he has for me? The answer to that question is there, somewhere in the darkness. I don't have the courage to go looking for it. I am crying while I am writing this. Am I crying for Charlie, or for myself?

Like I did when I was growing up, I try and escape by falling down a rabbit's hole. I have to leave for work now. I will write you another letter soon. Please do write and tell me if you have any news about Charlie.

Sincerely,
Maya

Sitting on the concrete floor of his tenement, Desai's thoughts turned philosophical. He knew he had to cross the Rubicon river through hell and high water. The die had been cast. Let the waters flow where they may now. Like the sages, seers and saints of the past, he heard 'The Call' reverberate in his brain.

Joan of Arc had heard those 'Voices' and so had Saint Augustine of Hippo, but on the other end of the spectrum there were people like Vlad III, The Impaler, who roasted children and fed the flesh to their mothers. He also cut off the breasts of women, and forced their husbands to eat them. After they had finished eating, he had them all impaled because the voices deep in his brain justified his actions. Through the good, bad and ugly annals of history no one had been able to determine if these 'voices' were a manifestation of madness or a spiritual awakening. 'What is truth? What is wrong? What is right?' Desai wondered. He could not walk a straight and narrow path anymore. D.H. Desai was turning into Charlie Strongbow. He was fighting to live, recapture, and retain a place he called home. The collateral damage that was inevitable, the moralistic questions that religion brought and the distinct possibility of death were swept into the gutter. Burning fanaticism gripped his daylight hours as he schemed and plotted the destruction of Cross Island.

Like Charlie, Desai started the next phase of his operation at the Victoria Docks. He had heard of the young barrel-chested, six-foot hoodlum, Karim Lala. Word on the street was that Lala was a petty crook involved with stealing merchandise from the docks; but what attracted Desai were the dark underground sounds that whispered that Lala commanded a small force of Pashtuns who carried out extortions and contract killings. Desai hoped that Charlie's smuggling enterprise would interest Lala. He began gathering information about the Pathan. He was going to set up a fight, stand in the audience, and watch the fire of his wrath burn Cross Island.

Desai's investigation had confirmed that Lala often played mediator in the troubled lives of Muslim couples headed for a divorce. Clad in his burqa, Desai made his way to Agiary

Lane and a house called Tahir Manzil. This was Lala's home in Bombay's Grant Road area. He was stopped at the entrance by a security guard who said that Lala was not at home. 'Come tomorrow,' was all the guard said, 'We will see if he is willing to see you. Lala is a busy man.' After four futile visits, Desai decided that if he could not meet Lala he would have to think of another plan. Finally after a week, Desai decided to try again. Lala was at home. He was ushered into a small living room. There were thirteen people waiting for Lala who was sitting in his terrace garden conducting business. He was told to wait in a room reserved for women. There were six women waiting to discuss their problems with Lala. After two hours, he was notified that Lala was now free. Desai walked out onto the terrace garden covered in his burqa. Desai had been told that Lala was known to talk in short staccato sentences. His informant had been right. 'Welcome. My simple home. What is problem?' Lala asked, 'Can I help. You understand. I will talk to husband. Hear other side. So please. Let me know. What I can do. I will do.' Desai started to take off his burqa and stopped abruptly. Lala was staring at him. Desai turned his head and looked at Lala's bodyguard. He was sure that the man had a concealed dagger under his loose Pashtun clothing. A sudden move would mean grave injury even death. 'I am not what I seem to be,' Desai explained in his normal voice. 'My life is in danger, so I have to use this disguise. I am going to remove my burqa so that we can speak freely. Do I have your permission to do so?' The bodyguard moved closer. Lala held up a hand and the man retreated. Lala nodded. Desai removed his burqa. Lala looked at him with his piercing black eyes, his face expressionless. 'Speak,' he commanded. Desai had carefully rehearsed his speech. Lala listened with quiet intensity. When Desai had finished, Lala rubbed his forehead, scratched his thick right eyebrow and ordered his bodyguard to get him a bottle of Chivas Regal Scotch. 'I know this Cha-lee,' he said. 'What he is doing. Cross Island. Not competition. Why I must interfere?' It was then that Desai sowed the seeds of expansion and power into Lala's brain. Lala, he explained, could take over Charlie's business. Desai lied and told Lala that Charlie was planning to get into the business of smuggling hashish and gold, which was Lala's domain. But Karim Lala was a man with both ears to the ground. 'Not true,' he retorted frowning, 'I would have heard. I understand. This falsehood. I understand reasons. Why you tell lies.' Lala snapped his fingers. His bodyguard poured two drinks from a bottle of Chivas Regal. Lala lifted his glass and said, '*Kha sehat walary*. Pashto for cheers,' he explained. While Lala drained his glass, poured himself another and sighed with contentment; Desai, who was not fond of alcohol, tentatively sipped his drink and quickly changed the focus of the discussion. 'They ruined my family life, killed my dog and destroyed my career. When this is over, I will be reinstated into the police force and I will not forget your help, if you are kind enough to offer it.' Lala was silent. Finally he stood up. 'Need to think. About this,' he explained, 'Must know more. Don't want. Politician problem. Policeman problem. Need one month. I am busy man. Come back. We will see.'

The fire burning inside Desai could not wait a month. When the next water carrier boat failed to arrive at Cross Island, Charlie knew that Desai was instrumental in the cancellation of the service. The search for the detective had been exhausting and futile. Desai had been here, he was seen there. They followed leads that disintegrated to frustration, and led nowhere. The reason for this illusion was the way Desai was operating. When he approached his contacts to deal with the water supply company, he did so without his burqa. He would then retreat to a deserted side street and cover himself in black anonymity. Charlie and his Cross Island people were chasing a grey shadow of the black night, whose reality changed when the light of morning arrived. They met people who had talked to Desai occasionally. They had touched him. Desai had walked down that street; he had stopped at the market to buy vegetables, turned there, at the second intersection, and then disappeared into another cul-de-sac. The people of Cross Island had to turn around and follow another trail of smoke that the wind blew into the bay.

Desai had become the ghost of Cross Island.

While the rest of the island worked on securing orders for the next consignment, Charlie, Willie and Thommo went through myriad 'trap Desai' scenarios. Charlie had managed to recruit another water company but with Desai out there, they knew that the next crisis was as inevitable as the tides that lapped the periphery of Cross Island. 'Remember, the Portuguese gold that I had told you about?' he asked them. 'Now is the time to find it.' 'We don't need gold, Charlie,' Willie scoffed, 'we need water.' 'You seem to have forgotten the conversation we had some time ago,' Charlie continued with stubborn insistence. 'Gold bars were buried here, on Cross Island. Remember, I told you all about Luis de Camoes, the Portuguese poet who was forced to leave Portugal. He left in 1553 for Goa aboard the *São Bento;* with a huge quantity of gold he had stolen from the treasury. You seem to have forgotten this story. This is not a fable, this is historical fact. The captain of the ship that was carrying the gold two-timed Camoes and buried the gold in a well here, which had a natural spring. If we find the spring, we will have all the fresh water we need. And we will also find the gold.' 'Assuming this nutty story is true, which I highly doubt,' Willie sneered, 'how are we going to find this well?'

'If the gold was here, the Indians would have found it by now,' Thommo added. 'Oh! They tried,' Charlie explained, 'for years, they dug up Cross Island; all they got was salt water. We are going to dig in a specific place, where the spring is, and we will find the gold and our water.' 'And how are you going to get to the exact spot?' Willie asked. Charlie smiled, stroked his beard. His eyes twinkled as he poked Willie in his chest. 'We are going to get a water diviner to help us find that bloody spring.'

Charlie contacted a farmer who had once used a famous water diviner to find potable sweet water. When the old water diviner was brought to Cross Island, he closed his eyes and made his first pronouncement. 'This is a place of bad poison,' he mumbled, 'Life cannot be sustained here.' Charlie translated what the diviner said. Dona Maria felt an involuntary shiver go through her body, Thommo laughed at the old man and Willie wanted to know why the old man had said what he had. They escorted him to The Rot Gut Café and offered him tea and snacks. Willie inspected the old man's Y-shaped water-divining rod which was a small sturdy branch of a tree. The old man told them that his name was Shiva and he was not uncomfortable being around spirits. But he cautioned, there were good spirits, and there also existed very bad ones that would enter a body and refuse to leave. For some mysterious reason, Shiva stared at Charlie with his wise eyes and said, 'You, especially you, know what I am talking about.' Charlie fidgeted. He wondered if the old man was referring to his schizophrenia. How did he know? Or was he addressing Charlie because he perceived him to be the leader of the group?

Shiva considered his gift special. Few people in this world, he explained, were bestowed with his unique ability, which he believed came from the Gods because of the good deeds he had done in his last life. His divining rod he said was a family heirloom that had been handed down from his great-great-paternal grandfather. It was found at Gangotri, the source of the great sacred river Ganges. 'How long do you people plan to stay here?' he asked. Charlie said he did not know. Shiva looked at the ground and said, 'I hope you understand that it is not up to you. There are forces here that will determine that. It is my duty to say these things.' When Charlie translated, Willie and Thommo laughed. Shiva then stood up and picked up his divining rod. He stated that he would need to do this alone. They watched him with interest and amusement as he began slowly walking around the island, pointing the tail of the Y of his diviner's rod at the ground.

Five hours went by. Charlie, Willie, Dona Maria and Thommo stayed at The Rot Gut Café, discussing the next consignment. They presumed that the old man was still walking about or resting somewhere on the Island. Willie said, 'Maybe he died and has gone to join the spirits.' Thommo laughed, but Charlie sat there grim-faced, thinking of the warnings that Shiva had uttered. They decided to go look for him but stopped as they saw Shiva in the distance, walking slowly to The Rot Gut Café. He sat on a chair, massaged his knees, requested a cup of tea and said, 'I found it.' Then he sipped his tea in silence, ignoring their questions. After he had finished, he led them to a deserted part of the island where the colossal water drums had been placed. Shiva raised his diviner's rod and the stick began visibly vibrating in his hands. 'This is where your water is,' he said. Charlie, Thommo and Willie stared at the site. This was the place where the now destroyed altar had been. This was where children had once been sacrificed. Shiva looked at them, seen the consternation on their faces and smiled. 'The innocent pure water of life is buried here,' he said in a whisper. 'Use it wisely. I must go now.' Charlie thanked and paid the old man and Willie ferried him back to the mainland.

Later, as they gathered around the place which the old man had said the spring was, Charlie said, 'Now, I know why the Indians never found this place. The altar always stood there, before we destroyed it.'

The next day the digging began.

Charlie's elation on finding the source of the hidden gold was repeatedly interrupted by the old man's warnings. There is something about that old geezer, Charlie thought. He stood to gain nothing from his warnings. He had not asked for extra money for further advice, or pressured them to leave. He just said what he had to say and had left. 'The innocent pure water of life is buried here,' he had said. 'Innocent'. 'Pure'...Was he talking about the sacrificed children? Or was he talking about plain old water?

That was an ominous sentence scrawled on a giant sign that needed to be deciphered.

Charlie went back to his shack. Dodo arrived. Charlie was glad to hear his voice.

***Dodo:** You think all that the old man said was plain old ignorant superstition, don't you?*

***Charlie:** I have a problem with grasping his far-fetched philosophy. Even if we find the water, I will still have my doubts. I really don't know why...it is not practical, logical or rational. It is not believable if you apply...*

***Dodo:** Talking about believability, listen to this. Moses stands before the bush on Mount Horeb. It is on fire, but the bush is not burning. And then, God begins talking.*

How believable is that?

Six hundred thousand fighting men on their way to the Promised Land, plus women, children and cattle, travelling from a confused square to a turning circle and back again. Israelites wandering and lost in the small desert in Sinai for forty years, eating manna from heaven.

Is there any sense of realism to this divinely orchestrated exodus?

A jealous Shiva cuts off the head of Ganesha. Replaces it with the head of an elephant. There is no pain and bleeding, no dying. Ganesha lives happily ever after; with the head of an animal.

Try logic here, see where it goes.

Prophet Mohammad in Seventh Heaven. Bargaining with God. Uses Moses as his council, to know about the number of times Muslims had to pray each day. God says, 'Fifty', Moses disagrees. Sends Prophet Mohammad back; again, and again and again. God finally consents. Five times a day is practical. Moses wants a further reduction. Prophet Mohammad refuses to go back. You would think the Prophet Mohammad would have chosen a safer sounding board. If you recall, old Moses failed to follow the Lord's Word to the letter, felt the wrath of God, never got to see the Promised Land. And here he is, openly encouraging dissent with God! Again! Don't you think Prophet Mohammad would have taken that into consideration before choosing Moses as his advisor? So why did he...?

Try figuring that out.

Hanuman desperately searching for the lifesaving herb Sanjivini that grows exclusively on Dronagiri Mountain in the Himalayas to save Lakshman's life. He cannot identify the plant species. He lifts the entire mountain. Carries it to the battlefield in Lanka. Lakshmana is saved.

Is there any rationality to this left-handed monkey business?

Jesus of Nazareth. Changes water into wine. Walks on water. Raises a dead Lazarus. Then comes alive after being crucified and buried, and then ascends into heaven.

How far-fetched is that? Even the Immaculate Conception pales in comparison!

Siddhartha Gautama. Reaches enlightenment. Demon Mara attacks him with armies of monsters. The about-to-be Buddha does not move from under the Bodhi tree. Mara sneers at Siddhartha, 'Who will speak for you?' Siddhartha reaches out his right hand. Gently touches the ground. The earth quakes and thunders, 'I bear you witness!' Mara disappears. The morning star rises. Siddhartha Gautama realizes enlightenment. Becomes a Buddha.

How believable is that earth-shaking story, Charlie?

Go on. Apply your theorems of practicality, normality and reason. You deserted Christianity and ruined your Hinduism, because you have absolutely no faith in anything living or dead. You are confused by what the old man said...but if you look beyond his words, you will hear the silence of his voice and see his message.

It's like understanding magic, Charlie. Once you decipher the sleight of hand, learn the art of cutting a woman in half, or disappearing in front of thousands of people; the hidden mechanism of hocus pocus becomes comprehensible. The old man's sentences come from thousands of years of belief. For him, there are no more questions, and what remains...well, he knows how it all works. The rabbit that is pulled out of a hat is real. The magician is real. The hat is real. The stage is real; the act is an illusion. If you are looking for an answer set in steel that you can touch, you had better stop...Remember, Pontius Pilate once asked Jesus of Nazareth: 'What Is Truth?'

There was no answer.

Dodo waited for the expected refutation to his explanation and left when Charlie walked to his bed in silence.

Victoria was getting ready to go to church on Saturday morning when she heard a knock on her door. It was the old postman, Vikram, who had delivered her mail for years, and sometimes did small chores for her. He smiled and said, 'A letter from Maya.' Victoria thanked him. She was surprised that Maya had written her another letter so quickly.

Dear Victoria,

Thank you for your letter. I guess Charlie must be alright, if you have not heard anything about him. I consider this good news.

In my last letter, I mentioned falling down a rabbit's hole. When I was told about my adoption by my foster parents, I was young, maybe thirteen- years-old. I began wondering what my real parents were like. When I was alone in my bedroom, I used to close my eyes and pretend to slip down a rabbit's hole like Alice. This would take me into a wonderful world. I guess smart people would call this a form of escapism. The Mad Hatter was Charlie, and Caitlin was the Queen of Hearts. I replaced Alice with Maya and had heart to soul conversations with the Hatter and the Queen. I used to watch in confused silence as Charlie would ask Caitlin intellectual questions and Catlin would scowl, 'Off with your head.' Just amusing nonsense.

But there have been many times, when we would have a picnic by a river and they would talk of family and love and the good times that we had all had, and I would feed the ducks, wondering which one was Dodo! It was, and still is comforting entertainment, and I always feel better when I return to the real world. Victoria, I hope you don't think that I am batty. I am sure if Charlie or Caitlin heard, this they would think that I am just silly.

I must confess that when you first wrote to me about Charlie's schizophrenia, it troubled me on two levels. The first: that Charlie was fatally afflicted, and the second, is schizophrenia hereditary? The first question made me sad; the second terrified me.

Doctors till date don't really know. What if this disease is already in me; waiting to destroy me? Maybe there were signs, and I have ignored them. It really is very unsettling and frightening. In my bitterness, sometimes, I think, besides giving me away, my father, bestowed upon me this gift of his afflicted bloodline. At other times, I can forgive, knowing that for once, this is really not his fault.

Last night, while I was lying in bed beside Neelam, I thought, what if I end up like my father? Like many of the questions in my life right now, I don't want to think of the answers. I just want to slip down the rabbit's hole.

Sincerely,
Maya

After five days of digging for water on Cross Island the men were tired, frustrated and disillusioned. There was no water, and certainly no gold. They blamed Charlie for his naivety and refused to dig any further. Willie took Charlie aside and privately counselled him to give up the idea; but Charlie was a stubborn man. He journeyed to the mainland and hired a borewell company. Willie grumbled about the financial waste. Charlie had lied to the company. He assured them that a team of geologists had tested the area for ground water and they had determined that an aquifer did exist on the spot where they were going to be drilling. A week after work commenced, the borewell company penetrated through two hundred feet of soil and rock and finally hit the aquifer. Now, Charlie walked around with the old 'I told you so' attitude and a glint of triumph in his eyes. Willie shook his head in amazement and said, 'Everyone here thought you were crazy. No one, not one of us believed you and now...Ah! Well we were all wrong.' People came up to

Charlie and patted him on the back. Charlie felt exhilarated. He felt good. This was a feeling that he had not felt for a very long time. He was a great asset to his people. They liked him and trusted him.

It took another three weeks for the company to set up the pipe, protective concrete grout and pump. Charlie talked to one of the engineers. He told him the story of the gold. The engineer laughed. 'We had to drill through solid rock to get to the water,' he explained, 'there is no way anybody in the past could get to that level and hide gold there.' 'The geologist you hired to find this water was right,' the engineer said. 'There was no geologist's involvement here,' Charlie explained. 'What do you mean?' The engineer asked intrigued. Charlie patted the engineer's shoulder playfully, smiled and sheepishly narrated the story of the water diviner. The engineer shook his head and laughed, 'You took a big chance here. If we hadn't found that aquifer, you would still have to pay for all that work. Luck is on your side, these so called water diviners are a joke.' After completing their work on setting up the borewell, the company drew water samples for testing and left. Two weeks later, they had the results. The Island now had an unlimited supply of safe drinking water. Now everybody congratulated Charlie again, and Willie apologized for being a 'doubting Thomas'. But Charlie just mused cryptically, 'There is another fresh water source on Cross Island and that is where the gold is.' Willie frowned, 'Let it go, Charlie,' he said in a chiding tone, 'we found our gold.'

Back on the mainland detective Desai was getting ready to meet Karim Lala. He was sure that the smuggler's greed would motivate him to destroy Cross Island. When he arrived at Lala's home, Lala refused to see him. An appointment was made for them to meet the next week. They met at Lala's hotel, the New India Hotel. Lala greeted him with an insincere smile. 'What you do. You do,' he said. 'Word I gave. To Cha-lee. I will not interfere.' Desai thanked him and walked out.

The next night Cross Island went into a state of shock. Thommo did not return from the mainland. Charlie suddenly entered a tunnel of depressive darkness again. The side effects of the experimental drug had begun to wag its vicious uncontrollable chemical tail. Hot flashes began ricocheting and clashing through his bloodstream. As they rushed through his veins, their short black fuses self-ignited. Pregnant and ready for delivery, they exploded in his brain like mighty firecrackers.

Willie stared at Charlie in horror. Fragments of what Dr Youngblood had said flashed through his stunned mind.

And then...the police found Thommo's body wrapped in a gunny sack. It had been dumped on one of the fishing boats moored at Ferry Wharf.

Thommo was walking that night through Ferry Wharf to get back to Cross Island when six men, armed with knives, surrounded him and backed him into a deserted construction site. They had been warned of how dangerous Thommo could be. They kept their distance. As Thommo rushed one side of the murderous circle, he stabbed one of them in the chest. And then, one of the thugs threw sulphuric acid into his eyes. Blinded by white hot flashes, Thommo snarled with pain and slashed at the darkness in futility. The acid had begun eating into his eyeballs and eventually, wracked with pain, gasping, and clutching his eyes, Thommo doubled over, and the circle closed in, cutting and stabbing till he dropped to the dirt. Thommo was already dead when they prised his stag-handle carving knife from his clenched right hand and plunged it into his heart.

Willie visited the morgue. He looked in shock and horror at the mutilated remains of his old friend and wept. He signed for the body and took Thommo back to Cross Island. They buried

Thommo with his Sheffield steel knife. Dona Maria, in tears, led the prayer service. As they placed a wooden cross on his grave, they grieved for Thommo, and cried in anxiety for their future, that had so suddenly become so insecure.

Dona Maria talked to Willie after the funeral. She tried to assure him that together, they could run Cross Island. What she did not know was that without the backing of Thommo and Charlie, Willie had lost his nerve. He listened to her in silence. He recalled Thommo's words about her Machiavellian ways and his heart hardened. 'She seems almost relieved that Thommo is dead and Charlie incapacitated,' he thought, 'Thommo was right. I have to get away from this madness.'

The next day, as the men went about the mainland getting orders for the next consignment, disaster struck again. Three of the men had to be rushed to a hospital with bleeding skulls. Stones had been hurled at them from dark corners. The police as usual had nodded their heads, filled out forms and politely informed Willie that they would 'look into the matter'. 'And what about Thommo's death? Do you have any suspects? This former Detective Desai is responsible. Why can't you people arrest him?' Willie wanted to know. The police officer, not pleased with Willie's aggressive tone, had looked at Willie with a stern face and said, 'We are looking into the matter.' Willie had stomped out of the police station in frustration and disgust.

Chapter 15

And in the End

The next morning, back on Cross Island, the men refused to work on the mainland. Willie had been up all night, thinking and planning. He called a meeting. 'This is the end,' he said with simple finality. 'We are going to distribute Thommo's share of the profits and then we all go our own ways. This was great while it lasted; but now, with Charlie and Thommo gone, there is no way that we are going to survive. You all might as well go out there and enjoy the money that you have made here. I wish you all good luck. I will always remember what we did here.' After he had finished, Willie walked to The Rot Gut Café and started to drink whisky. Dona Maria sat beside him and wept like a child. The next day Willie started the process of contacting everybody involved with Cross Island. He sent messages to Southampton, paid off any debts they had incurred, visited the docks and held meetings with dock bosses, and in three weeks Cross Island was ready to roll down and move on.

Willie summoned a representative from the travel company Cox and Kings. The company arranged for all travel papers, freight transport, bank transfers and passports. Dona Maria wanted to stay with Willie but he had other plans. He told her, 'I cannot go back to England and I do not want to move to Portugal. These are foreign places to me. India is all I know. I am going to go to the Kullu valley in Himachal Pradesh, buy myself an apple orchard and retire. I know an English bloke who has done the same thing. I sent him a telegram. It's that simple. I'm going to live there, die there. You and me, it will not work. There is a flood under the cracked bridge we stand on.' They talked about Charlie who had disintegrated into drowsy involuntary movements he had no control over. Muscle spasms and tremors wracked his body. His face had turned into a death mask that drooled.

Willie and Dona Maria visited Charlie's friend Victoria. 'I am taking Charlie to England,' Dona Maria told her. 'Charlie had once mentioned that you were in touch with his daughter. It is our request, if possible, that maybe you can contact his daughter Maya, wherever she is, and tell her that her father will be at Saint Bernard's Hospital, at Uxbridge Road in Southall.' Fernandes looked at them in silence. Willie handed her a paper with the postal address of the hospital. She did not ask what had happened to Cross Island or to Charlie. She knew the answers. They wished her well, said goodbye and left.

When the door shut, Victoria walked to her easy chair, held her head in her hands and wept for her friend. She had always known that Cross Island would bring disaster. Now the life of her friend Charlie had come to an end; and the only living soul that he cared for, was a world away, unaware of the tragedy that would arrive in a letter. 'This was no way to tell a daughter that her father had lost his mind,' Victoria thought. 'How sad,' she mumbled, 'how very sad.'

Now, plans to leave Cross Island went into overdrive. Most of the men were going back to England; a few had decided to take a chance on living in Bombay. The girls wanted to tour India and then leave for Ireland. Dona Maria, it was decided, would drop Charlie off at Saint Bernard's Hospital in England; and then journey back to her farm in Portugal. Willie handed her a large leather satchel containing Charlie's share of the money of Cross Island. He had exchanged the rupees for pounds in Bombay's black money market. 'Give that to the hospital,' he instructed her. 'With that, they can set him up in a private room for the rest of his life. God knows there is more than enough there.'

There were long, tear-filled goodbyes and promises to keep in touch, and then in four weeks, all that was left on Cross Island, were the lonesome figures of Charlie, Willie and Dona Maria. Before they left, Willie and Dona Maria stood before Thommo's grave and said goodbye to their friend. They packed Charlie's meagre belongings and stuffed them into a duffle bag. As Dona Maria was walking out of Charlie's shack, she noticed the small wooden replica of *Sea Princess Maya* sitting on a shelf. She grabbed the boat and shoved it into the bag. They loaded *Sea Princess Maya* and rode away from Cross Island. Willie turned back to look at the island as the boat was halfway to Ferry Wharf, he held up his hand in one last farewell. Dona Maria did not look back.

Willie turned to Dona Maria when they landed and said, 'It is better this way. We both need to find something. I don't know what it is, but I hope that we do. Thank you for giving me your address in Portugal. I'll send you a letter once I settle down.' Dona Maria hugged Willie and sobbed. Willie looked at Charlie, held his shoulders and whispered, 'Goodbye my friend. Goodbye.' Tears filled his eyes and dripped down his cheeks. 'I will miss you, Strongbow,' he mumbled, his voice trembling with profound sadness. It was the only time Willie had called Charlie by his last name. Charlie gazed at him with eyes that had lost all comprehension. Willie kissed Dona Maria on her cheek and took a taxi to the train station. Dona Maria held Charlie's hand and guided him into the vehicle that would take them to the airport.

Three weeks later, a man and his German Shepherd boarded *Sea Princess Maya* that had been abandoned at Ferry Wharf. He started the engine, checked the fuel gauge, turned the boat around and headed for Cross Island. He walked around the island aimlessly, inspecting the shacks and the borewell, walked into the store house where some of the merchandise that had not been delivered lay, and sat in the shade of The Rot Gut Café to get away from the merciless sun. He then walked to the place where Thommo was buried. He stared at the mound and the crude wooden cross on which was carved: *In Memory of Timothy 'Thommo' Blackwell. R.I.P.*

His young bitch sniffed the dry mud, bent her hind legs, lifted her tail, and urinated on the grave. The man smiled.

BOOK III

Chapter 1

Balls-Up in Blighty

Dona Maria arranged for an ambulance from Heathrow airport to take them to Saint Bernard's Hospital in Southall. She handed Charlie over to the staff with a letter that Willie had written detailing in common parlance Charlie's schizophrenic history and some of his personal information. She waited while a doctor read the letter. 'How did this man get hold of Chlorpromazine?' he demanded, 'This is illegal and dangerous.' Dona Maria said she had no idea. 'Does he have any money or family?' he inquired. She looked at the doctor and said, 'Charlie Strongbow has two daughters, Maya and Doris. He used to talk about them. Nobody knows where they are or what happened to them. They were given up for adoption when they were babies. He has no money. He is a pauper.' The doctor nodded and asked her to fill out a form. A nurse appeared. They sat Charlie in a wheelchair and placed his duffle bag on his lap. Dona Maria knelt before him, put her hand on his shoulder and whispered, 'I wish you well, Charlie. Thank you for all the great memories.' Charlie looked through her and began to drool. As they wheeled him away, she stood still and watched the wheelchair disappear through the doors of a ward. Dona Maria held her right hand up in one last goodbye.

Fearing a backlash from the Chlorpromazine that Charlie

had been self-medicating himself with, the doctors set a rigid medical routine for Charlie the same day, and hoped that he would recover a semblance of his mind and motor skills. They inundated his system with powerful doses of sedatives collectively termed by psychiatrists as the 'Chemical Cosh'. Insulin injections were also to be administered to Charlie six days a week for two months. This was the Insulin Coma Therapy. They began by injecting Charlie with small doses of insulin and gradually increased the dosage to one hundred and fifty units which produced a coma that lasted an hour. Charlie would be brought out of the coma by a glucose injection. After approximately sixty comas, if the doctors deduced that Charlie had benefited, the dosage of insulin would be gradually reduced and then terminated. If Charlie's condition stayed the same, in a timeframe determined by the doctors, they would add Convulsive Therapy to his treatment. Minute, controlled electric currents would be propelled into his brain through his cerebral cortex via electrodes placed on his scalp while Charlie was under general anesthesia. This would trigger a brief 'therapeutic seizure'. The common consensus among medical experts was that brief seizures caused by Convulsive Therapy created positive changes to the complex chemical circuitry in a brain, and this reversed some acute schizophrenic symptoms. This induced alternative state of somnambulistic consciousness was now going to be Charlie's life till the doctors detected an improvement.

It took six months of intensive care for Charlie to begin the first tentative steps to a partial recovery. He was consigned to a ward on the ground floor which had a window that looked out to the garden. On sunny days, they walked him out to a garden bench where he sat for hours talking to the squirrels. There were times when his schizophrenia took complete control and the doctors feared he would die. Like every patient at the hospital, Charlie had good days and ugly times, but as the months passed by, he began a steady recovery. He started asking rational questions. 'What happened? How did I get here? What is this place? How long do I have to stay here? Where are all my friends from Cross Island?' He began remembering, talking normally, and the tremors that had seized his body retreated. He could now walk in the garden with assistance and supervision. The hallucinations still arrived but the 'Chemical Cosh' doses and insulin had made them manageable. He would talk to the nurses attending him and like most patients, he had a favourite. She had recently joined the hospital as an intern and she was the only one who took time from her busy schedule to talk to him. She told him how he had got to Saint Bernard's Hospital. 'Ahaaa...Dona Maria,' Charlie had exclaimed. 'Is she your wife?' the intern asked. For the first time since he was admitted to the hospital, Charlie laughed. 'No, no...' he said, 'just a friend.' The following week, as Charlie was sitting in the garden, the intern walked up to him. She had finished her shift and was leaving for home. She sat beside Charlie. 'Your recovery seems to be going well,' she observed, 'I am glad that you are feeling better.' 'What's your name?' he asked her. The intern smiled, 'You can call me Maggie; everyone does.' Charlie, who needed someone to talk to, began telling Maggie about Cross Island. She listened without interrupting as he described why he had decided to move to the island. But she could not stay long. She had a bus to catch and supper to cook. She promised him that they would have other conversations. Charlie also liked the psychiatrist who was in charge of his case. Dr Harry Trucker had worked in Bombay for a short time and he often traded stories with Charlie.

Back in Bombay, Victoria received a letter from Maya.

Dear Victoria,

Forgive me for the time lapse in writing to you, but your last letter was devastating.

Thanks to you letter, I now know where Charlie is. I always wanted a father, that I could live with, go to the park, sit on a bench, feed the squirrels, and play on the monkey bars.

And what do I say to him, now after all these years? I forgive you? I love you? Even while writing this, the sentences sound trite and phony. Our daddy-daughter days are gone, Victoria. He is too far away from where I am. The journey is too long, the destination dangerous.

I see Charlie these days, in flashes of a dream at dawn. I see him, like a negative image of an old photograph, sepia toned and dusty. I am not quite asleep and not fully awake as I watch this, my father...I remember once, standing in a parched field. It began to rain, and that aroma of earth that wafted from the mud...how do you describe that rising smell? You inhale and exhale, close your eyes, and then it is gone. But the memory remains, you can touch it, almost...but you cannot hold it. I see Charlie like that Victoria.

The shroud that surrounds the word 'orphan' is a thick, sad black garment. I wear that often these days. I wish he had died in Bombay; so that I would not have to go through with this. Perhaps I say this out of self-perseveration and desperation and selfishness.

There are nights and days, when I sit alone, and a kaleidoscope turns in me, and I wonder if schizophrenia is part of my reality too; a gift from my father, something to remember him by! I am too scared to get myself checked out by a doctor. I don't want to know...Something tells me that I should leave this all alone, forget that he still exists, let him die with the madness of his life; and then there are the whispering voices of reconciliation...I am not sure of anything anymore. I have started a new job, the salary is good, but I may have taken a risk that I may regret for the rest of my professional and personal life. I don't want to talk about it till I know how it will, or will not work out.

Maya

Dr Trucker had noticed that Charlie and the intern talked sometimes. He summoned her to his office and said, 'I know that you and Charlie have long conversations. I want to warn you; he is a man who is at the edge, like so many of them here are. Be careful of what you say to him. His mind is like an old door with a cracked hinge. It can snap at any moment. I have read the letter that was left behind by the woman who brought him here. The letter talks about his daughters Maya and Doris. Apparently Charlie is fixated on Maya. I don't know why. Now, I obviously do not know where his daughters are, but if they are in England, and turn up here, they must not be allowed to meet with him without my consent. The reason being, that if Charlie, upon meeting his daughters, gets into a state of anxiety, as he obviously will, it may trigger horrible schizophrenic attacks. Acute anxiety is known to do this to patients like Charlie. This could pull the trigger and send him permanently over the edge. It can be sudden, total and irreversible. There is a diagnosis termed "Brief Reactive Psychosis" that has demonstrated without a doubt that stress can sometimes be fatal to people like Charlie. I hope you understand the severity of all this.' The intern nodded thoughtfully and thanked him. 'Keep on talking to him about general things,' Dr Trucker advised, 'the psychotherapy is good for him. Let him ramble on if he wants to talk about his past and present experiences, his thoughts, feelings and relationships. Please report a summary of these conversations back to me as it may help with my private psychotherapy sessions with him. I hope that at some stage his negative cognitive patterns will turn into healthier positive beliefs.'

The next time Charlie and the intern talked, he told her about his daughter Maya. Maggie wondered why he did not talk about Doris. Through the months, Charlie developed a good rapport with Maggie the intern, who would graduate to the nurse level in a year. But Charlie's mind now occasionally began slipping into a fantasy world which the doctors stated was a 'normal association' with schizophrenic patients, and as predicted by the doctors, Charlie had days when he felt and acted normal. But when the bad days arrived, he played with the small wooden replica of *Sea Princess Maya* and sailed into a revolving kaleidoscopic world, whose changing patterns no one could decipher. On his good days, Charlie began writing letters. The first one was to Maya.

Dear daughter,

I don't know if forgiveness is possible here. But I write, in hope and despair, as my life is fading. I don't know who you are, and at the same time, I know you. Maybe what I just said does not make sense; from what the ward boys tell me here, nothing I say makes sense anymore. They are crude unfeeling blokes, these ward boys, but that is what life has offered them, and I guess making fun of mad men is their entertainment. I understand. I think of you often. I don't know what love is, Maya, but what I feel for you, I think comes close to what I have heard, when people talk about this thing called love. I am going to try and justify what I did to you, why I did it...I am not asking you to try and understand. I am just saying listen to what I have to say. You can throw this into the gutter later. In many ways, it has ceased to matter to me, and in many ways, it is all that I hope for, that maybe, you will understand. You may find this all confusing, but that is part of my life right now. For whatever it is worth, I hope that you find me, so I can look at you and you can look at me, and then, you can tell me to go and burn in hell or maybe, you can learn to forget and we can talk as father and daughter, just one time, before my end comes.

I don't deserve anything, anymore. Good and bad. I have had my share. There is a woman here, a nurse in training, who tells me that sometimes she has seen me crying, sometimes I laugh for no reason. My life is full of some strange times, most of which I cannot recall. It does not matter. I guess I am not making sense again. Maybe another attack is in progress. I never know these days, suddenly voices start speaking. It is terrifying and it scares me. There are nights, when I am alone. In the darkness, I see you, and I talk to you. You are real then, for me. And I can talk...of what is remaining of me. I live, knowing that reason has passed by me. I am not normal, Maya; at least that is what the ward boys tell me.

I remember the day we gave you away...I was...

I cannot write anymore, a ward boy has come, he tells me it is time for my bath.

Your Father

Charlie Strongbow

Charlie handed the letter to Maggie. She read and re-read the letter, placing her finger on the lines, deep in thought. She handed the letter to Dr Trucker. 'Why is he writing to his daughter, when he knows that there is no address?' she asked Dr Trucker. The doctor smiled and said, 'Charlie is writing because for him it is a catharsis. He is delusional; he thinks you will post the letter to Maya. On his good days, he knows in the back of his scrambled mind that there is no known contact with her, but his delusions override these rational thoughts. It is complicated, Maggie. I hope he continues writing. It will do him good.'

In a corner of the recreation hall, Charlie discovered a small library that had been obscured by a cupboard. These were novels that people had donated to the hospital through the years. No one read these books that lay in dusty piles on the floor. Charlie found a tattered copy of Fyodor Dostoyevsky's *The Idiot* in the middle of one pile. He smiled. 'An appropriate title for a place like this.' Sifting through the dusty books, Charlie discovered *Alice's Adventures in Wonderland.* 'Ahaaa...Dodo...' Charlie muttered. He wiped the dust off the fairy tale and took it back to his ward.

CHAPTER 2

Cry of the Blackbird

Maggie often tried to engage Charlie in conversation that would divert his attention. One afternoon, she came to Charlie. 'I have some news for you,' she said. 'King George VI, The Emperor of India, has died and Elizabeth Alexandra Mary Windsor is to be our new Queen Elizabeth II.' Charlie stayed silent, looked away, an indefinable oceanic look in his eyes. 'Just wanted you to know…this is a historic British day, and I know you were born in India and lived there…' Maggie mumbled. Charlie was sitting hunched on a chair in the garden. He ignored her. Finally he looked at Maggie. 'What day is it?' he asked? 'Wednesday,' she said. 'What date?' Charlie wanted to know. 'February sixth,' Maggie confirmed. 'What year?' Charlie whispered. 'Nineteen fifty-two,' she said. Charlie lapsed into silence again. Maggie turned to leave, but Charlie stood up and placed his right arm on her hand. There was a look of resignation in his eyes. 'I am lost in time…Maggie, I don't even know where I really am…this is not my country, you understand? It does not matter to me,' his voice moaned the infinite sadness he felt for what should have been, could have been. 'I should have died at my home in Bombay where I belonged,' he said in a low voice. 'When you mentioned this new Queen's middle name, Alexandra, all I thought about was the Alexandra, Prince's and Victoria docks in Bombay. That's all it means to me.' Charlie looked at the squirrels, then looked up to the sky, grimaced, sat back in his chair, covered his eyes with the palms his hands and began to cry. Maggie placed a supporting arm around his heaving shoulders.

Maggie reported the incident to Dr Trucker, but as time went by, despite all odds, Charlie began to get better. Dr Trucker had been monitoring his medication carefully and Maggie did all she could to see that he was comfortable. He spent his days reading, or sitting in the garden talking to the squirrels about Cross Island. Hallucinations came and went, but their severity was curtailed by his medication. Charlie kept away from the other patients. He waited in anticipation every day for either Maggie or Dr Trucker to come and talk to him. He hated the ward boys with passion. They treated the patients like sub-human beings and laughed at their afflictions. He felt lonely on 'Visiting Days' when families of some of the patients came in. The routine of institutionalization had created a comfortable padded circle that Charlie went around mindlessly. It had been a long year and a half since Dona Maria had dropped him off at the hospital; but for Charlie, years, months, weeks, days and time had absolutely no relevance in his walled incarceration.

One morning, as Charlie was sitting in the garden talking to three baby squirrels, giving them peanuts and pointers on life, and explaining the dangers that could come, Dodo arrived. Charlie smirked.

***Charlie:** Ah! Old friend, where have you been?*

***Dodo:** I've been to London to see the Queen. How do you feel?*

Charlie pondered the seriousness of the question, turned his head and looked at the old, abandoned chapel and the two gatehouses with porter's lodges. He stared at the original boundary wall that still stood along the canal. A bird was perched there. Suddenly, it took off. Charlie and Dodo watched as it disappeared.

Charlie: *I wish I had the freedom of that bird. But here I am, with this death sentence. What I have done to deserve this, is best left to be answered by people who are smarter than me. It's a little like karma, I guess. The poor sod who suffers, has no idea what he did in his last life. He goes through his life like a mule, and the poverty of his desperate existence makes him do bad things to survive; the wheel turns, and his next life gets worse. Look at me. I am afflicted by a disease that I have no control over. There is no cure. I was born with this curse, like the untouchables in India.*

Perhaps I don't understand, maybe I am just ignorant, and frankly my mind is not considered normal...but I think about these things sometimes. But never mind all that nonsense. Here I am, jailed for life. I can escape, but where will I go? I have no home, family, or faith. I am a pauper. It is an insulting end. Do I have a choice? Sure, I do. I can try and escape, but where do I go...? I can kill myself, or I can stay here. This is what is written for me, my destiny is now chained to this mad house.

Dodo: *I understand how you feel. There is nothing I can do or say to help. Like you, I am serving a life sentence, so I had better go. Charlie if there is any truth to reincarnation; we should be born birds in our next life. It would be nice to have wings, to fly... away...*

Charlie scattered the rest of the peanuts on the grass, sighed, and walked to his ward.

It was Monday morning. Dr Trucker's assistant handed him his mail. Most of the correspondence was from other doctors whose addresses Dr Trucker was familiar with. There was one piece of mail which had been posted from Cheltenham. Doctor Trucker unsealed the envelope and began reading the short letter addressed to him.

Dear Dr Trucker,

My name is Doris Strongbow. I was informed, through someone who works at Saint Bernard's Hospital, that you have a patient by the name of Charlie Strongbow. I am his daughter. You may give him my address, if you deem fit. But I do not want to meet with him. I am hoping that you will abide by my wishes. The reasons for my decision are complicated and sad, and I do not have the emotional strength to explain. I need to hear from him. There will be no response to his letters. I do not wish to explain why.

P.S.

He knows who I am.

Yours Sincerely,

Doris Strongbow

He sighed and placed the letter in a tray on his table. The letter that had been left behind when Charlie had been admitted to the hospital had mentioned two daughters named Doris and Maya. His first thoughts were: 'Is Doris schizophrenic? Is she really his daughter?' He had heard of women who would write to criminals in prison professing everlasting friendship, love and lust. 'What if this woman was one of those unhinged specimens? It could shatter what was left of Charlie's mind! Why had she written to the hospital? And why did she not want to meet him or answer his letters?' Dr Trucker's first impulse was to destroy the letter but he had been ingrained with old school English protocol. It would be morally and legally wrong, he told himself, if he destroyed this letter, or withheld it from Charlie. At the same time, he wished to keep a professional distance from Charlie's personal life. He had other patients to look after.

Finally, two weeks after the letter arrived, Dr Trucker called Maggie into his office. She was now a certified nurse and Dr Trucker could legally confide in her. He asked her to be seated and handed her the letter. He watched as Maggie read the letter, turned a whiter shade of pale and began crying. Dr Trucker was startled by her reaction. He stood up, walked from behind his desk and patted her on her shoulder, 'Now, now, Maggie,' he said gently, 'Please don't get emotional. We will try and work this out.' Maggie apologized for her outburst mumbling, 'This is so sad. Oh! This is terrible. This is a horrible woman.' Dr Trucker turned and went back to his chair behind his desk. He leaned forward and said, 'Maggie, you know that we should not get emotionally involved with our patients. That is one of the cardinal rules, right?' Maggie nodded wiping her eyes with a handkerchief. 'We do not know,' Dr Trucker explained 'What happened between Charlie and this daughter of his. So it would not be right for us to make judgements.' Maggie apologized for calling Doris 'a horrible woman.' Dr Trucker nodded and continued. 'I am going to go against medical judgement and take a chance here. What I need for you to do is ask him casually about this daughter Doris. He trusts you, I see that. There are days when Charlie is almost normal. Ask him about Doris, if and when he talks about his past. You can tell him about this letter. Let me know what his reaction is. You have the right to refuse; in that case, I will have to do so myself.' Maggie said that she would be glad to help and do anything that contributed to Charlie's well-being.

At her home, feeling pensive, Maya decided to reply to Victoria.

Dear Victoria,

Thank you for your reply to my last letter that was filled with a trail of tears. I am so glad that your health is good and you are keeping busy with your social work.

I know you grieve for my father and you are saddened by the position I am currently in; but what is written in chalk on the slates of our destiny, is carved in stone for our lives. I have learnt to accept this. There are no 'What Ifs?' anymore. That boat sailed a long time ago; it sank somewhere between the English Channel and Cross Island.

Forgive me if I don't write frequently. These letters burn holes in my heart. I am trying to lead my life away from Charlie and at the same time, he is always there in my mind. I see him, night and day; his deep blue eyes, tinted by the flashing darkness of his madness. He is far away, but in many ways, so am I. There is no comforting domestic promise of tomorrow in this relationship, there never was; maybe that is how I can deal with this. I am trying to maintain a psychological distance from Charlie and where he is at right now; because that is the only way I can retain a semblance of my sanity.

Maya

Maggie, when she met with Charlie, watched him the way a chess player watches an opponent. She tried to measure the intensity of his current mood and read his mind. It was not easy, because between his silences, Charlie oscillated between surly moodiness and vacant glances that told her nothing. He rambled on about Cross Island, then forgot what he was talking about, and asked the squirrels obscure questions about their domestic life. Maggie was hesitant to interrupt him as he talked about Victoria, Willie, Thommo, Dona Maria and a detective named Desai. For three weeks she tried to get him into a conversational position where she could quickly ask him about his daughter. Suddenly, one Saturday evening as they were sitting in the recreational hall, Charlie asked her if she was married and had children. Maggie smiled and told him that she hoped to marry someday and have a family. 'I hope that I can have a girl,' she said, 'I like little girls; but a boy would be fine too. Who knows, it could happen.' Charlie was silent for so long, Maggie thought of leaving. As she adjusted her uniform and fidgeted, Charlie looked at her and said, 'I could have had a family. But the times were not right. I have family somewhere. Two daughters. Doris and Maya; God knows where they are now. I think Doris is in England, somewhere. Maya, don't know, maybe India, England, maybe anywhere in the world. My friend Victoria knows where Maya is, but she would not tell me.' Maggie sat still. Charlie went silent again. She waited, looking down at her clenched fists that lay in her lap. Finally, he whispered, 'I got a message once, in India, from someone connected to Doris. They told me that she wished that I would get a bad disease and die a horrible death. Her wish is coming true, I think. So, I left her alone. For my own peace of mind, I let her go. Maya is the one I hope to meet. Maybe she feels differently. I don't know. Maybe I should write a letter to Doris, try and explain…who knows; who cares…I don't know.'

Instinctively, Maggie felt that now was the time to tell him about the letter that Doris had written. Charlie sat there, frozen. His deep blue eyes looked up to the sky; he rubbed his beard, twisted his fingers, shuffled his feet, massaged his thighs vigorously and grunted like an animal whose spiked yoke is cutting into its hide. He did not say a word. He continued grunting, eerie flaming throaty sounds that seemed to be coming from the foundry of hell that was melting his soul.

Suddenly, Charlie stood up and began pacing. Maggie stood there, paralyzed from the neck down. Only her terrified eyes moved imperceptibly, watching, wondering if a violent volcanic eruption was on its way. The question, 'What have I done?' screamed inside the cavity of her chest, as her breathing grew fast and short. Charlie stared at Maggie; his eyes were like twin flame throwers. She thought that he was going to attack her. Dr Trucker, who was on his way out, stopped to observe Charlie's frantic reaction. He approached him and said in a calm conversational voice, 'Charlie let's go talk to the squirrels.' His statement shifted the load that was tipping a precarious scale in Charlie's mind. The coiled spring in his mind unwound, the rigidity in his body posture loosened; he stopped pacing and headed for the garden, where he sat and talked to the squirrels. He asked them about their families, and how their sons and daughters were doing, suggested guidelines to squirrel morality and offered tips on parental guidance. Maggie and Dr Trucker sat away from him on another park bench. He did not look at them. They listened in silence.

Finally, Charlie grew silent, pensive. Dr Trucker took him by the hand and led Charlie to his ward. He gave him a strong sedative, and waited till Charlie was asleep. Dr Trucker patted a visibly upset Maggie on her shoulder, 'You did nothing wrong,' he counselled, 'Charlie's reaction was not abnormal. He will be fine tomorrow.'

The next morning, Charlie gave Maggie a letter that he had written to Doris. He appeared groggy. He told her that he could not sleep and had woken up to write. He said that he did not want to eat his breakfast and asked for permission to get back to bed and sleep. After Charlie had retired to his ward; Maggie started reading:

Doris,

This is your father, Charlie Strongbow. They tell me that you wrote a letter...I have tried to forget about you. That is the truth. I am too old to lie anymore, and on some level, I just don't care what you think of me. I am writing to you from a mental asylum in England. The wish that you made may years ago has come true. I have a bad disease that cannot be cured and I may die a horrible death. I hope that this letter finds its way to you, wherever you are. Now you can have the satisfaction. Your wish has been granted.

I want to tell you about your mother. She was a decent woman. I knew her for a short time. She died shortly after you were born. I do not remember how or why. I remember that she always wanted a family. She thought that I was the man who would give her this. But then, I was not capable of doing this. I am not sorry. I was young and ambitious and I wanted to be rich and powerful. Your mother always smiled at troubles in her life and said that life would get better. She was a good woman but she was wrong. Yes, she was kind and wanted the small things in life. She wanted us to go to England and settle down. I did not want that. In many ways her death ended the frustration and disappointment that would have come had she lived. I was angry when she died. I did not know what to do with you, so I gave you up for adoption, knowing that you would have a better life. Under the circumstances, I think I did the right thing. Maybe you disagree with me but it is too late for that discussion. I am dying and I don't know where you are. I think the hospital knows where you and Maya are, and they will not tell me. Anyway I am suspicious of everything, so maybe they don't know. Maya is your younger sister who was also given up for adoption. Yes, that is the kind of father I was, if that is what you can call me. You can call me a bastard, but I did my best for you and Maya. If you had stayed with me after your mother died, you would have had a horrible life. By giving you away, I gave you a gift.

I do not have any regrets and right now regrets do not matter. They are not going to change anything. I don't know if you have any contact with Maya, or even know that you had a sister, but if you do know where she is, please ask her to come and visit me. Maybe I am an old fool for asking you to do this.

My mind is not what it used to be. There is a lot of confusion. I write when I feel normal—whatever that means. It is only at these times that I can remember the past. Yesterday, your name came up and so I decided to write. I am not going to ask for forgiveness because I think there is no wrong done here. If you can walk in my shoes you will understand. I hope that you are happy wherever you are. I have nothing to offer you. My good wishes, I know, will not matter to you considering what you once said about me. I understand how you feel and do not wish that you die a bad death.

Your Father,
Charlie

Dr Trucker watched Charlie closely, waiting for the break that would snap what remained of his reason and reality. He adjusted his medication and asked Maggie and the other nurses to report Charlie's behavioural patterns to him. Charlie now withdrew from everyone. He doodled in his notebook, drawing stick figures of a boat sailing into the sunset, surrounded by twenty-four birds. He drew islands and oceans, ships wrecked by storms and added strange foot notes to each sketch. He talked to Dodo often in the darkness of his room. He began writing letters to Doris regularly. In four weeks, he had scrawled eighteen letters. He also wrote letters that were addressed to 'The Ward Boys', while others were marked 'For Squirrels', 'To Dr Trucker' and 'Maggie'. Many of his letters were mumbled lines that consisted of crippled words, impossible to decipher; some detailed his justifications to his Cross Island experience and life in India. As the months went by, he continued writing letters. Now many of them were for Maya, some explanatory, some dismissive and some garbled; most of his letters to Maya culminated with the plea, almost begging requests, to see her one more time. He handed the letters to Maggie. He believed that she would mail them. She cried often as she read about Charlie's life, and then handed the letters to Dr Trucker who was pleasantly surprised that many of the letters sounded so 'normal'. 'They were clearly written by a man who felt a great inner urgency to explain his actions, to tell somebody where he had been, what he had done and why he had done what he did,' Dr Trucker thought, 'It is like he is seeking redemption, maybe praise. He cannot say it. Writing is the only way his mind can handle what he really feels, of what he let happen in his life.'

Finally, Dr Trucker who had been thinking of what he could do with the letters made up his mind. He stuffed them all into five large envelopes and mailed them to Doris Strongbow in Cheltenham.

On an everyday basis, Charlie still communicated with Dr Trucker and Maggie but his sentences were cryptic, non-committal and brusque. He continued writing letters that took him back to his past. On one level, Charlie, aided by his medication, understood where he was, and why he was here at the hospital, but there were days and nights when the kaleidoscope turned suddenly and his mind jackknifed into a dark paranoid whirlpool. There were also near normal times when he felt discarded, alone and scared, and nostalgia was the only vehicle that led him away from the hospital and the solitary confinement he felt he was imprisoned in.

He wrote a letter to Willie.

Dear old friend,

I am sitting here in this nice English garden talking to squirrels out of boredom and waiting for the sun. Of course, the ward boys think that I am insane; maybe they are right. I am in Saint Bernard's Hospital. It is somewhere in England. I don't know where it is. They have often told me of the location, but I forget; it does not matter, because I do not leave this place. In India, they call places like this 'Mad Hospitals'. There are days when I remember things; this is one of those unfortunate days.

They tell me Dona Maria brought me here. I wonder where she went after that. Willie, I don't remember saying goodbye to you or anyone on Cross Island, and it bothers me sometimes that I cannot recall this. There is a nurse and doctor here. I like them. They are kind people. The nurse's name is Maggie, it is her pet name, she tells me. I don't know what her real name is, but it is not important. And then there is Dr Trucker who has been to India and is familiar with Bombay. Maggie the nurse, I am sure, often wonders why I write all these letters. On my good days, I wonder myself, because there are no addresses where they can be sent to. But writing makes me feel good; I can keep in touch with my past without sounding silly or stupid, which in my condition, I am entitled to.

The good thing is that I don't remember much of the attacks when they come. The medicines that they give me help, so I don't really suffer, but after an attack that can sometimes last for days, I can feel my body, or what is left of it...it is a feeling of your blood being drained from you, slowly...it is horrible, but I have to live with that. I sometimes wish I would die. I am too scared to take my own life. I wish, sometimes, that I would just pass away in my sleep. Then all this madness would all end. At other times, I don't mind it here, with Dr Trucker and Maggie and my squirrels. My hope is that Maya will come someday, but as the months go by, as years pass, my hope is fading like my mind and body. Still, I wait...sometimes I cry.

Our days on Cross Island and at the docks are all I have now. Maybe I write, hoping that some day after I am dead and gone, someone will locate people like you who I write to, and give them these letters. It is the hope of a mad man, but again, I am entitled to that.

I often think about you, Thommo and Dona Maria. Did you go back to England? It would be nice to see you again. I know that Dona Maria liked you and maybe the two of you are living in Portugal on her farm, milking cows and growing things like farm people do, drinking wine and thinking of the good old days in Bombay.

I remember the girls, from The House of Tarts. There are times when I stare at the little replica of 'Sea Princess Maya' that sits on my desk in my room here. Yes, I have it with me. Dona Maria must have packed it in my bag. I would like to thank her for that. If she is with you please thank her for me. Willie, remember four and twenty blackbirds? That is our story, Willie. It is a good one. I don't know what happened to my share of all the money that we made at Cross Island. I thought about that money when they told me I was a pauper. When I first heard it, I was insulted, but here, money is of no consequence, so it does not matter. I was just wondering, that's all.

Do you think of the old days, Willie? I wish we were still at Cross Island, drinking whisky at The Rot Gut Café and planning the next operation. You know, I don't blame that Detective Desai for doing what he did. It had to end at some time, we all knew that. I don't remember leaving the island. All I know is that I was at this hospital suddenly, far away from Cross Island.

They are very organized here. I meet other patients at breakfast, lunch and dinner but we don't really talk, there is nothing that I can say to them and I guess they feel the same, who knows. There is a recreation hall where they sometimes play music, and patients play cards and take part in silly games the nurses organize. I thought of you one day as I was playing cards. You would not like the card games here as we are not allowed to gamble.

Maybe if you do get this letter, you will come and see me.

Bring Dona Maria. We can sit in the garden and pretend that we are back on Cross Island. Maybe you can smuggle in a bottle of whisky. We can get drunk, and then perhaps when I am dead drunk, I may recall the times when I was alive; and maybe, I will remember our last goodbye. I miss you, Willie. I miss everybody.

Your friend,

Charlie

It was a month after Dr Trucker had sent Charlie's letters to Doris that he informed Maggie of what he had done. 'She is his daughter,' he explained. 'She has a moral and legal right to those letters.' 'Did you also send the letters that Charlie wrote to Maya and other people?' Maggie asked. 'Yes,' Dr Trucker confirmed, 'I sent her everything, even his letters to the squirrels. Since Maya is not here, and Doris is the only living family member we know of, Doris has a right to all her father's writings. And I wanted to remind you,' Dr Trucker continued, 'If Doris were to change her mind and come here to the hospital to see her father, she should not be allowed to see him. Charlie would go into a dark anxiety phase from which he will not recover. His nervous system will go into overdrive if she were to confront him. The same goes for his other daughter Maya.' Maggie nodded sadly; and left Dr Trucker's office.

Chapter 3

A Grave Father and Child Reunion

Charlie was reaching the fifth year of his incarceration at Saint Bernard's Hospital. A weary resignation surrounded him. His dream of meeting Maya or Doris was now a fractured hope that hurt when he thought about it. Depression came and went accompanied by anxieties and suspicions. Dodo arrived infrequently. Charlie shuffled from garden to recreation hall, to the ward, and then back again. The frame of his once magnificent physique had bent with age, bitterness, sorrow and suffering; and his spotted skin resembled browning leaves in autumn, waiting to die and fall. His alpha-lion mane thinned to grey dangling limp tendrils hung in defeat; and his once luxurious beard and moustache had withered into a sparse shrub. Charlie's deep blue eyes now reflected the vacant wasteland of his mind. They seemed to be perpetually focused into the far distance, squinting, waiting for someone or something to arrive.

It had been almost two years since Victoria had heard from Maya. She had almost given up hope that Maya would write again. Suddenly a letter arrived...

Dear Victoria,

I apologize for not writing and replying to your many letters. The fact is I have nothing more to say about Charlie and my life. My friends tell me that I am depressed, maybe I am...maybe my mind is following the mind of my father...

When I got back home from work last evening, I made myself a cup of tea. I then sat by my window the overlooks a beautiful garden and thought, Charlie in all probability wants his little girl back; and I want a daddy. It is a sad unfinished circle. I looked at a flower in the garden and thought how perfectly the leaves on the plant compliment the flower's petals; but then, I said to myself, it will not last long. Pretty as it is, that flower, will be dead in a week, and at some point in time, the leaves will die.

How will this all end, I don't know. I have nothing more to say right now. I wish you well, Victoria, and hope that one day, I will have the fortune of seeing you again. I was too young to know you when I was given away for adoption. The fact that I was 'given away' brings an inconsolable sadness. Charlie is where Charlie is; and I am where I am. There is no real connection, the distance is too wide.

I do not want to talk about this again. I know you will understand.

I have to stop writing now.

Maya

Christmas eve, 1955. Dr Trucker told the doctors, nurses and some of the patients that he had resigned his post as psychiatrist at Saint Bernard's Hospital to take on another job. He apologized for the last-minute news and confided that he had informed the hospital Board of Directors three weeks ago of his decision. This was going to be his last day at Saint Bernard's Hospital. He talked to Charlie and wished him well. Knowing that Charlie liked to write letters, Dr Trucker wrote down the address of the hospital he would be working at, and asked Charlie to write to him. Charlie spiralled into a black depression. He wrote a letter to Maya.

Dear Maya,

I cannot go on anymore. I do not expect you or anyone to understand. I don't know if you will see this letter, but I feel I have to say goodbye to you before I leave.

Dr Trucker, my friend, is leaving the hospital. Now all I have left is Maggie and the squirrels. I do not want to be around when Maggie decides to leave. There are times when I have secretly hoped that Maggie would take me to her home. I would live with her. Maggie is like my daughter, that's how I feel...because we have spent so much time together.

Yesterday, after Dr Trucker left, I was walking in the garden and I came across a squirrel that had died. It frightened me. I cannot explain why.

I waited for many years to see you.

It does not matter anymore.

I must go now.

Your Father,

Charlie

A ward boy noticed Charlie, an hour after midnight, with a towel tied around his neck, standing on a chair trying to loop the towel around the ceiling fan. He called for help. They subdued Charlie, injected him with a sedative and moved him into the emergency ward. The next day, a groggy and furious Charlie showed signs of extreme antagonism. He kicked and screamed and had to be sedated again. When Maggie arrived for her morning shift, they informed her of Charlie's suicide attempt. She rushed to the emergency ward. Charlie was fast asleep. She looked at him. 'He looks so small, so defenseless, so sad,' she thought. She sat in a chair and watched him. Dr Trucker's replacement walked in and checked his pulse. 'He is going to be alright,' he said, turning to Maggie, 'I wonder why he suddenly tried to take his life.' Maggie had not read his letter, but she was reasonably sure that Dr Trucker's leaving had something to do with it.

In the days that followed, Charlie began to sink. They had restrained him because he often exhibited sudden explosions of violence. One afternoon, as Maggie sat by his bed, Charlie appeared calm and clear-eyed. 'So this is how it all ends,' he said with profound bitterness, 'tied to a bed like a bloody mad dog.' Maggie looked down at the floor and bit her lower lip. Tears welled up in her eyes, her voice trembled with sadness. 'You're going to get better,' she reassured him. 'Then, we can sit in the garden again, and talk to the squirrels.' Charlie grimaced and said nothing.

The next day, he asked Maggie to get his little boat from the cupboard in his ward and told her to place it on the nightstand by his bed. 'You have never talked about yourself,' he said. 'What did you do before you came to work here? Where were you born? What about your family, your mother, father, brothers, sisters?' Maggie appeared uncomfortable. 'It is not really important,' she explained, 'there is nothing remarkable about my family. They are plain old middle-class English people. Maybe one day, I will tell you my story. Now you must get some rest. I will see you tomorrow. You are going to get better, so don't worry.' As she was leaving Charlie said, 'You know Maggie, if only my daughter Maya were here...all I have of her, is this wooden boat...This is a replica of the boat we used in Bombay, I named it after her. I like you, Maggie. If I could, I would adopt you, make you my daughter, but I guess it is too late now for that kind of thing. And, I have nothing to give you but my madness and poverty. Once upon a time, I was a rich man...' Maggie smiled, touched Charlie gently on the shoulder and left the ward with tears in her eyes. She wished Dr Trucker was still there. He would know what to do with the questions that were burning inside her. Was this the right time to tell Charlie? Would the shock kill him?

The next morning, Charlie's chest began heaving as anxiety attacked his blood and scrambled his brain. He moaned like a desperate, incarcerated animal, crying for its lost paradise of freedom. As the doctor sedated him, Maggie watched in stricken silence. She asked for permission to sit by him. She sat in a chair, looking at his emaciated body. An hour later, as his breathing became laboured and his limbs jerked in sudden spastic motions, she summoned the doctor, who checked his heart, and asked Maggie to watch over him. 'I will be back in half an hour to check on him,' he said. Fifteen minutes after the doctor had left the ward, Charlie opened his sedated eyes. He turned his head, looked at *Sea Princess Maya* sitting on the nightstand, then shifted his gaze and stared at Maggie. He tried to say something. His mouth moved in a grotesque soundless movement, there was a horrible gurgling sound from his throat. Maggie walked over to Charlie, put her right hand on his shoulder and caressed it. His arms twitched, his eyes closed, his mouth opened. She asked a ward boy to get the doctor, who arrived and placed his stethoscope over the heart of the motionless body.

Charles Lorcan Strongbow was dead.

Maggie sobbed. Grabbing the wooden replica of *Sea Princess Maya*, she stumbled out of the room. They buried Charlie the next morning in Pauper's Cemetery on the hospital grounds. Maggie was the only attendee. As the grave diggers began to cover his cheap casket with earth, she pulled *Sea Princess Maya* from her pocket and dropped it on his coffin. She started crying as she turned to leave. As she made her way to the gate of the cemetery, she heard the grave diggers singing 'Friggin' in the Riggin',' a salty old sea shanty. She turned her head to see them shovelling dirt on Charlie and smiled through her tears as she heard the bawdy words. 'Charlie would have liked that,' she thought. She waved once, a silent last goodbye, and walked out.

Back in the garden of the hospital, she sat on Charlie's bench and watched the squirrels. A ward boy approached her with two letters; the farewell letter that Charlie had written to Maya and one addressed to her. 'We found these under his notebook,' he said. Maggie nodded her thanks. She sat back and read the letter that Charlie had written to her aloud to the squirrels. She then folded the paper and placed it in her pocket. It began raining. The squirrels scurried away. Maggie sat there, still, barely moving, irrationally hoping that this trembling excruciating physical agony would somehow fill the stark emptiness inside her. Maggie, her back hunched, arms resting on her thighs clutching her bowed head, clawed fingers gripping the skin of her skull whispered the end of Charlie's letter: *All these words I write seem to arrange themselves into death sentences. That is the story of my life.*

The next morning, Maggie arrived at the hospital and met with the Matron. She told her that she was resigning her position. The Matron was sorry to see her go. 'Oh Maggie,' she exclaimed, 'you are so good with our patients. I wish you would stay, but I guess you have to follow your future. I wish you well.' Maggie thanked her. 'You have to fill and sign this form of resignation,' the Matron continued. 'Here it is. Please use your full first name, a middle name if you have one, and your surname,' the Matron advised, 'it is a governmental requirement, for the records, you know. We also need a current forwarding postal address and telephone number, if you have one. Please do use your full legal birth name.'

Maggie began writing on the form. She glanced over it to make sure that she had filled in all the slots, and at the bottom, where it said 'Signature', Maggie signed her official birth name, stared at it and smiled, said goodbye to the Matron, and walked out of the hospital.

EPILOGUE

In Memoriam

A year after Charlie died, Maya visited Victoria in Bombay. They stood at Ferry Wharf and gazed across the bay at Cross Island. In Victoria's home, they talked about Charlie Strongbow. Victoria wept inconsolably as she listened to Charlie's tormented life at the asylum. Victoria died on Good Friday, 19 April 1957.

Maya returned to England and her adoptive parents. She had often thought of contacting and visiting her sister Doris in Cheltenham. She never did. After Doris died, her only son Danny, finally tracked Maya down in Boyd Avenue, Southall, West London, where she lived with two Himalayan cats, Hobson and Jobson, and her memories. They communicated and met frequently, till Maya passed away on Guy Fawkes Night, Wednesday, 5 November 2014. Southall is heavily populated by people of South Asian descent. It is generally referred to as 'Little India'. Why she preferred to live and die there is an interesting psychological query.

Danny Strongbow chose to stay a bachelor, married to demons he could not divorce. Savaged and shattered by schizophrenia, he hung himself from the ceiling fan in his living room in Chelsea, on Thursday, 22 December 2016.

They are all gone now: Charlie, Victoria, Doris, Maya and

Danny. At Saint Bernard's Hospital, the mental asylum in Southall, England, squirrels still scamper through the grounds; and in the pauper's graveyard located at the western part of the cemetery area, Charlie Strongbow is still there in 'The Garden of Remembrance' underneath a cracked dirty flat stone with his *Sea Princess Maya.*

Like they were in life, they lie in death, two souls, a heartbeat away from each other.

Acknowledgements

Thanks to Titus Fernandes from Bandra, Mumbai, who worked at the Bombay Docks for thirty-one years as a Supervisor. Thank you for explaining the intricacies of the finely tuned web of organized corruption at the Bombay Docks, and making time to take me to the Bombay Docks and Ferry Wharf innumerable times. I want to extend my appreciation to you for explaining how the complicated international underground routes worked, and the *modus operandi* of past audacious corruption that was a day and night occurrence behind the walls of the three wet docks: Prince's Dock, Victoria Dock and Alexandra Dock. This novel would not have been possible without your detailed explanations and 'inside information'.

Sincere thanks to Editor Ujwala Samarth from Pune, India, for reading and editing the first raw skeleton draft before it turned into historical fiction. Thanks to Radhika Shenoy, Editor at Speaking Tiger who worked on the final edits, suggested editorial changes and deleted some of the historical clutter which lay in the path of the plot and story.

A debt of immense gratitude is also owed to Latin Scholar, Historian and Editor, John Goulding from Shrewsbury, England, who undertook this endeavour with extreme reluctance. His initial refusal was not that he disagreed with the subject matter or writing; as I discovered later, J.G. does not trust or have faith in humanity anymore, is unapologetically cantankerous, and rarely seeks voluntarily human relations; it's a long story of betrayals and bitterness, but he consented to look at the manuscript, eventually. His meticulous editing of the final manuscript led to its current form. This novel would not have been possible without his knowledge, wisdom and intimidating explanations.

I also wish to thank classmate Mahesh Vyas, from Saint Andrew's High School, now Managing Director & CEO, Centre for Monitoring Indian Economy Pvt. Ltd., Mumbai, for reading the final manuscript, checking dates and suggesting editorial changes.

The publication of this novel would not have been possible without the help of Anurag Basnet who graciously connected me to Editor Radhika Shenoy; *muchos gracias* Anurag. And to old friend Hartman DeSouza; thank you for your suggestion that led me to read and study historical fiction author E.L. Doctorow's writings, especially *Ragtime*. It soothed the edges of this literary journey, made me understand the complexities of a historical fiction novel and helped in directing the tedious research and fact checking involved in finishing this manuscript. I also owe a debt of gratitude to the Asiatic Society Library in Mumbai for granting me access to newspapers and magazines from the 1940s and 1950s.

Bibliography

These are some of the books and material I referred to for historical authenticity and guidance while compiling this novel.

Allana, G. *Quaid-i-Azam Jinnah*. Ferozsons Ltd, Lahore, 1967.

Ambedkar, B.R. *Riddles in Hinduism: The Annotated Critical Selection*. 1954. Navayana, 2016.

Auden, W.H. 'Partition', *City Without Walls*. Faber, 1969.

Bolitho, Hector. *Jinnah: Creator of Pakistan*. Quaid-i-Azam Academy, 1954.

Bourke-White, Margaret. *Portrait of Myself*. Simon and Schuster, 1963.

Campbell, J.M. *Statistical Account of the Town and Island of Bombay*. Government Central Press, 1893-1894.

Chittar, Shantaram D. *The Port of Bombay: A Brief History*. Bombay Port Trust, 1973.

Cottineau de Kloguen, Denis Louis. *Historical Sketch of Goa*. Asian Educational Services, 1988.

Dellon, Gabriel. *An Account of the Inquisition at Goa, in India*. Bower, Archibald, 1819.

Dwarkadas, Kanji. *Ruttie Jinnah: The Story of a Great Friendship*. 1963.

Emperor of Hindustan, Jahangir Memoirs of the Emperor Jahangueir. Translated from Persian by David Price, Printed for the Oriental Translation Committee London. 1829.

Fonseca, José Nicolau da. *An Historical and Archaeological Sketch of the City of Goa: Preceded by a Short Statistical Account of the Territory of Goa*. Thacker & Company, 1878.

Freeman, Henry. *The East India Company: From Beginning to End*. CreateSpace Independent Publishing Platform, 2016.

Gandhi, Mohandas K. *The Story of My Experiments with Truth*. 1927.

Garmon, William W., PSYD, FPPR, FICPP. *Understanding Schizophrenia*. Outskirts Press, 2010.

Gazetteer of the Bombay Presidency. Government Central Press, 1894.

Godse, Nathuram. *Why I Assassinated Mahatma Gandhi*. Surya Bharti Prakashan, 1993.

Hicks, Lady Pamela. *Daughter of Empire: My Life As a Mountbatten*. Simon & Schuster, 2014.

Jinnah, Fatima. *My Brother*. Quaid-i-Azam Academy, 1987.

Khan, Yasmin. *The Great Partition: The Making of India and Pakistan*. Yale University Press, 2007.

Khan, Yasmin. *The Raj at War: A People's History of India's Second World War* by. Vintage, 2016.

Morgan, Janet. *Edwina Mountbatten Biography: A Life of Her Own*. HarperCollins, 1992.

Mother Teresa. *Come Be My Light: The Private Writings of the 'Saint of Calcutta'*. Brian Kolodiejchuk, ed. Doubleday, 2007.

Nair, P. Thankappan. *A History of Calcutta's Streets*. Firma KLM, 1987.

Nayar, Kuldip. *Scoop*. HarperCollins Publishers India Private Limited, 2006.

Nehru, Jawaharlal. *The Discovery of India*. Meridian Books,1946.

Nehru, Jawaharlal. *Towards Freedom: An Autobiography*. The Bodley Head, 1936.

Pepys, Samuel. 'Mughal Emperor Nuruddin Salim Jahangir's Letter to James I- Selling India to the British', *The Diary of Samuel Pepys*. Henry Colburn, 1825.

Reddy, Sheela. *Mr and Mrs Jinnah: The Marriage That Shook India*. Penguin Random House, 2017.

Scholberg, Henry. *Bibliography of Goa and the Portuguese in India*. Promilla & Co., 1982.

Scott, Paul. *Staying On*. Heinemann, 1977.

Winokur, George, M.D. and Tsuang, Ming T., M.D. PhD. *The Natural History of Mania, Depression, and Schizophrenia*. American Psychiatric Publishing, 1996.

Wolpert, Stanley. *Jinnah of Pakistan*. Oxford University Press, 1984.

Wolpert, Stanley. *Nine Hours to Rama*. Random House, 1962.

Wolpert, Stanley. *Shameful Flight: The Last Years of the British Empire in India*. Oxford University Press Inc, 2009.

ALSO IN SPEAKING TIGER

THE DRUNK BIRD CHRONICLES

Malay Chatterjee

'With an unlikely cast of nawabs, missionaries, maharanis and an English-teaching raven, this is an exhilarating, audacious work of fiction.'

—Gautam Bhatia, author of
Punjabi Baroque and *Malaria Dreams*

Allegro Armstrong Braganza, the eponymous avian chronicler of this novel, is immoral, immortal, irreverent, intelligent, irritable and often drunk. Born in the forests beyond Shillong, he was a foul-mouthed friend of the eccentric Englishman Gareth Armstrong; then coarse companion to his daughter Rachel who married a talented Anglo-Indian piano tuner named Emilio Braganza; and finally avuncular anchor to five subsequent generations of this expansive British-Goan family who travel across India and the globe to further their various quests—Orlando in Cambodia studying the architecture of the Angkor Wat, Bella learning translation in Portugal, Maria in Almora furthering her dance ambitions under the tutelage of Uday Shankar, and Asifio in New Delhi continuing the family's thriving music shop in Connaught Place. Through shifting tides of fame and fortune over a hundred years, it is Allegro who remains their constant and reliable port of stability.

Wickedly funny and full of surprises, Malay Chatterjee's *The Drunk Bird Chronicles* is a sparkling debut that will be read and enjoyed for years to come.